GAMBLING ON A DREAM

M. E. COOPER

This is a work of fiction. Though this story uses some famous people and historical locations, names, characters, places, events, dates and incidents are products of the authors imagination. Any resemblance to actual persons, living or dead, or actual events is purely coincidental.

Copyright © 2025 M. E. Cooper
All rights reserved.
Imalooga Press

ISBN-13: 979-8-9853720-4-5

To Dean
1964 - 2024

Chapter 1

T he neon sign in the diner window was flickering 'pen'. Off and on, the O no longer lighting up. Pen, yes, that's what he should do, pen his own songs, not play those written by someone else. His plan had been to take the bus to Los Angeles and chase the dream of stardom. It was not finding himself here, after having spent the night sitting in a police station interrogation room on the wrong side of Las Vegas.

Chapter 2

Neil was about to give up on his dreams. Give up on everything else that mattered to him in life. He had been trying to find a way out of his backwards hometown, to no avail. However, every time he tried to leave, something always stopped him. Hearing all about Sun Records and the guys that were recording with Sam Phillips. Elvis! For Pete's sake, had made his first record there and look at him now. Surely if someone from Tupelo Mississippi could make it, then why couldn't he? After all, Forrest City Arkansas wasn't near as far from a city that may hold the key to his dreams. Yet, every time he tried, it felt like life threw a curve ball, causing him to take two steps back.

First granddaddy Joe died. Okay, that was a big deal. He admired Joe even more than his own father. Joe supported and encouraged his dreams of music stardom; he even bought him his first guitar from the Sears and Roebuck catalog. His death was completely unexpected. An accident on the tractor had left him in the field for two days before anyone realized he was missing. When they found him, the bugs and animals had already gotten to the body, leaving behind a mangled and barely recognizable corpse. The best they could do to honor him was to clean him up as best as possible and bury him on the land he so loved.

Without Joe's encouragement and his unwavering confidence in Neil's talent, the guitar sat in the corner of the room for weeks on end, collecting dust. One afternoon, while wallowing in his self-pity, Neil realized he wasn't doing anything that would have made Joe proud. Picking up the guitar, he started writing his own songs again.

The obstacle of actually getting to Memphis still stood in his way. Because his daddy didn't understand the point of this musical dream Neil was holding onto, daddy held back the keys to the car for anything more than a trip into town. He kept an eagle-eye on the odometer and the gas gauge, too. Neil knew he didn't have enough saved yet to pay for both the gas and the cost of making a record.

Momma getting sick was the next life event to knock Neil back off his game. With her being unable to work, he picked up extra shifts to help supplement the household income. Even being able to hold a little of the extra money back for his savings. It still wasn't enough to get him to Memphis. Momma bounced back quickly. The worst seemed to behind them, when one night momma got sick again. This time, it was even worse. In the hospital for a month before the doctors finally declared there was nothing left they could do for her. When she passed, Neil threw himself back into his songwriting, letting out the emotions of losing the two people closest to him.

One evening while strumming his guitar and working on another new song, daddy came storming into Neil's room. Grabbing the guitar from his hands, he marched outside and threw it in the fire he had burning, all before Neil had the chance to react to what was happening. Rushing out, not thinking about the consequences, he started to make a grab for the burning instrument, but it was too late. All that remained were the strings, knobs, and a few fragments of charred wood. Standing over the remnants, he watched as the pile smoldered. Making a vow to himself that he would leave this place, go somewhere new, and start over again.

Deciding Memphis was just too close to home, he declared it would have to be somewhere he wouldn't be known. Leave the demons of the past in Forrest City and start a new life. Maybe he'd even adopt a new name. Anything to help cut ties to this life holding him back.

Chapter 3

Gathering the few personal items that held any value to him, including his songwriting notebook, he shoved it and his clothes into a backpack, setting off in the middle of the night.

'I should'a done this long ago,' he thought, taking one last look at his childhood home. 'Momma's gone, Grandpa Joe is gone. Daddy doesn't care. There's nothing to keep me here anymore. My dream is out in the world somewhere. I'm gonna find it. One way or the other.'

The five-mile walk into town felt tedious and unending. Yet at the same time, it was exhilarating. He was determined to let nothing stop him this time. Not the pebble that kept creeping into his scuffed up sneakers, or the growling in the depths of his stomach. He knew he would have enough time to eat once he got to the bus station. Pushing down that pain down too, he kept going. After the third time of trying to shake the pebble out, he gave up. 'Let it serve as the reminder I need why I'm doing this. Let it keep nagging at me. I'll leave it until I get to Los Angeles if I have to.'

As Neil strolled in to town, the sun was coming up over the rise of the fields. Life in Forest City began to stir. Roosters crowing, announcing it was time to wake up. Tractors groaning in protest as their owners tried coaxing them to life for another day's work. A newspaper truck lumbering down the street, stopping to drop a bundle of papers on a corner as a delivery boy came pedaling up. Stopping just long enough to pick it up and shove them into his bag. Neil watched the boy hop on his bicycle, steering with one hand, the other reaching into the bag, expertly folding the paper then tossing it onto a waiting porch or stoop.

He wondered what dreams the paperboy might be chasing. Was he saving the nickels and dimes he got as holiday tips? Planning to buy a new bicycle? Was he hoping to find his way out of town, just as Neil was? Did he want to chase down a bigger dream, more than this town was capable of providing?

Shaking his head to clear the tiredness trying to overtake him, he made his way down the street, arriving at the diner next door to the bus station. Opening the door, he breathed in the smells of breakfast permeating the air. Looking around, he found Bernie, grease stained apron tied around his waist, back in the kitchen. Mabel, the ever-present wise cracking waitress, stood behind the counter, brewing coffee and shouting at one of the other girls. Probably telling them to hurry it along. Mabel was always shouting at someone. 'Was she going deaf?' Neil wondered. Best to be careful not to suggest that to her; he'd probably be on the receiving end of an earful and then some too, if he did.

Sliding into one of the booths, he waved at Bernie and nodded when Mabel asked if he wanted coffee. Walking over, cup in hand, she set it down, looking at him, then the backpack at his feet.

"Heading out somewhere?" She surmised sarcastically.

"Running down a dream," Neil replied.

"You'll be back," her only retort before asking what he wanted to eat.

Satisfied with his order, Mabel hollered back at Bernie, as she took coffee to the other customers trickling in.

Neil tried pushing her demoralizing words out of his head. Everyone in this town was always discouraging the younger generation. Trying to make them stay. Go to work on the farms or at the factory in the next town over. The world was a big, scary place, they would say. It would stomp on their dreams and spit them back out again. Most of his friends believed this to be true and stuck around. A few found the confidence to leave and join the military, sending home postcards from the exotic locales where they found themselves stationed. One or two left. Having seemed to have disappeared. Never to be heard from again. Those, he believed, were the ones that found their way and made something of themselves in the world. Deciding to never look back or return.

Bernie interrupted Neil's thoughts by shouting from the kitchen. "Bus'll be along later than usual. It seems the driver had a bit of dust up with someone who didn't want to follow his rules."

Neil shook his head. He was certain this meant that the driver had someone he didn't like on board. And, for no good reason other than he was a bigot. Instead, he was giving them a hard time. "I guess whoever it was decided to stand up for himself. Good on him," Neil muttered under his breath. That was something else he would be happy to leave behind. The racism and hatred that permeated this town. Neil couldn't understand why people found it necessary to think less of someone just because of the color of their skin.

Finishing his breakfast and gathering up his belongings, he left money on the table to pay the check, giving Mabel a bigger tip than usual. Knowing she would have some mocking comment to make, he slid out of his seat, making his way out the door before he could hear it. As he walked over to the station, he found he could hear faint strains of new lyrics floating around his head.

Chapter 4

"Bus 512 departing for Los Angeles, gate number 3," the loudspeaker blared as he walked in the door.

The voice of the ticket agent booming and echoing off the tile walls and rundown lockers drowning out the melody in Neil's head. What he heard instead was "hopes and dreams departing now, leaving you behind."

'You keep procrastinating,' he thought to himself. 'Here you are, writing your songs despite everything that has tried to beat you down. It's time to find and follow that passion that used to burn so bright in your heart.'

Seeing all the people milling about the station, he knew there was nothing in this town he could do to make a living and be happy. What could he do to change that? He didn't have the support of family or friends; they were all continually telling him to grow up. Be a man and find a proper job. His now ex-girlfriend was always telling him to follow his dad into construction. "That's where the money is," she would constantly say. Finally, realized all she wanted out of life was the money, a house, a car, two kids, and the white picket fence. No. That was not what he was envisioning for himself.

Shaking away the memories, he overheard a shrill voice arguing with Fred, one of the station employees. While he couldn't hear the specifics, he felt compelled to go step in. He knew most everyone that worked here. As a result, he couldn't figure out why Fred, one of the most generous and gregarious people Neil encountered, would argue with a customer. That he was even raising his voice with someone. That was an event out of the ordinary and worth investigating.

Placing his notebook back in his backpack, he slung it back over his shoulder. He wasn't about to leave it just lying around. Small city or not. This was a bus station after all and no matter how trusting you may be, common sense sometimes must prevail.

"Fred, what's going on, man? Need some help here?"

"Nah man, thanks. Everything is under control. This little lady here was just leaving." Fred said, turning his attention to Neil.

"I am not!" she exclaimed. "I am getting on that bus and you can't stop me. I have a valid ticket that allows me to travel wherever I choose."

Neil turned to see the woman standing in front of Fred, first noting her dark unruly hair and that one strand that kept falling across her face. The more agitated she got, the harder she tried to push it away. It was then he caught sight of her eyes; the color of the pines that populated the countryside. He thought to himself, 'a man could get lost in that forest searching for the secrets that lay deep within.'

"I'm sorry, miss, I can't let you on that bus. First, you

have to go to the ticket window. Present them with your voucher and then follow the procedures. Just like everyone else. Once you've done that, then you may go wherever your little heart desires." Fred said, straightening his back, his deep voice dropping that much lower.

Hoping to help diffuse the situation, Neil offered to take her bags and walk with her over to the ticket window. Relenting, she smiled sweetly at Neil, thanking him for his chivalry as she handed him her suitcase.

"I'm Sharon. Nice to meet you." She said, offering a hand to shake.

"Nice to meet you, too. I'm Neil. So where are you headed, anyway?"

"I'm trying to get to Los Angeles. I start a new job next week. I need to get there as soon as possible. I have to get settled in before I don't have any spare time left."

"What about you? Are you headed somewhere? Or just here for the entertainment factor."

"I am the entertainment factor," he joked. "Normally I'd be here playing my guitar for the folks passing through. I walked in this morning knowing there's something more for me out there. Now I find I'm faced with taking that first step, trying to find out what it is. And I'm having second and third thoughts."

Without missing a beat, she offered. "Why don't you come with me? It sure would be nice to have the company. Maybe this is just what you need. To jump start that dream again."

What a random suggestion from a total stranger reigniting the resolve he had last night. Could this be the reminder he needed? Showing him he didn't have a reason to stay? Was this opportunity staring him in the face? The nagging voice in his head, the one he kept trying so hard to drown out, told him he was crazy. He'd never amount to anything. Why was he even considering this? Still a much softer voice, one he could barely discern over the shouting voice of defeat. In his head, simply asked, "why not?"

Before he could continue the argument in his head, he replied. "Sure, okay, let's go." Just like that, he decided he was ready. The look of surprise on her face was telling him that was not the response she was expecting. But she simply replied, "Great."

Proceeding to the ticket window, she presented her voucher, requesting two tickets to Los Angeles.

"I can't let you pay my way," Neil said, attempting to interrupt the transaction. Before he could protest any further, he saw the agent give her a quizzical look before looking back at the voucher. He shrugged, printed two tickets, pausing before handing them over.

"Something wrong?" Sharon inquired.

Neil watched the agent glance at her, back at the voucher, then at her again.

"Gate 3, bus leaves in 15 minutes," he said, sliding the tickets and voucher back over the counter.

"Thank you," Sharon said, picking up her bag and beginning to walk away. "Aren't you coming, Neil?"

"Yeah, um, okay." He said. Considering what had just transpired, he thought. 'That was a little weird.' Then again, this wasn't turning out to be your ordinary day, either.

Boarding the bus, he kept a tight hold on his backpack while Sharon allowed her luggage to be stowed below. Realizing she obviously didn't have the same concern about the validity of her ticket or the purpose of his trip, he began to think maybe he shouldn't be either.

'Maybe that's just what I need to do. I need to have the confidence that everything is working in my favor now. When I get to Los Angeles, I'm going to find where I fit in.'

Neil watched the ever-changing landscape of the country pass by in a blur as he tried to settling into his seat. Not that there was much to see out the dusty window. Open road, field after field of corn, soybeans, and wheat. Once they were out of the city, traffic became nonexistent. The only unexpected slowdown they encountered was caused by a herd of cows that decided to take up residence in the middle of the road, much to the driver's consternation. After that brief delay cleared, he found they were on their way again, heading towards the first stop on this new journey.

Not having anything else to do, Neil looked over and saw Sharon reading through what looked like a manual, making notes in the margins. Figuring it must have to do with her new job and the logistics of getting set up in a new city, he didn't think it would be appropriate for him to interrupt.

When it appeared she had finished, he turned toward her asking, "why?"

"Why what?"

"Why me? Why did you ask me, a complete stranger, to accompany you to Los Angeles? It seems rather a risky proposition, don't ya think?"

"Call it a gut feeling, I guess. You seem like a nice enough guy, polite, decent. And you looked like you were ready to be out of that place, too. Was I wrong? Did I make a mistake in asking?"

Neil turned his head away. Letting his gaze wander over

the scenery buzzing by, he started to say something, but stopped himself. "No," was his only reply.

No more explanation, just two simple letters, short and to the point. As he turned back to face her, he saw her tilting her head to the side, reaching out as though she was going to tap him on the shoulder. She quickly withdrew her hand, leaving them both sitting in silence.

The hum of the tires on the asphalt provided the sound-track for their journey over the next hours. An occasional child crying broke the monotony of an otherwise boring existence. Neil closed his eyes in an attempt to nap. But couldn't find that comfortable position that would allow himself to drift away. He replayed the previous day's events over and over in his mind. His thoughts scattered, not coming in any chronological order. They were flying through his head as though they were a bird, given some-thing to increase its speed. Unable to decide on a heading or destination, criss-crossing about until finally collapsing.

Peering over at Sharon, he watched as she sat stock still, staring straight ahead, no discernible expression on her face. He wondered what could she possibly be thinking? Was there a chance she was having doubts about inviting him along? Maybe he should get off at the next stop, offer to return home and let her continue on her journey. Before he could make the suggestion, the driver announced, "First stop. 45 minutes folks. Bathrooms, food, stretch your legs. We're pulling in to gate B. Departing again in 45 minutes."

Neil quipped, "boy he has the personality of a door-knob." Thinking to himself, this must be one of the most mundane jobs ever. Seeing the same scenery every day. The only changes to look forward to were the weather and the faces of the passengers.

Stretching, he extricated himself from his seat, following the rest of the passengers off the bus and into the tiny station. Walking in, he wondered why the driver made such a point about which gate they would depart from. With only two choices, it was obvious. They were the only bus at the station. Wouldn't it be clear which gate they should use to re-board?

Ambling over to the lunch counter, Neil stood perusing the board of meal options. The gravity of what he had done settled in his stomach, much like the pebble in his shoe. The thought of picking up and leaving without much of anything was rapidly dawning on him. Rummaging through his wallet, he found sixty three dollars, his driver's license, and an old business card, worn and faded. Along with the sixty-eight cents in change, he realized he was going to have to budget himself accordingly. At least until he was able to figure out how he was going to survive this escapade.

"Fried egg sandwich and a black coffee please" was what he settled on when the waitress with a hairnet and an old faded apron finally took his order. Looking at her, he thought she was the epitome of what you would expect to find in a run-down station like this. Maybe he'd have to write a song about her, too.

Cracking her gum, she asked, "are you sure that's all you want, honey?"

'Want?' he thought. 'Well, no. It's not really what I want. What I really want is to find success with my music. I want to find love. I want to order more food because I'll be hungry in an hour. I want so many things. But that's all that they are. Just wants.'

"Yes, ma'am, that's all for now. Thank you." With a

shrug of her shoulders, she turned, hanging the ticket for his order in the kitchen window. "He won't be the tipper that breaks the bank today," she mumbled, pouring his coffee. Looking back over her shoulder, she saw him slouched on the stool. Seeing that her boss wasn't looking, she slipped a piece of cherry pie into the bag with his sandwich.

"That'll be seventy-eight cents darlin'."

He handed her a dollar. "Sorry, it's not much, but keep the change."

Watching as he strolled back towards the bus, she stood shaking her head in wonder before turning to the other waitress next to her. "That boy has something about him. I can't place it, but I'm guessing we'll be seeing him again someday," she said.

Settling back into his seat by the window, Neil started opening the bag just as Sharon came back on board.

"Oh, what d'ya get?" she inquired.

"Nothing much, fried egg sandwich and coffee, and huh, a bonus. A slice of cherry pie. Couldn't really afford more than that. Not until I figure out what's next."

"Well, what is next?"

"I don't know. I thought you might be able to tell me. After all. You were the one who instigated this journey."

"Well, I can only speak for myself. Like I said earlier, I'm starting a new job in a new city. A fresh start, if you will. What you're going to do, though. Well. That's up to you. I kind of thought you had a plan. Seeing as how quickly you agreed to go. It seemed as though you needed that final push to get you off the fence."

In that moment, sitting in stunned silence, Neil realized he had no idea what was coming next. What was he thinking? Getting on a bus with a total stranger, leaving every-thing behind, and by everything, he meant everything except what he had with him right now. This must have been the stupidest, most asinine thing he's ever done. Who did he think he was? That he could just hop on a bus with a stranger? Without a plan? Did he think things would just magically work themselves out? What a fool he was. If he got off now, then maybe he could use the rest of his ticket to return home. Back to normal. Back to his insignificant life. Seeing the countryside passing by again, he knew he had lost that chance. The next stop would only put him another eight hours further away from what had been safe and that much closer to his new future. Maybe that's what he should focus on instead.

Chapter 5

Continuing on for what seemed an eternity, he felt as though he was trapped on this journey. It was only when they stopped at the stations along the route did he find moments of quiet, away from the obnoxious ramblings of the driver and the various noises of the passengers. Fortunately, somewhere in the middle of nowhere Texas, they switched out drivers, reducing some of the noise. Neil found he was able to get some sleep.

The bumps and rattles of the road kept him from falling into anything more than a light doze at first. It wasn't until when they crossed over into Arizona he must have fallen asleep hard. He dreamt of what he hoped was awaiting him in Los Angeles. Visions of movie stars and studios, the sunshine and bikini-clad girls. The clubs and all the music he would hear on the Sunset Strip swirled in his sleeping mind.

Arriving for a scheduled stop in Las Vegas, he woke up. Following Sharon into the terminal, he took this as an effort to shake out the cobwebs and stretch his legs. Coming in through the doors, he noted the driver talking with two police officers as he pointed in their direction.

"What's going on?" He asked Sharon, inclining his head toward the men.

"Dunno," she yawned. "Probably looking for someone who skipped on their tab at a casino, maybe."

Seeing as she didn't seem too concerned, he continued walking until the officers walking toward them stopped them.

"Sharon Taylor?" One officer barked.

"Who wants to know?" She flatly replied.

"We have a warrant for your arrest. Theft of services. Come with us, please." The second officer said to her, reaching for his handcuffs.

"Theft of what services? I have no idea what you are talking about. And I'm not going anywhere with you. I have to be back on that bus in less than ten minutes in order to make it to Los Angeles."

"No, ma'am, you aren't going anywhere. And your friend here isn't either."

"Wait, I don't understand," Neil interrupted, grabbing a tighter hold of his backpack.

"Your girlfriend here didn't pay for your tickets back in Arkansas. So, by connection, you are an accomplice to her theft. But you must have someone in your corner, because the agent back at the originating station isn't willing to press charges against you. Just her."

"But," Neil started.

"Sir. Please. Gather your belongings and come with us. We'll get this all sorted out at the station." The first cop instructed as his partner fastened the cuffs around Sharon's wrists.

Looking back and forth between Sharon, the driver, and the officers, Neil nodded in agreement. Reboarding the bus, he gathered her things as the driver retrieved Sharon's bags from below.

"Sorry son. I don't know what she's dragged you into. But consider yourself lucky the company isn't charging you for this, too."

"How am I supposed to get anywhere now? I don't have enough for the fare to return home or go on to Los Angeles."

The driver simply shrugged his shoulders, calling to the remaining passengers it was time to depart.

Standing there dumbfounded, Neil was left wondering what he was going to do next. Gaining his composure, he found the officers waiting outside, Sharon already in the backseat of the patrol car.

"You'll need to take a taxi and meet us at the station, son. We can't have the two working out your story, sitting in the same back seat." The second officer said, getting into the passenger side of the car. "Make sure you get there soon. Otherwise, we'll have to issue a warrant for you as well."

"Yes, sir." Left unsure of how he was going to pay for anything. He was hoping a taxi ride wouldn't cost too much. Exiting the bus station, he was now face to face with the reality of being in a strange city. Looking off to the left, he was astonished at the expanse of desert stretching out before him. Off to the right, he could see casino signs and Las Vegas strip. Walking over to a waiting taxi, he explained his predicament, hoping the driver would take pity, along with the shortest route possible.

Neil arrived a few minutes after the arresting officers

did. The desk sergeant directing him back to the squad room. Here he was told to wait until someone was available to take his statement.

Waiting in the hard chair, his backpack at his side, Neil's knee began bouncing to the beginnings of another song running through his mind. Reaching into his bag to pull out his notebook, he saw the officer coming towards him.

"Sorry to have kept you waiting. But this friend of yours. She's in a heap of trouble. What can you tell me about her?" The officer asked, pulling his notebook out of his pocket.

"Not much really." Neil replied.

"Sorry? She seems to think you two have known each other for years."

"Um, no. I just met her today, well, yesterday I guess. Or whenever it was that the bus left Forrest City. It's all a blur. I was trying to be nice and help her out. As her way of saying thanks, she said she had a voucher that allowed her to travel anywhere and take a guest along. I jumped at the chance. Foolishly, I suppose. Why should I even have thought that something that good, even on the off chance, was possibly true?" Neil replied, dejected and realizing the enormity of the situation he was finding himself in.

"Son, she's a known con. She's got warrants out on her in half a dozen states. You sure you didn't know any of this?" The look on the officer's face telling Neil he was finding it hard to believe that Neil wasn't somehow involved.

"No sir. Not one bit. I left home the night before. I was hoping to make my way to Memphis first. You know that's where Elvis got his start. Anyway, no. I thought it was just a misunderstanding between her and Fred at the station. Like

I said, I offered to help. Once it was all sorted, she asked if I wanted to go to Los Angeles. As her guest. I thought this could be the break I was looking for. I didn't consider maybe it was too good to be true. So I went. I Guess I should have given it another thought or two."

"Yeah, I'd say so. She's facing a lot of charges and is going to be held. She's been telling a convincing tale, saying that you knew exactly what was going on. But I can't charge you at the moment. The agent back in Forrest City vouched for you. Said you're a good kid. You didn't know her from Eve. However, that being said, you're gonna have to stick around here for a while. Until we get this all sorted out. Looks like Memphis, Los Angeles, or wherever, just aren't going to be in the cards for you right now."

Explaining he had little in the way of money, the officer offered Neil a few suggestions of cheap places to stay. "Find a job if you can, too. I can't say how long this will all take." As the officer took charge of Sharon's belongings, he continued. "At least you still have your stuff. You said you're a musician, maybe you can make some use of that. Plenty of places around here have bands. I'm sure one of 'em needs another player, singer, something."

"Yes, sir. Thank you. I guess once I'm settled, I'll let you know where you can find me."

Gathering up his belongings, he walked out of the station, head hanging down. Looking every bit the part of the hound dog Elvis sang about.

"This is not what I had in mind. At all." He said to no one. Crossing the street, hoping to find a place to stay.

Chapter 6

Finding the first three motels with no vacancy, he came across a place where they had a room he could afford, at least for a couple of days. Overwhelmed by the events of the past days, he let himself into the room. Falling onto the bed, not bothering to take off anything but his shoes. Exhaustion fast overtaking him, he slept fitfully for a few hours. After tossing and turning, he decided it was time to get undressed. Returning to bed the rest of the night, he was plagued by nightmares of what could happen next.

A knocking on his door woke him the following morning. Stumbling out of bed, he answered the door with a gruff, "what?"

"Sorry sir. Just wanted to see if you wanted your room cleaned this morning?" The housekeeper said, taken aback at his attitude and appearance.

"Right. Sorry. What day is it? Or rather, what time is it?" He asked apologetically.

"A little after 10, sir. I'll just come back in a little while," the maid said, pushing her cart to the next room.

"Thank you," he muttered.

Closing the door, Neil turned to face the room. Taking in his surroundings, he saw it wasn't much. A bed, dresser, chair and lamp in the corner. For now, it was enough. It met his basic needs. And it was cheap. Washing his face and dragging a comb through his hair, he looked at his reflection. Hoping it wouldn't take longer than a week, he decided he could stay that long. Maybe then he would find his way out of this situation he was now mired in.

Making his way down the stairs to the parking lot, he saw the coffeeshop next to the motel. Taking in his surroundings, he was finding Las Vegas vastly different from what he was used to finding in Forrest City. Here it was bright, noisy, and a constant energy in the air. Gone were the fields, country mornings, and night skies filled with stars. Oh, there were stars here, painted on the sign for the Atomic Diner. Stepping inside, he noticed the theme of the menu was spaceships, mushroom clouds, and atomic symbols. Finding an empty booth, he slid into the seat, perusing the menu, shaking his head at the corny names they gave their meals. A brief explanation about the atomic testing that took place in the desert gave him the history behind the diner's odd theme.

Neon signs reflecting in the windows, flashing lights atop the slot machines in the corner next to the cigarette machine, and posters for current and past shows plastered the walls. All the tourists that had been here before him had worn down the cheap vinyl of the seats and the formica table tops. How many of them were chasing down their dreams of fame and fortune? Or were they just after the quick fortune they hoped Lady Luck would bring them?

Knowing he didn't have the time or money for gambling, this entire trip had already been a crap shoot for him, he made a point to bypass the slot machines. Stuck here, in a town where he knew no one, the odds stacked against him. Trying to convince himself this was just a stop on the way to bigger and better opportunities in Los Angeles. Maybe he could find a job. One that would pay him enough where, after a couple of weeks that he could then afford a ticket the rest of the way.

Finishing his breakfast, he started walking to the register to pay, wondering where he could find a job. When he overheard three guys at the counter muttering about how they had just lost one of their players.

"Can you believe he just ran off with her like that?"

"Yeah, boss is gonna flip his lid when he finds out."

"How we gonna play without him? Not to mention, he took the guitar too. That wasn't his for the takin' man."

Without giving a first or second thought to who these guys were or where they played, Neil jumped into the conversation. "I'm sorry, I don't mean to interrupt, but did I hear you saying you need a guitar player?"

The biggest of the three swung his head around, laughing in Neil's face. "Who do you think you are, jumpin' in our business? Go on, now, get."

"Now hang on a minute, Clarence," another one interjected. "This kid's right. We do need a guitar player. At least let's find out. Who are you, kid?"

"Neil. Neil Evans sir. Sorry, I didn't mean to intrude. I just, well. I just arrived here yesterday and I'm looking for a gig. I was about to head out. Then heard ya'll talking and well..."

"Humph. Some southern boy we got here." The one they called Clarence replied, looking Neil up and down. "We don't need your kind, son."

Feeling the iciness and disdain dripping from Clarence as the other two shrunk back into their seats, Neil replied.

"I mean no disrespect, sir. For the record, I may be from the south, but I don't abide by that mentality. I'm trying to find my way out of that cesspool and chase down my dreams of playing with a band. Sorry to have bothered you. Good luck with your search. I hope it all works out for you."

Turning to walk out, he stopped when he heard one of the others call out to him. "Neil Evans. Be at The Crossroads casino, three o'clock this afternoon. We'll see what ya got."

Looking back over his shoulder, Neil nodded to the three men, biting his lip. He sprinted back up to his room, not wanting to say anything more that could change their minds. Now he had to figure out where to find a cheap guitar.

After showering and changing his clothes, he went down to the lobby asking if there was a pawn shop close by and what was the best way to get to The Crossroads. The front desk manager gave him a couple of recommendations within walking distance for the shops, but said a taxi would be the quickest way to the casino since it was on the other end of town, along the main strip.

Counting his change and the fact that Lady Luck had been on his side so far today, Neil decided he would try his luck with a slot machine in the corner. Even if he won a couple of bucks, it would be enough to cover the cab fare. Putting in the nickel, he pulled the lever and said a quick prayer. Three cherries in a row popped up as the machine paid him out a small jackpot for his nickel investment. Taking this as a good sign, he made his way out in search of a new guitar. Hopeful of the opportunities it could bring.

Arriving at the casino just before three, he found the sights and sounds just as overwhelming as he was expecting. Flashing lights and ringing bells greeting you as soon as you stepped through the doors. Somehow, coming in from the broad daylight, it seemed a little less glamorous than it did at night. As though the city was exposing what went on by giving him a peek at its underbelly.

With his guitar case in hand, Neil made his way back to where he was told to be. Walking into the unknown, or who to ask for, he found the club room. Coming face to face with Clarence, along with the other two guys from the coffeeshop he saw two more guys that hadn't been with them that morning.

"Well, well, if it ain't Arkansas in the house," Clarence boomed as the others laughed. "Didn't think you'd actually show up here. Guess you were serious after all."

"Yes sir. I told you, I'm looking to play. And I'm ready." Neil said, trying to find his confidence as he stood facing the five men sitting on the stage.

"Okay then. Come on up. Let's hear what you can do. This here is Leroy on drums, Duane on bass, Vernon on piano and Joe on horns. We've got others that come and back us up from time to time. But this here is the core of the group. Guest singers come and go. At the boss's whim, so don't worry none about that right now. We need someone who can play and roll with whatever is thrown our way. You think you can do that?"

"Yes sir, I can."

"Alright, enough with the sir. I'm Clarence. Let's see what ya got."

Joining them on stage, Clarence started by calling out a Frank Sinatra song. Having expected a standard like this, Neil started playing. Halfway through the song, Clarence shouted out another one. This time it was Twilight Time by the Platters, which Neil played to perfection. Thinking he would stump Neil, Clarence called another song, this one dating back to 1943. That Old Black Magic by Glenn Miller. Again, Neil performing as though he had been playing with them for years.

Impressed at how quickly he was adapting to whatever was thrown at him, Clarence nodded as he looked at the rest of the band. Vernon bowed his head in acknowledgement, Joe smiled, and Leroy gave one thumb up. A slap on the back from Duane was enough to show to Neil that he got the job. Indeed, maybe his luck was changing, his dream a little closer in sight.

Chapter 7

After a week of rehearsals with Clarence and the Tru Tones, Neil received his first paycheck. Having earned enough, he found he could to move out of the noisy motel he was staying in and into a small furnished apartment he could rent month to month. From the brief interaction he had with the building manager, he guessed they housed a lot of people who didn't stick around long. At least this was a place he could call his own, even for a little while.

Only having one day off a week, always a Tuesday, was fine with him. It wasn't as though he was going out on the town or doing much more than playing and eating. Knowing he didn't want to tempt fate again, he stayed away from any sort of games of chance after his one and only win on the slot machine. His focus had to be on saving enough money to make it to Los Angeles. He wasn't done chasing this dream of his, even though it would now take a little while longer.

Playing with the band turned out to be a great deal for

all involved. He had proven his talent and honor both, and had gotten to be friends, or at least acquaintances with the guys pretty quick. Even Clarence, after a couple of days of riding him pretty rough, relented and accepted him as a member of the band.

During rehearsal on Monday, while hearing Neil grumbling about how he hadn't had a good home-cooked meal since arriving, Duane turned to him.

"Tell you what. If it will shut you up, what do you say to you coming over for dinner tomorrow night? My Rosie is an amazing cook. And trust me, if she knows I made you this offer, she won't take no for an answer."

"Duane, no really. I'm just grousing. And I'm not looking to be an imposition. I guess I'm just missing my momma's cooking and well, her too. No one said being an adult would be easy."

Laughing, Duane shook his head. "Nah kid. It's all good. I wouldn't have offered if I wasn't serious about it." While scribbling on a cocktail napkin, he continued. "Here's the address. We'll eat around six. Come on over any time before that. And be sure to bring your appetite."

Grinning, Neil nodded. "Okay, you don't have to tell me twice. I'll be there."

Arriving at Duane's the next evening, he was met at the door by a young boy, no more than five years old.

Crouching down to his level, Neil said, "Hello. I'm Neil. What's your name?"

Before the boy could answer, Duane walked up, patting the boy on the head. "That's Joe. He doesn't say much. But he's a great kid."

"Nice to meet you, Joe. That was my grandpa's name, too. And he was a great man as well. And

Duane, thank you again for having me over. Based on what I'm smelling I can already tell I'm in for a good meal."

"Oh yeah. Rosie is one hell of a cook. That's why I stay married to her. But don't just stand here in the door. Come in, man."

Walking in, Neil looked around at the tidy home. It was a little place, but obviously a loving family lived here. Toys in the corner, records sticking out on the shelf, Duane's bass leaning against the doorjamb.

"Sorry, Duane. I almost forgot, these are for your wife." Neil said, handing over a bouquet of carnations and daisies. "Momma always told me you don't go to somebody's home empty-handed. And well, yeah."

Before Duane could accept the flowers, Rosie walked in to announce dinner was just about ready; they were only waiting on one more guest.

"Neil, this is Rosie, honey this is the young fella I was telling you about."

"Neil, it's lovely to meet you. Please have a seat. Tell Duane to fix you a drink. I'm sure Frank will be here in just another minute or two. In the meantime, I'll go put these in water. They are lovely. Thank you."

Excusing herself back to the kitchen, Duane and Neil settled down in the living room.

"Duane, you didn't mention someone else was coming. I hope I'm not intruding."

"Naw man. Franks a good friend. He works at the casino. You'll usually find him running security, but sometimes he'll fill in as a pit boss or anywhere else he's told to go. I think you'll like him. In fact, you remind me a little of him."

As if on cue, the doorbell rang as Duane excused himself to go answer.

"Frank, come in. Someone here I want you to meet."

"Duane, good to see you again," Neil overheard. That voice, sounding so familiar. But no, it couldn't be. Just as quick as the thought crossed his mind, he looked over to see someone walking in, who he hadn't seen in years.

"Uncle Frank? What are you doing here?" Neil exclaimed, jumping up from his seat.

"Neil? Duane, is this who you wanted me to meet? Why didn't you tell me it was my nephew?"

"Nephew? Man, what? You two are related?" Duane said. Looking back and forth at both men in disbelief.

"Yeah man, Neil is my sister's son. I haven't seen him since her funeral." Turning to Neil, he grabbed him in a bear hug and squeezed until Neil thought he would pass out.

"Uncle Frank, I can't breathe," he gasped.

"Right. Sorry. It's just been so long since I've seen you. And here of all places. What are you doing in Las Vegas, kid?"

"You wouldn't believe me if I told you."

"Well, you can regale us all with the tale over dinner," Duane announced as Rosie called out, they should all come to the table.

Sitting down at a table filled with food, Neil's stomach let out a loud growl. The smells had been intoxicating. But the sight of all this wonderful home cooked food was almost too much.

"Sit, please, and dig in. I made plenty enough to go around," Rosie said. "Now, did I hear that you two are related?"

"Yes ma'am," Neil laughed, "but I had no idea Uncle Frank was here in Las Vegas or that he was the Frank that you said would be joining us for dinner."

Smiling, Frank looked around the table, his gaze settling on Neil. "So. You want to tell me how you wound up here?"

In between bites, Neil briefly explained the story of his fight with his father, making the spontaneous decision to walk to the bus station, unsure of what exactly he was going to do next. Choking back the lump that he found forming in his throat, he paused. Resuming his story, he shared his encounter with Sharon and her offer of a ticket that should have gotten him all the way to Los Angeles.

"It turns out she was some sort of con woman or something. The voucher wasn't legit, after all. Thankfully, Fred, back at the station, was nice enough to take pity. Not pressing charges against me as well. But now I'm stuck until I can get this resolved with the cops. Eventually I'll make it to Los Angeles too, I guess."

"Why didn't you write? Tell me this was going on?" Frank asked. "I would have helped you out in a heartbeat. I know your daddy can be a stubborn mule sometimes. I still don't understand how my sister stayed married to him all those years."

"I don't know. I guess I thought you were busy with your own life and didn't want to burden you with any more of my problems. You were so nice to buy me that guitar and then daddy destroyed it. I guess I just couldn't. It didn't feel right asking again. It was more than you needed to do Uncle Frank."

"Neil, you know you can always count on me. And now,

well, since it seems we'll be working together, let's drop the uncle title. Alright?"

"Sure, unc… sorry, Frank. So what is it you do at The Crossroads?" Neil asked, taking another helping of the roast Rosie was offering.

"Oh, a little of this. A little of that. Not sure how much you've seen of what goes on around there. But every day it's something different. I guess I just haven't made it in to see the band since you joined, though."

Jumping into the conversation, Duane added, "Yeah, we've been keeping Neil on his toes. Rehearsals every day to make sure he's up to speed on the material. Gigs six nights a week. He hasn't had much time for anything else."

"Good. Good…" Frank replied. "Now that I know you're here, maybe one of these evenings I'll try to drop in and catch part of the show."

Something about the distracted way Frank said good unsettled Neil. It was as though Frank had something more to say, but he wasn't telling.

After finishing their meal, Frank, Duane, and Neil moved into the living room while Rosie brought out dessert and coffee.

Turning his attention back to Frank, Neil asked, "I thought you were still in New Orleans? How did you wind up here in Las Vegas?"

Taking a deep breath, Frank looked down at his feet before answering. "It was after your mom's funeral. I got back to New Orleans and it just didn't feel like home anymore. I can't quite explain it. The city was losing its appeal. And no, I never thought I'd say that about New Orleans. Our family has so much history there. We've been living in that city for what seems like forever. Then on top of that, I had a falling out with Victor. It was bad. I won't bore you with the details, but let's just say it was the last straw for me. It made the decision to leave that much easier. When I found out about the goings on in Las Vegas, I thought, why not give it a gamble? Not that I am enjoying the actual gambling part, but the music, all those big names that come through are honey to my ears."

Hearing this made Neil smile. Growing up, uncle Frank had always encouraged his musical dreams and was responsible for his varied taste in music.

Frank quickly glossed over details about how he wound up with a job at the casino. "It took me a few weeks to find my feet. Unlike you kid, who just happened to walk into a job the day after you arrive. But I digress. I worked at a couple of places. Short term, mostly dealing at blackjack tables. It was just enough for me to find my rhythm. Figure out how things worked around here. The first place, I lasted all of two days. But I will say in those two days I saw all the ways to not treat employees or customers. I got out of fast. Now I can happily say that place is no longer in business. Nor are the owners, from what I've been told. But that's just speculation." Taking a sip of his drink, he waved away the questions he knew Neil was about to ask.

"The next place was better. Definitely a step up. I stayed there a few months. I won't bore you with a lot of details. Got to deal blackjack and poker, manned the roulette wheel for a while and even had a short stint on the craps table. But I found I was happier when I could pitch in for the security team. Walking around the place. Keeping an eye on things. Attention to detail is one thing when you're face to face with just a few the gamblers, but it's a whole other level when you are overseeing the entire floor. You learn how to judge people. Their mannerisms are always the biggest tell. But if I'm being honest, that's also the best part of the job. You see all kinds of folks coming through. You thought Bourbon street at Mardi Gras was the place to people watch. Here, it's like that every day and night. Biggest perk so far though has been the shows. Clarence and the guys are fantastic. And the names we have come through, they are why I stay. Where else can I see and hear that caliber of music and get paid to do it?

It's crazy hours, as you have found out. And yet I wouldn't have it any other way. Speaking of, I hate to cut this short, but I do need to get going. Duane, thank you again for the invite. Rosie, as always, you've outdone yourself." Turning his attention to Neil, "and what a stroke of luck that we should meet up here like this. Never in my wildest dreams did I think you'd wind up here. Memphis or Chicago, sure. Los Angeles even. But here. Just one word of advice, kid. Be careful who you find yourself involved with. You'll come across some shady characters in this town who will use you for whatever they can and not give you a second thought when you take a fall. As you've already learned."

"Yes sir. I understand," Neil replied. Noting the genuine concern in his uncle's voice.

Getting up and stretching, Frank continued. "Alright. Now I have got to be getting back to work. Neil, you've got my number. You call if you need anything. I'm sure I'll see you around the casino. Oh, and stay away from those show-girls. They'll drag you into a heap of trouble faster than you can say blackjack."

Chapter 8

Arriving back at his apartment, Frank walked in, surprised to find Sharon sitting on his couch.

"Sharon? What trouble have you gotten yourself into this time?"

"Frank, honey. Is that any way to greet me after I've been gone for so long?" She purred.

"Oh, don't you honey me. You're lucky I sent Redd down to the station to get you out of jail. I should have just left you there. Especially now that I found out more information about that little stunt you pulled."

Standing, making her way to the small bar Frank had in the corner, she began pouring drinks. "Whatever are you talking about? I told you everything."

"No, Sharon, you didn't. You left out one very significant detail. That guy you dragged out here with you, he's my nephew."

Setting the bottle back down hard on the counter, Sharon turned, eyes wide open in disbelief. "Who? That kid? He's what? Oh, you're just being funny."

Closing the distance between them, he took the glass from her hand. "No, Sharon, I'm not kidding around. Neil is my nephew. My sister's son. What are the odds you'd wind up in Forrest City? And he'd show up at exactly the same time? This is bad Sharon. This is really bad."

Stepping back, Sharon stammered. "Well, how was I supposed to know who the kid was? He just helped me with my bags and diffused the situation that could have gotten worse had he not stepped in."

Frank glared at her as she continued.

"Okay, yeah, I got pinched once we hit the station here. The cops didn't charge him. So see, it's no big deal. And look at it this way. You get to have a family reunion. And he's that much closer to Los Angeles now. Who knows? Maybe he'll give up on that idea. Come work with you too?"

Trying to control his temper, Frank snarled. "Don't even suggest that. No, he can't know what I've gotten myself into. Hell, he doesn't even know I've changed my last name. Thankfully, Duane didn't mention my full name at dinner. As far as he knows, I'm still Frank Batiste. Not Frank Barnes."

"But -"

"No, Sharon, no. He can't know I'm going by a different name here. He needs to keep his head down and stay out of trouble. It's bad enough he's working at the Crossroads. This move to Los Angeles needs to happen, the sooner the better. You, on the other hand. You are going to have to keep a low profile for a while. And we can't be seen together. Not at work and definitely not here. He's got my number now and I'm sure it won't be long before he shows up here as well. I love that kid like he was my own. But he just can't know who I really am or what I've gotten myself into."

Chapter 9

Redd Doyle was tasked with the responsibility of making sure the band knew the boss wasn't happy about the fact that they lost their guitar player. Now he found himself tasked with running a background check on this new guy they had seemingly picked up off the street.

Stopping by the dressing room, he asked Clarence for more information. In typical Clarence fashion, he answered, "I don't know much about him. He's from some town in Arkansas. He thought he was going to Los Angeles, but wound up here. Kid is a damn excellent player. But, that's all I can tell you. Maybe ask Duane. He had him over for dinner last night. But why the sudden interest now? He's been playing with us for a few weeks now."

"It's just due diligence. Mr. Costa has been busy with other casino business until now. You guys aren't exactly high on his priority list. But he still likes to know who he's got working for him. So okay, I'll talk to Duane later. See what he has to say. Thanks for the help." Redd replied, holding the door open as the rest of the band strolled in.

Known around the Crossroads, Redd was always trying to see things from everyone else's point of view. Despite being one of the largest guys on the security team, working with Frank and the others, he was always the one guy the band guys and the showgirls could depend on. Had it not been for his connections to the Costa family through marriage, he probably would have found himself working a regular nine-to-five job somewhere. Living in a nice little house with his a wife and two kids. Maybe even a dog.

Returning to Nick Costa's private suite, he shared with the owner and boss of the Crossroads casino what little he had found out so far. "I've got one of the guys running down other background information on this kid, too. As soon as I find out anything else, I'll be sure to give you the full report, Mr. Costa."

With a nod and wave of his hand to dismiss him, Redd quickly left. Well aware, the most important detail of his job on the security team was keeping an eye on all the money flowing through the games. The second next important task was to keep those in charge aware of any changes in personnel.

Tonight, Mr. Costa would be entertaining VIPs at his table in the clubroom. Redd was told to make sure everything was in order. Hence the reason for the sudden need to run a background check on the new kid.

Clarence, back in the dressing room, was reminding the band that Mr. Costa and guests would be in the house tonight. Pointing out the fact where they would be sitting would offer a full view of everything that went on in the room.

Neil found himself more nervous than usual. This was his first time playing a show for an audience as important as this one. He had to be sure to leave a good impression. He didn't want to do anything that could possibly mess thing up for him or his uncle. Since he was unsure if anyone else besides Duane knew of his connection to Frank.

Taking the stage, Clarence counted them in, starting with "All My Tomorrows". Finishing the first song, Neil saw his uncle Frank and three other gentlemen he had never seen before walk in and take seats at the reserved table. If it wasn't apparent he was nervous before, the sweat covering Neil's brow was a sure sign that he was now.

Taking a deep breath to steady his nerves, he drilled his focus in on the chart in front of him. The fear of reprisals kept him from playing any wrong notes. Just before walking on stage, the other guys in the band had given him a heads up about how hard Nick had the potential to be. He was going to make sure to not give any reason for him to lose this job.

Finishing the set on a high note, the band returned to the dressing room. A knock on the door revealed a delivery of a bottle of champagne. The note simply saying, "Good job, boys." Neil felt his breathing return to normal as the rest of the guys in the band passed the bottle around.

Clarence turned to him and said with a slap on the back, "well I guess you met Nick's approval. So that's all that was left. Welcome to the band, son."

Neil laughed, shaking his head. "I don't think I've ever been more nervous. I was sure I was going to play the wrong note. Heck, the wrong song, even when I saw him and the others walk in."

"Nah, man. We had your back. Nothing was going to go

wrong. You've more than proven yourself these past few weeks. Shoot, the day we met you, you showed us what you had, jumpin' in our business like that."

Vernon, usually the quiet one of the bunch, added his two cents worth. "Yeah man. You solid."

Looking around at the guys, Neil smiled. "Thanks. All of you. I didn't think this would happen this fast, but wow. Here I am."

"Yeah, yeah. Just don't let it go to your head, big shot." Clarence joked. "Alright. Parties over. We got two more sets to play. Let's get back to it, fellas."

Walking back out on stage, Neil surveyed the rest of the room. More people had wandered in. He saw couples taking a break from the tables, businessmen away from their families acting like they were single men again, and even what looked like a few families. None with small children. That was definitely something you wouldn't find in the casinos.

He saw a table with what looked like two couples at a business dinner, accompanied by a young redhead about his age. Was she the daughter of one of the couples, maybe? She appeared to be bored out of her mind, twirling a strand of hair around her finger while alternately playing with the food on her plate. Briefly catching her eye, he smiled, but couldn't tell if she had actually seen him or not. Mentally kicking himself, he reminded his brain and his heart that he was here to play music. This was to be his stepping stone. Allowing him to move on to bigger and better things, he had to focus. Falling in love was not in the cards for him now.

Chapter 10

"**O**h, my aching neck."

"You're not kidding. And my feet."

"I can't wait to slip into a warm bath. Just stay put until the water is cold."

Typical of the conversation overheard in the showgirls' dressing room after the nightly shows. They put in the required hard work every night. The headdresses alone weighing up to twenty pounds. Not to mention the heels they had to wear? Even at 2 inches, it felt like they were on stilts.

"Hey, Patsy, throw me my robe, will ya?" Monica hollered from behind a dressing screen.

"Incoming!" Patsy replied, balling up the slinky piece of silk, its colors reminiscent of a painting you'd find in a museum.

Audrey was trying to stifle a laugh with little success. She was always laughing, it seemed, no matter what anyone said. And it wasn't a delicate giggle, either. She had a belly laugh that once started, she just couldn't quit.

"What's got you in stitches tonight? Huh?" Monica asked as she came out from behind the screen. Her silk dress hugging her curves in all the right places.

"Incoming. I don't know why that struck me so funny. Maybe it's been the tests they've been doing out in the desert this week. It rattles my place sometimes. I always think it's the end of the world when I see one of those clouds. How soon before it really happens?"

"Seriously Audrey, how can you laugh at that? It's a serious thing they're doing out there?" Patsy chastised.

Raising an eyebrow and looking over at one of her best friends, Audrey replied, "because if I don't laugh, I think I may cry. I lost my dad in the big war, and every time they test, I'm reminded of that. And what this world has become. And kids in school, practicing their duck and covers. It's just heartbreaking."

Moving over to hug her friend, Monica nodded. "I'm sorry, honey. I know. We all lost someone in that awful war. If it makes you feel better to laugh, then I say, by all means, laugh. We could all use some humor, I think. Hey, who's up for drinks and maybe we can catch the end of Jerry's show, too?"

"Now that sounds like the best idea I've heard all night." Audrey replied, hugging her friend in return. She didn't know what she would have done had it not been for the support from these girls. They had been working together now for two years. They were tighter than sisters, sharing everything; secrets, love stories, break up tales, and even clothes. Despite the glamorous appearances, the pay and the working conditions were anything but.

The casino supplied the costumes, but the shoes, stockings, and makeup were all provided at their own expense.

Stockings, because they wore through them so quickly, often became a premium purchase that they couldn't always afford. Continuing to lobby the show producer to have management at least pay for half of that expense. There were occasions when they would be generous and give them all two new pairs. But those times came few and far between.

Since they were going out after having finished their show, the girls could wear their own clothes, not having to worry about dressing the part.

Monica would be sure to turn the heads tonight. Capturing the attention of the guys. Patsy, on the other hand, was opting for her capris and a twinset that she had worn into work earlier that evening. The casinos would be cold. Even though the summer night temperatures were still hovering around 80 degrees. She wasn't one who liked to be chilled artificially. How she longed for the fall and winter nights. When it was cool outside and they could bundle up in the sweaters and furs that admirers had gifted to them.

Audrey finished changing into her skirt and sweater, removing all the stage makeup. Now she looked as though she wasn't much older than a high school student. This choice of clothing only accentuated that as well. All that was missing now was a ponytail to complete the look. After Monica, the guys immediately gravitated to her. Was something about the schoolgirl look they liked? Or was it just her fresh face? Whatever it was, she was never lacking for male attention either.

Patsy, waiting by the door for the others, almost lost her balance as Sharon burst in.

"My god, where have you been?" She cried out as she regained her composure.

Hugging all of her friends, Sharon explained. "I got pinched by the cops just as I got back here. Some smart Alec in Arkansas apparently didn't believe my voucher charade. It took them a while to catch up and then find me. But the cops were waiting when I got off the bus. I Almost thought I was going to make it. All the way to Los Angeles this time, but…" she trailed off.

"Oh honey, I told you this was going to happen one of these days. Did Frank come bail you out?" Monica chimed in.

"No. I tried to manage it myself, but I wound up having to call Redd. When I tried to surprise Frank at his place, well, let's just say, he wasn't happy to see me. Turns out this kid I invited to come along with me was, get this, his nephew!" She exclaimed.

A chorus of what's rang out, along with the questioning looks all directed at her.

"Yup. There was this guy. He just happened to come into the station while I was there. One of the workers there was giving me a hard time when I tried to buy my ticket. Apparently, the southern gentleman persona is really a thing. This kid came over to my rescue. Girls. The look he had in his eyes. I could tell he just wanted so desperately to leave that podunk town. When I invited him to come along, figuring he'd turn me down, he actually jumped at the chance. Seeing this as my chance to deflect attention and deciding he'd make good cover, I managed to finagle two tickets. I'm guessing that was my downfall. Had I stuck to the plan and only tried only for one, I probably would've gone unnoticed."

"Wait, Frank has a nephew? And he's here?" Monica was intrigued. "Does he look anything like Frank?"

"Whoa, slow down girl. Yes, Frank has a nephew. From Arkansas. I don't know all the details. Whose side of the family he's on and all that. But the kid is good looking, I'll give you that. But Frank said, hands off. He doesn't want Neil knowing anything about what he's doing here. The kid thinks he's on the up and up. And Frank intends to keep it that way. He doesn't want the kid getting into any trouble. I guess he's a musician of some kind."

"He wouldn't happen to be a guitar player, would he?" Patsy asked.

"I think so. Why?"

"Because the band just hired a new player. From what you're saying, it sounds like it could be this Neil fella. So how exactly is Frank going to keep it a secret from him that he's connected if they are both working for Nick?"

Sharon just shrugged her shoulders. "I guess that's for him to figure out. But enough about them. What's the plan for tonight? Are we going out or what?"

Chapter 11

Settling into his routine of work, practice, and sleep, Neil found little time for much else. His thoughts wandered back to the red-headed girl he noticed in the crowd one night. There with her family, she was unlike any of the other girls he had come across around this city. Most appeared to be just as made up as the strip was at night. Flashy and glamorous, but come daylight, the cracks began to show. Not that you didn't encounter some great beauties in the daylight. Yet life was so different here than it was back in Forrest City. He was finding it to be one of the hardest things to acclimate to. The hustle and bustle, the constant barrage of sounds, sights, and smells. He reminded himself, a relationship was not what he needed to get wrapped up in. Not if he was going to chase his musical dreams. Find a way out of here.

Now, when he found himself restless at night. He was no longer kept awake by the neon lights illuminating his room, but by the thoughts of all he observed and overheard in the casino.

The casual gambler, a pretty obvious character to spot. He and his family were passing through town, heading somewhere else on vacation. You would find him in front of a slot machine, dropping in a few nickels. Or maybe if he was feeling adventurous, he'd venture over to the blackjack table or roulette wheel. He'd lose ten, maybe twenty dollars at the most, then call it a night. His wife and kids waiting for him upstairs in the room. Neil was guessing this trip was more about making memories with them.

Then you had the hard core gamblers. They were the ones that you'd come across sitting in a chair when you arrived for work in the afternoon. And they'd still be in the same spot in the early morning hours when you leaving for the night. They were the ones the casino girls would always hang around. The men always hoping a pretty girl would bring good luck. It seemed like they were interchangeable arm candy. He was sure these guys couldn't tell you the names of the girls. When their luck took a turn for the worse, one girl would be sent on her way. Only to be replaced by another one. Neil had noticed it was often the same girls night after night. Were they on payroll here at the casino he wondered? Maybe they were off duty showgirls trying to make a few extra bucks. There was still so much he didn't understand. About the way this place and the city at large operated.

At least once a week he would make a point of meeting up with Frank for lunch or dinner. Whatever meal they could squeeze into their competing schedules. Frank always seemed to be busier than him. He never let on exactly what was taking up his time. He would tell Neil one day he was overseeing the gaming tables, making sure all the dealers were playing on the up and up. Another day, he was in charge of security. Working in some back room. Hidden away from guests and employees who didn't have any connection to that side of the business.

Frank was evasive when Neil asked where he was living. His excuse always was how small of a place he had. But he was hardly ever there, so it didn't matter. One benefit of his job, he said, was a reserved staff room available in the hotel. Often his long hours would prevent him from being able to go home, so he'd crash in the room, take a shower, grabbing an extra suit and change of clothes that he kept in his office.

At first, Neil thought maybe this elusiveness was due in part to the security sensitivities of Frank's job. He tried understanding why Frank didn't want to discuss those sorts of things with him. It didn't concern him or his job as a band member. But one night when he was on a break, while crossing the casino floor, he had overhead a conversation between two other guys he had seen frequently working with Frank. Guessing they were some sort of security from the way they were dressed and patrolling the place, he diverted his path, trying to keep a safe distance.

Hearing Redd saying something about "the boss" not being pleased with Frank's latest heist. 'Heist?' Neil thought. 'But isn't he supposed to be taking care of security? Why would he be on the opposite side? What could Frank be up to?' He wasn't about to interrupt them to ask. But who else could he trust enough to raise these concerns with?

Before he could dwell on these thoughts any longer, he noticed a woman walking deliberately towards them. She sure looked an awful lot like Sharon, he thought. But what would the woman who conned him, leaving him stranded here, be doing at the Crossroads? Shouldn't she still be in jail? Inching his way closer, hoping to hear more, he did a double take when he heard her mention Frank's name. What was that she said? Was she asking where Frank was? How does she know him? Now he had even more questions.

Debating whether to follow her, he watched as she walked towards the elevators. Maybe she was just a regular in the casino? Surely that's how she knew Frank. Or perhaps it was just a sheer coincidence. Just as it had been him winding up here. Perhaps Las Vegas wasn't as big of a town as he first thought it was.

Lost in these thoughts, he didn't notice that she stopped walking, causing him to crash straight into her back. "Oh, sorry. Excuse me," he started.

"Yes. Well. Excuse you," a voice said in reply.

Catching sight of Frank approaching, Neil saw a look on his face showing something was terribly wrong. Facing the back of the woman he ran into, he looked back at Frank when he heard the woman's voice saying, "right, let me get out of your way. You seem to be in a hurry to get somewhere."

Stepping up to the both of them, Frank asked, "everything alright here ma'am?"

"Yes, sorry. I just stopped to adjust my shoe and this gentleman plowed into me. I don't think he was watching where he was going."

At a loss for words, Neil nodded until he could find his voice. "Um, yes. Sorry. I wasn't paying attention. The band was just on a short break. But I need to get back to work now. Again, I'm sorry."

Frank looked at Neil. Then back at Sharon. He could see

she was trying her best to keep her face turned away from Neil. "I'll take care of her, Neil. Go on. Get back to the club. The band is probably waiting on you."

"Yes, of course. Sorry again." Neil said, slowly making his way back toward the hall. Glancing back over his shoulder, he got a good look at her. Now he was sure that was Sharon. The same woman he met and shared the bus ride with.

Unable to hear their conversation, he could see the urgency on Frank's face. Certain now that they had some connection, he wondered what could it be? Why wouldn't he tell me he knew her when I told him about how I wound up here?

Keeping his suspicions to himself for the time being, he vowed to find out more. There was more going on and he wanted to know why Frank was being so secretive.

Chapter 12

"What are you doing here, Sharon? I thought you were told to stay away from the Cross-roads." Frank hissed.

"I had to stop in. Take care of a few things. The girls have been calling and leaving messages. I couldn't leave them hanging. I thought I'd be able to get in and out quickly. At least without being detected. The band was supposed to still be playing. How was I supposed to know they were going to be on break? Or that Neil would come out here?" She started sobbing, while trying to regain her composure and sweet talk Frank at the same time.

"You need to get out of here. Now. And just hope he didn't recognize you. I don't think he got a good look at you. But would he remember your voice? Did you two talk while you were on the bus?"

"I don't know. Not much. I mean, he was pretty lost in thought or sleeping the entire trip. I think he was having doubts about what he'd done. But he seems to have fit in pretty well here. Don't you think you ought to tell him what you're up to now? Maybe even involve him, too?"

"No. He can never know. His mother didn't know about all that I was involved in when I was living in New Orleans, and I can't have him knowing what I'm doing here, either. As far as he's concerned, my last name is still Batiste too. He doesn't know I'm going by Barnes out here. Or that I can't go back to New Orleans any time soon. It's bad enough he's working here. I don't think he knows about the level of involvement of the connected families here, and I'm doing my best to keep it that way. Even the guys in the band have been kept in the dark about this latest plan."

"But you're going to need my help, right? I'm still a part of this plan, am I not?"

"I don't know yet. Redd and Michael are handling details right now. They keep me appraised of what's going on until I need to get further involved. So no. Your part is done."

"Your not getting cold feet, are you? This is going to be one of the biggest jobs any of you have pulled off. Nick is really not going to be happy if anything happens to foul it up."

"I know. I know. The magnitude of this is huge. And I know Michael thinks we should involve the band. And if it weren't for the fact that Neil is with them now, I probably would have. But like I keep telling you, I can't have him knowing what's going on. If they can maintain deniability, all the better. Then I hope the cops will go easy on them. I can't let anything happen to Neil. I just wish I could get him out of here."

"Well, he was heading to Los Angeles. Maybe you can

give him the bus fare? That way he could the rest of the way there?"

"He'd never take it. The kid is too proud. It's a trait that runs deep in the family. He's got the talent to make it. But he'll want to do it on his own. Also, he'll ask too many questions. Why am I trying to get rid of him so quickly? Now that we've just reconnected?"

"What about getting one of the girls to distract him? I don't think Audrey is involved with anyone right now. What about introducing the two of them?"

"Maybe. I don't know. I'm afraid if he gets involved with her, then he might want to stick around longer than any of us want him to. No. He needs to come to the idea that he needs to go. And soon. On his own. Speaking of going. You need to get out of here."

"And just what am I supposed to do, Frank? I have bills to pay ya know. I don't work, I don't get paid. And I, or rather we, still have the police to deal with."

"I get it. But there is too much riding on the outcome of this. Any little mistake, the whole thing could be blown. Do you want to be on the wrong end of Nick?"

Sharon knew he was right when she saw the serious expression on Frank's face. The last thing anyone wanted to do was to get on the wrong side of Nick Costa. "So, what do you suggest I do?"

"Regarding the police, you need to deal with that one. This was your screw up. It's yours to fix. As far as you working the casino floor, tell you what. Check in with Clarence. Find out their schedule. Avoid being seen during any of the times that Neil might be out on the floor. Then you can probably pull this off. In the meantime, I'll talk to him, tell him to hang out backstage or in the club room between sets, instead of coming out on the floor. I can convince him it's a casino policy. That way, he comes to work and leaves again. That should give us all some cover."

"Fine. But Frank, be careful. He's a smart kid. He's bound to find out what's going on. Sooner or later."

"Let's hope for later. Much later."

Chapter 13

Making his way back to the dressing room, Neil couldn't shake the idea that his uncle was hiding something more about his connection with Sharon from him. But what could it be? The fact that he was in Las Vegas and not New Orleans? That had been a surprise. To be sure. But then again, Frank was single. He always did like to travel. The idea he was here looking for a new adventure was plausible. But what role did Sharon play in his life?

Should he talk to Audrey and ask her if she knew anything more about Frank and his relationships? Or would that seem odd? Why would she share any information with him? After all, she didn't know him either. Maybe he should just focus on playing music. Save up enough to purchase a ticket to Los Angeles. Hopefully, he'd have enough left over to get him settled. Until he could find work.

As if fate was looking out for him, it showed up as both he and Audrey came out of their respective dressing rooms.

"Hey honey, how's it going this evening? You look a bit down." She smiled at him.

"Hey Audrey. I'm fine. Just thinking about stuff."

"Stuff, huh?" She laughed. "Sounds really important and deep."

Neil looked at her and shrugged. "Yeah, not really. I guess it's just me still being the new kid around here. Seems there's a lot I don't know."

"Maybe that's for the best. Some things around here are better left unknown. If you know what I mean," she told him, patting his arm.

"Do you think, maybe - " Neil started to say when he heard Clarence calling him. "Sorry. Never mind. That's my cue to get back on stage."

Before letting go of his arm, Audrey stopped him, saying, "hey, let's meet for coffee later. I think you could use someone to talk to. I may not have answers, but it could be fun. Meet me at the coffee shop when your next set is done."

"Yeah, sure. I'll see you then."

Making his way back to the stage, he knew he had to set aside his thoughts of anything not related to music. His brain was on adrenaline overdrive. Was he reading more into situations that weren't anything other than what they appeared on the surface? Hopefully, meeting with Audrey could shed some light on the inner workings of the casino. In addition to the people here, and Las Vegas in general. He had only heard stories about the city before he arrived, never thinking he'd find himself fully immersed in them, though.

After the second set, Neil stopped in the dressing room, discarding his jacket. No sense drawing more attention to himself than necessary. The entire walk to the coffee shop, he wondered how much Audrey would be willing to tell him. Or was her motive behind the meeting to see if she could be the first to turn his head and heart?

Walking in, scanning the room, he didn't recognize her at first. She was sitting in a back booth, dressed in her street clothes. 'What did you expect? She'd come in dressed in full costume?' He scolded himself.

Settling in across from her, he indicated to the approaching waitress two coffees. He didn't want anyone to hear their conversation, in case somehow something got back to Frank.

"So. How long have you been in Las Vegas? A few weeks?" Audrey asked, blowing on her coffee before taking a sip.

"Yeah, not long in comparison to everyone else, that's for certain. Not sure how long I'll stay either. I mean, don't get me wrong, I'm enjoying playing with the guys and catching up with my uncle has been great too. Aside from that. This isn't what I was dreaming of when I left home."

Laughing, Audrey set down her cup and took Neil's hand. "Honey, no one expects to wind up here. Somehow, you just do. Some leave, a lot stay, others just disappear into thin air. Maybe they get vaporized in those crazy tests out in the desert. Who knows? But you? No. I know you won't be here long. You've got too much in your future to keep you here. And honestly - " stopping mid sentence, she glanced around before her continuing, "the less you know, the better off you'll be."

"What do you mean?" Neil questioned.

"I mean, I know you love your uncle, but sweetie, he's mixed up with some not so good people. We all are. Just a lot of us don't know it. Or don't want to admit it, anyway. What I can tell you is a lot of the rumors you've heard are true. This place. This town. Is run by, well, you know. Even if you don't know them personally. The politicians. The cops and those in charge. They all put on a good front. But they also look the other way. In a lot more cases than not. And if you want to survive, I suggest you do the same."

"But then, why are you still here? Surely you could go somewhere else, do something else?"

"Neil, you're young and so naïve. Unless I find some rich guy who wants to sweep me off my feet and take me away from all this, I'm stuck here. Sure. I'm working to save money for school, but even once I save enough and decide what I want to do, I'd still be stuck here in this city. Instead, I figure why not make some good money, have fun while I'm at it? I can still dream, but I know what my future holds. And it's not going to be one like Marge's either."

"Why doesn't someone in charge do something about it? You know, the…"

"Shush, don't say it out loud. Yeah, I know who. But like I said. Those in power want to stay in power. And in order to do so, well, here we are again. Full circle. You need to think about what your next steps are going to be and how soon you're going to get out of this town."

Audrey continued on a little longer. Detailing some people Neil had seen but didn't know. She explained the hierarchy of Nick, Frank, Michael, Redd and others.

"Now you have a little bit better understanding. And like your uncle has told you too, keep your nose clean. Stay away from the tables. And oh yeah, stay away from us girls, too. We'll only break your heart." She said, scooting out of her seat. Leaning down, she gave him a kiss on the cheek.

"Thanks for the coffee and the company. See you back at it tomorrow night." Audrey waved as she made her way out of the coffee shop.

Neil, finding his mind wandering, stayed seated, trying to take in all the information that Audrey shared when he spotted Redd and Frank entering. They appeared to be having a heated discussion. Neil knew he shouldn't come in the middle of. He didn't think Frank noticed him when they passed his booth as he overheard him saying, "I'll take care of it, Redd. Nick has nothing to worry about. Plans are in motion. The job will get done. Soon enough, the necklace will be in his safe. No one will suspect a thing. Blame will fall on the courier, maybe one of the cashiers. But there won't be anything linking it to Nick, the family, or any of us."

Chapter 14

S crambling and trying not to be noticed, Neil was trying to get out of the booth and the coffee shop. Feeling as though the room was spinning, he was hoping he wouldn't run into anyone else. He wanted time to gather his thoughts. He didn't think he'd be able to hide the evidence of the chaos that was running through his head at the moment. What was his uncle up to? Were they actually talking about stealing a necklace? Why would Frank take part in something like that? And Nick and the family? What was that all about? He saw Nick Costa and knew he knew he was the owner of the casino. But what family? Audrey had explained a bit about the mob connections existing. Was that who Frank was referring to? Surely the Crossroads wasn't one of those places. And Sharon? Was she involved in this, too? Had she been involved since he first met her back in Forrest City?

'Good grief, what have I gotten myself into now?' He wondered, making his way back down the hall to the dressing room to grab his jacket. Should he ask any of the guys in the band? Or would they just laugh him out of the room? How could he have been so naïve? First, he gets conned into taking the bus with that woman. Then he winds up taking a job at a mob run casino. What next? Is he going to take the fall for a job that his uncle is planning? No. None of this made any sense to him. He had to talk to someone, but who could he possibly confide in? And should he warn Clarence? If what he heard was true, could the band be in trouble, too?

While it had only been a short time that he'd been playing with them, these guys were becoming like family to him. It had been a rough start. Clarence giving him the hardest time, making assumptions about his prejudices before he even got to know Neil. Assuming because Neil was from Arkansas that he must be a card carrying bigot. That was the farthest thing from the truth. By the end of the second week, Neil felt like he had proven himself. As both a musician and as a human being who cared about others. Now, at least Clarence was only getting on his case about his guitar playing and nothing else.

Duane had been the most gracious one. Taking Neil in. Having him over for dinner, introducing him to his family and inadvertently reconnecting him and his uncle. Uncle Frank. Maybe he should just go straight to the source and ask him. He must have misheard what Frank said. Was he just making assumptions on only a half of a conversation? After all, wasn't Frank part of the security team? Maybe he was trying to avert something from happening. Yes, that had to be it. Frank was trying to get ahead of someone that had plans in place to try and steal the necklace and was just trying to protect the casino and its owner.

Calming himself down, splashing water on his face, he

jumped when the door flew open. The rest of the band pouring in. "Alright guys, last set. Let's make it a good one. The tip jar already filled up once this evening. Let's try to get overflowing for this one." Clarence called out.

"Ready boss." Leroy called while giving Neil a side eye. "Dude! What's up with the wet face? Trying a new look?"

"Ha, ha. No. Just played hard during that last set and need to cool myself down." He replied.

"Quit the jawing and let's go. There's money to be made. We don't get it by standing around back here." Clarence barked.

After a raucous last set, Neil returned straight to the dressing room as the rest of the band mingled in the crowd. Packing up his stage clothes and guitar, he decided he would go find Frank and ask him outright. Hadn't grandpa Joe and uncle Frank always taught him honesty was the best policy? Now was the time to put that policy to the test. Of course, Frank would tell him it was nothing. He was just overreacting to something. Or that it was all just a big misunderstanding. That's it. Just a misunderstanding. Neil convinced himself as he made his way into the casino. By the time he got around to finding Frank, he was sure he had misheard the entire conversation. That nothing illegal was going to happen.

Spotting his uncle in a roped off area by the baccarat table, Neil observed Frank keeping a watchful eye on the dealers, as well as the players. 'It must be a tough job,' Neil thought. 'All that responsibility. Having to monitor so many moving parts all at once. Why hadn't Frank found a regular job and settled down?'

When Neil saw Frank smiling at his approach, he knew Frank had no idea of all of his questions. This wasn't the place to bring them up, either. Walking up to the rope, he slapped a goofy grin on his face and called out, "Frank!"

"Neil. Great to see you. How's things?"

"Good. Good. I just finished for the night."

"Great man. You settling in okay?"

"Yeah. I think Clarence has finally accepted me. The rest of the guys have been great, too. All this playing is really honing my skills, too."

"Fantastic." Frank replied, as he continue keeping a watchful eye on all the activity.

"Listen, uncle Frank, sorry, Frank. Do you think we could get together and talk?"

Hearing the unease in Neil's voice, Frank moved closer, looking at his nephew. "Neil? You sure everything's okay? You didn't get yourself into trouble here, did you?"

"No, nothing like that. I've been avoiding any sort of gambling. I'm trying to save every penny I can so I can get to Los Angeles. No, it's nothing. I just had a few questions. Thought maybe we could chat." Trying to hide his discomfort. He didn't enjoy fibbing to his uncle.

"Alright. Tell you what, why don't we meet for breakfast, say around 9:30 tomorrow. I've still got to finish some work here. And you look like you could use a good night's sleep."

"Sure, 9:30 tomorrow. At say, the Atomic Diner?" Neil laughed. "I know, corny name, but I found they've got some pretty good food."

Frank smiled at the thought of his nephew finding the Atomic Diner as serving good food. "Right. Atomic Diner, 9:30. I'll see you then, kid."

Chapter 15

Watching Neil leave, Frank took the time to consider what his next steps should be. He could tell something was bothering Neil. He didn't think Neil would know anything about what Frank and the others had been planning. Having seen his nephew and Audrey in between sets in the coffeeshop earlier, he wondered if something was going on between them? Maybe he had gotten into trouble some other way. With no other family around, he was just turning to Frank. Or maybe it had something to do with that run in with Sharon? Did he recognize her after all? Damnit. That woman was supposed to stay away from Neil. 'If she's been back around him again, I'm going to have to do something with her,' he thought to himself. When he saw Nick coming his way, it snapped his attention back to reality in a heartbeat.

"Frankie boy. How are you this evening?"

Nick Costa was an imposing man. Not in physical stature, but in the demeanor he projected. He could enter a room full of the top name stars and all eyes would immediately turn to him. Something about the man made you give him your undivided attention. Whether it was the perfectly tailored suits he wore, the hair that was just never quite perfect, but yet somehow always in place, or the piercing eyes. For Frank, it was definitely the eyes. They could look at you in that moment and know whether you were telling the truth. They could size you up, knowing exactly the man you were and what you had the potential to become.

As long as you didn't do anything to get on the wrong side of him, Nick Costa could be your best friend, your guardian angel. But one wrong step to cross him, and well, unless you got out of town right away, things did not go well for you after that.

"Nick. Great. Things are running smoothly. Everyone seems to be having a good time."

"Good, good. Glad to hear that. Walk with me, will you?" It was not really a question. When Nick suggested you walk with him, you did, no matter if it was in the opposite direction of where you were going or taking you away from your regular responsibilities.

"Sure Nick."

Strolling down the hall, approaching the main casino floor. Nick stopped, looking around, satisfied with what he saw. Gamblers at the tables and slot machines, waitresses delivering drinks, lights flashing, noise humming, a good night indeed.

"So tell me, was that your nephew I saw you talking to just now?"

"Um, yeah. Neil."

"Neil, right. How's he settling in?"

"Pretty good, I think. He's been playing with the band

for a few weeks now. As far as I know, he's just playing, eating and sleeping. I haven't seen him at any of the tables."

"Uh huh. And what about the girls? Has he been bothering them at all?"

"No. No sir. I don't think he's even considered any of them. He's a pretty shy kid when it comes to the girls. Had his heart broken pretty hard back home. No, if I had to guess, I'd say he's keeping clean. I'm supposed to have breakfast with him tomorrow, though. I can find out more if you really need me to."

"No, Frankie, that's fine. I just wanted to check. Make sure he was settling in okay. You know. We have to look out for all of our employees here. We don't want any of them caught up in anything they shouldn't be. If you know what I mean?" Nick turned and looked Frank in the eye, his tone challenging Frank to consider carefully what his next words might be.

"Of course, Nick. I understand. And as far as I know, he's keeping his nose out of everyone else's business. Like I said, eat, sleep, play guitar. That's pretty much his life right now. If anything should change, well, I'll take care of it. You can count on that."

"Good to hear. So tell me, how are our other plans coming along?"

"Everything is coming along just fine. Redd and I were discussing it earlier, and I don't see any obstacles that might present themselves. My only concern is…"

"Concerns? Frank, now is not the time to be having concerns. Didn't you just said there weren't any obstacles? Now you have concerns."

"No sir. Not concerns really. Bad choice of words on my part I guess. I just don't want to see any of the guys in the band get in any trouble. That's all. Especially now that Neil is with them. He is family, after all. He doesn't have any clue as to what I do here. I'd like to keep it that way."

"The boys will be fine. As long as they are on stage playing, doing what they normally do, they should come out of this unscathed too. They're just cover Frank, remember that. If all goes well, as you seem to be assuring me it will. Then everyone will be just fine. Your nephew will be none the wiser either. Capiche?"

"Yes sir."

"Good. Now. I'm starving. How about we get a drink and a bite?"

Chapter 16

Waking the next morning, Neil found himself more nervous than usual about his breakfast with Frank. He knew he had nothing to be worried about. Yet he still had a nagging thought that wouldn't leave him be. Feeling as though Frank was holding back. Why had he left New Orleans and come to Las Vegas? Sure, he had said the music brought him here. But with Memphis being so close, even Chicago and the music scene in either of those cities, Las Vegas just didn't strike him as a music lovers' destination.

Had it not been for uncle Frank and all he had done for him, Neil might not have even been here today. Well, playing guitar, that is. Frank had always encouraged Neil when it came to music. Sharing his extensive record collection with him every time they'd visit. He was responsible for introducing him to artists like Billie Holiday, Charlie Parker, Hank Williams, and even Aaron Copland. There was no genre he hadn't didn't have some exposure to. It was always uncle Frank and grandpa Joe, both pushing him to chase his musical dreams. More than anything, they both wanted to see him get out of Forrest City.

Get out, he did. Though winding up in Las Vegas hadn't been what he had foreseen in his plans, he figured he could have done worse. Thankfully, the police didn't bring any charges and were now leaving him alone. He had told them all he could about Sharon. Even if it wasn't much. Running into her at the casino had been a strange turn of events. He found himself thinking that Frank must know her somehow. But how? Why? What was their connection? Just another one of many questions to ask him about at breakfast, he thought.

A quick glance around the one-room apartment satisfied him everything was where it should be. It wasn't much of a place. But at least he could afford it and it came furnished. Just one less thing he had to worry about spending any money on. Besides, how would he get that stuff to Los Angeles when he was ready to move? It wasn't like he had a car or truck he could use to move anything. No. If he was getting to Los Angeles, it would be by bus again. Though this time he'd pay for his own ticket, making sure it was a valid trip.

Looking over at his guitar, he was overwhelmed by the memories flooding through his mind. Memories of momma and home. Perched on its stand where it belonged, he could feel it waiting for him to pick it up and start writing again. Without giving a second thought, he walked over, picked it up, and strummed a few chords. He had the beginnings of a new song building in his head. Feeling the weight of the instrument in his hands, the pressure of the strings against his fingers, this helped take the edge off the nerves that had been intensifying. Trying to calm himself as much as possible before breakfast with Frank, he played a few more notes. Now he felt a little more prepared for what the day may hold.

Arriving at the Atomic Diner a few minutes early, he slid into a booth back in the corner. Hoping this would offer them some privacy and a chance to talk without interruption. Right at 9:30 Frank came striding in the door. Looking like a man ready to take on the world. He exuded a confidence Neil hoped someday to possess, too. He still looked up to him as a role model. Despite all the unknowns of what or who his uncle was involved in.

Neil waved him over as the waitress came by with a cup of coffee. "Two please," he said as Frank slid into the seat across from him.

"Good morning Neil. I see you're bright eyed and bushy tailed this morning."

"Good morning to you too, unc-, uh, Frank. You certainly are chipper this morning."

"It's a fine day. I'm here with my favorite nephew for breakfast. What more could a man want?" Frank replied, all smiles.

Ordering two mushroom cloud specials in an effort to send the waitress away, Frank wasted no time diving right in to the conversation.

"So, what's on your mind Neil? You seemed a bit out of sorts last night. Everything okay? You haven't been losing money at the slot machines, have you?"

"No. No," Neil insisted. "Nothing like that at all. It's just well..." he trailed off, unsure of where to begin.

The waitress returned, filling their coffee cups, while informing them their food would be out soon. Frank nodded before turning his attention back to Neil.

"You're wondering about the woman you bumped into aren't you?" Frank asked.

"Well. Yes. But -"

Frank cut him off, saying, "Before you get too far ahead of yourself, I admit, I haven't been completely upfront with you about everything. Now, don't go asking questions yet, just hear me out." He paused to take a sip of the coffee, considering his next words carefully.

"As you may have already guessed, I do know that woman from your ill-fated bus trip. Yes, Sharon. No, I didn't know that she had been in Forrest City. The fact that you two wound up on the same bus and that she supposedly paid for your ticket, that was all news to me. The last time I saw her, she was on her way back to New Orleans. I thought she was still there. Never in my wildest dreams did I think you two would ever meet. Why would I?"

"But, I don't understand. Who is she to you? You say you knew her in New Orleans and she was here too. Was she your girlfriend or something?"

"Or something. Yeah. We worked together at a place down there. When I left, she stayed behind. A few months after I started at the Crossroads, she showed up. I don't know how she found me."

"But I still don't understand why did you wind up here in Las Vegas, Frank? It just seems like such an odd place to choose. I mean, sure they've got music out here. But I would have thought you would have wound up in Chicago, or New York, Memphis even."

"Like I told you over dinner at Duane's. I came out for a change of pace. I was about ready to leave again when one of the guys I knew from this club in New Orleans contacted me. He was looking for someone to take over their security team at The Crossroads. It seems the last guy they had working wasn't so secure, shall we say. I figured, what the heck, I'd give it one more chance. I went for a visit one night. Liked what I saw, and who I met. Deciding to stay was a simple decision."

Interrupted by the waitress delivering their food, Neil took his time considering the story his uncle had been telling him so far. Nothing seemed unbelievable and didn't conflict with what he had told him before. It all made sense. Frank always had an eye for the women. There was no lack of eye candy around here.

"So tell me about the Crossroads then. I don't know much about it. Or any of the casinos, really. I've been so busy rehearsing and playing with the band every night. I haven't had time to do anything else."

"What's to tell?" Frank said in between bites. "People come in. They spend way too much money on the games. Most go home with nothing left in their pockets, but they are still full of good memories of shows, girls, free flowing drinks, and good food. A few will win big sometimes, but for the most part, it's all harmless fun. Where else are you able to just walk down the road and see the likes of the Rat Pack, Don Rickles, or even Dorothy Dandridge. Not to mention all the stars that come for a visit. They'll come at any given time for a night of fun and frivolity. Just wait until you see Marilyn Monroe walking in the door. Then you'll understand."

"What about the owner, Nick Costa, I think is his name? I haven't had a chance to meet him. I know I saw you with him and some other guests one night in the club when we were playing. What's he like? And what about these rumors I hear about the casinos being run by the mob?" Neil was trying to be as casual as he could, but when he mentioned Nick's name and a mob connection, he swore he could see a flash cross Frank's eyes.

"Mr. Costa is a good guy. I've known him for a while now.He's a family man, a good boss, and always fair to the staff. Unlike some places out here, where you'll still run into bigots like you're used to dealing with back home, he doesn't consider any of that when it comes to who works for him. You do your job well, he rewards you. You don't. Well, here's the door."

Frank paused a moment, weighing his next words and lowering his voice. "As to any mob connections. Well, Neil. Be careful who you say that around. This town has ears everywhere. Despite it being a 'bright lights, big city' it's still a small town when it comes to the gaming world."

Neil looked at his uncle, taking in what he just heard. "But uncle Frank -" he started.

Holding up a hand to silence him, Frank admonished Neil. "No buts Neil. I mean it. Keep your head down. Do your job, save your money, get out of this town as quick as you came. This is no place for someone like you. You've got big dreams, and I want to see your name headlining, surrounded by those neon lights on the marquee some day. If you stay here. That's not going to happen."

Pushing his plate away, Neil looked at Frank. He could tell Frank was holding back. Was he involved with the mob and trying to protect Neil or was he just genuinely concerned for his nephew, wanting him to find success pursuing this crazy dream of his? Mustering his courage to ask the hard question, he took a deep breath then blurted out, "are you involved with them?"

Frank looked at his nephew. Reminding himself, he had

always been honest with him whenever he asked any tough questions. Neil had asked many over the years. But now, he was faced with a crisis. He couldn't very well confess his connections to the mob. Both here and back in New Orleans. Especially not in such a public place. What if he did? Would Neil take that information to the police? Or worse yet. Would it get back to Nick? That would lead to even more dire consequences. Possibly for both of them. Determining his best course of action was to tell a partial truth, he suggested that he and Neil take a drive.

"We can't discuss this here. I'll pay the check and meet you out at my car."

Chapter 17

Settling into Franks 1959 Thunderbird convertible, Neil noted the car, like everything else out here, was flashy too. A sleek, red convertible, the tail fins giving it that extra look of style. As Frank put the white top down, taking full advantage of the sunshine and warm temperatures of the late April morning, Neil chuckled to himself at how clean and polished everything was. Frank always cared about how everything looked. Watching the heads turning as they drove up and down the streets of Las Vegas. Neil saw Frank exuding confidence, as if to say he didn't have a care in the world.

This drive was the most Neil had seen of the city since his arrival. He had been relying on the bus, taxis, and rides from coworkers ever since he found himself here. For the briefest of moments, he considered buying a car, but that would wipe out his savings. He wasn't ready to commit to that expense, especially if he wanted to get to Los Angeles.

Admiring the interior, the soft leather seats, the polished wood trim, he reached over to tune in the radio. An Elvis song playing made him stop on a station as he settled back to enjoy the ride.

"Where we off to, uncle Frank?"

"Anywhere you want Neil. How much of the city have you seen?"

"Nothing. Other than my apartment, the diner and work. I've been keeping pretty much to myself."

"Well then, let me show you the sights." Putting on his best tour guide voice, he started, "Over here on your right we have the Sahara, home to the Conga Room. Over on your left is the El Rancho. And of course, you have the Stardust. The Desert Inn and last, but not least, the Sands. Where all the big names wind up."

Neil laughed as Frank continued his tour guide spiel.

"As you have already noticed. There are a lot of places around here trying to capitalize on the atomic testing that goes on out in the desert. Why people plan vacations around coming out to watch bombs explode in the desert is beyond me. But you'll see beauty pageants where all the girls are dressed up as different atomic elements and mushroom clouds, and of course the specials at the restaurants, well those you've already discovered."

Neil interrupted, "What can you tell me about Audrey?"

"Tell me you're not getting involved with her," Frank admonished.

"No, nothing like that. I swear. We just had coffee between sets the other night. I was curious about her as a person. How someone as smart as she is could wind up working as a showgirl."

Frank glanced at Neil, trying to gauge the change of direction of the conversation.

"She's a good kid. I think she's trying to save up some

money so she can go to nursing school, maybe? A lot of these girls only do it for a little while. It's not a career path. It's more of a stopover on their way to other things. Mostly, I think they're looking for their ticket out. Like you, they're all chasing a dream. So is Los Angeles still your dream, kid?"

"I think so. The glitz and glam here is nice. As is the steady paycheck, but I don't see sticking around if I want to make it someday. But I still question. Do I have the talent to make it in that cut-throat town? Maybe I should stick around here for a while? Keep playing with the guys. It is a good gig, after all."

Turning to look at Neil, Frank admonished him. "Listen to me, kid. If you're not careful, this town will suck the soul right out of you. What you don't see is what goes on behind scenes, the neon lights, feather boas, headdresses and all the games. There is a whole other side of this city. I don't want to see you getting involved in. And don't you ever question if you have the talent. Believe me, you do. I've heard a lot of the greats over the years. You keep playing and practicing and you'll be on your way soon enough."

Nodding, Neil looked over at Frank. Trying to muster the nerve to address the topic he kept dancing around. "Well, Frank, that's something I wanted to ask you about," Neil started. "I'm not sure how to begin."

"Just ask. You know I won't hide anything from you."

Taking a deep breath, then slowly letting it out, he considered how to phrase his next question.

"Is there something else you're not telling me?"

"What do you mean?"

"The other night. Well, a few things that happened. Of course, you were a part of the run in with Sharon. But you told me you didn't know her. And now you tell me you do, yet somehow I feel like you're still not telling me the whole truth. You've never lied to me before, Frank. Why start now? Aren't you the one that always told me to tell the truth? Even when it hurts?"

Frank kept his eyes on the road in front of him, not saying anything. He gripped the wheel tighter in an effort to control the emotions that were bubbling inside of him.

Seeing that Frank wasn't going to say anything, Neil continued.

"Then I overheard a conversation between Redd and Michael. I think he was the other guy. They were talking about a plan for the 'boss' and also mentioned you in the conversation. It didn't sound like something on the up and up. Then I saw you and Redd having a rather intense discussion in the coffee shop, and well, it got me wondering."

"Wondering what?" Frank asked, noncommittal in his tone.

"Well, you're always warning me about the seedy side of this city. Even today as we're driving around, you seem to be reiterating the idea that I need to keep my nose clean. Why are you pushing so hard? Is there something you've gotten mixed up in? Are you in trouble uncle Frank?"

Deciding he should put an end to this line of questioning without other distractions, Frank saw a sign for a gas station just ahead. How could he tell his nephew that yes, he was in fact tied in with the mob? To the same mob he had just been warning him about. It would shatter any positive notions that Neil had of him, likely even ruining their relationship. Could he risk that?

"I need to get out and stretch my legs a minute. Mind keeping an eye on the fill up while I do?"

Looking at Frank, Neil wondered what was he up to? Why was he avoiding answering the questions? Or was there something more going on that he couldn't share?

"Sure. No problem." He replied, watching Frank walk towards the station while the attendant hustled over to fill the tank, check the oil, and clean the windshield.

Neil was now certain Frank was hiding something. He saw him fumbling in his pocket for change when he got to the payphone in the corner. He could see it wasn't a pleasant conversation by the frown crossing his uncle's face. Even with it being too far away to hear anything. Who could he be talking to? And what were they saying? Lost in these thoughts, he didn't see or hear Frank come back to the car until he heard the car door close.

"Ready to see some more?" Frank asked, a little too cheerfully.

"Sure," Neil replied. Realizing he wasn't going to get any answers to his questions that day.

"Let's head over to check out the atomic testing grounds, then. Maybe we can figure out what all the fuss is about." Frank said, repositioning his sunglasses and turning up the radio, signaling an end to their previous conversation. As Frank eased the car back on to the road, Neil leaned back in his seat, considering what he learned and what questions remained.

A short while later, a giant billboard proclaiming this was the hotspot for atomic testing vacations, welcomed to the town of Indian Springs. Check in with the visitors' center for more information if anyone was interested in observing a test the sign instructed.

Looking around, Neil saw it was smaller than he expected. All the houses looked the same, with their perfect yards, white picket fences, and American flags flying. Further off in the distance he could see low buildings, clustered together, surrounded by fencing. 'Must be the military base,' he thought to himself.

Frank pulled into a parking spot in front of an official-looking building. The sign out front indicating this was the location for the chamber office, visitors center, and sheriff's department all in one. "Let's go in. We'll see what information we can find here." Frank suggested, getting out of the car.

Walking into the lobby, a bubbly receptionist greeted Frank and Neil. She gave them a detailed narrative of all that Indian Springs had to offer. Unfortunately, no testing would take place today, so they wouldn't get to see that "terrific sight", as she liked to describe it. Of course, they were always welcome to come back again.

Thanking her, Frank held the door open for Neil as they headed back out to the car.

"Sorry. That was a waste of a drive out here, uncle." Neil said.

"Nonsense. It gave us a chance to spend some time together. That's what this day is all about. Get you out. It gave you a chance to see some sights that you haven't yet had a chance to experience. Let's head back to the city, we'll pick up your clothes and guitar, and then I'll drop you off at work. I'm guessing you're playing again tonight?"

"Yeah. That sounds good." Neil replied as he took one last look around the tiny town. Still baffled at why anyone would plan a vacation or even live here.

Chapter 18

After their tour, which amounted to just a leisurely drive around Indian Springs, Frank dropped Neil back off at the Crossroads, telling him he'd catch up to him later. He said he had a couple of errands to take care of before he could come back to work. As he was heading inside, Neil avoided the casino floor as much as he could while making his way back toward the dressing rooms when Audrey stopped him in the hall.

Smiling at her, even with Frank's admonishment still ringing in his ears, he did his best to keep their interaction short. He had to make it clear to her and any of the other showgirls, his only goal here to play his guitar and save up his money. He didn't plan on sticking around this crazy town any longer than was necessary.

"Hey, Neil. Where ya been?" Audrey asked as he approached the door to the dressing room.

"Audrey, oh, hi. Uh, Frank took me out for a drive to show me around the town. Seeing as how I haven't seen much since I got here."

"Oh, that sounds fun. Hope he showed you some good sights."

"Yeah, it was enlightening for sure. Sorry, I don't mean to be rude, but I really have to get in and start getting ready for tonight's show." Neil said, pushing open the door.

"Sure. Okay," Audrey replied with a tone of dejection. "I guess I'll see you out on stage later, then."

"Right. See ya," Neil said as he stepped across the threshold of the dressing room.

Fully aware now, word had gotten around to most of the staff that he was Frank's nephew. He was going to do his best to maintain a businesslike relationship at work. Even with this new found status granting Neil access to places where he wouldn't otherwise be able to go, he thought maybe he should also now make it a point to avoid going to Frank's office unless he was called.

While rummaging through his gear bag, he found he didn't have his keys and wallet in his gear bag. Thinking maybe he left them in Frank's car, he figured this was going to have to be one of those times when he'd have to go uninvited.

Approaching the office, Neil could hear raised voices. It sounded like Redd was worked up about something, his voice punctuating the air. Stopping just outside the door, he decided it was best to wait until it sounded like the situation was calming down. He absolutely didn't want to walk in on the middle of something. Or make everyone else any more agitated.

When he heard Frank saying, "Okay, look, I get that you're concerned that Marylin is bringing in her own security too. But it will actually work to our advantage. They'll all be focused on keeping her safe, and keeping the adoring fans away from her. This frees us up to post our security in other places around the casino. We'll have clear access to the rooms and safe. No one will be the wiser."

Startled by what he heard, Neil tripped, bumping loudly into the door, pushing it open.

Apologizing when everyone in the room turned to see who came in. "Um, sorry. I see you're busy. I'll come back later,"

"Neil. Hey man, what's up?" Frank asked. The look on his face indicating his concern about how much Neil may have heard.

Neil shook his head as he looked at Frank, then Redd, then Michael, then back to Frank again. "It's nothing Frank. It can keep for now."

"No, we were just finishing up here. Redd, you and Michael go tell Nick everything is taken care of. We'll work out the rest of the details next week. By then we have the rest of the information we need. Got it?"

Michael, being a man of few words, just nodded. Redd started to say something. Seeing the look on Frank's face took a beat and replied, "yeah, boss. Got it."

Turning his attention back to Neil, Frank nodded at the chair that Redd had just vacated. "What can I do for my favorite nephew?" He said, trying to lighten the heavy mood permeating the room.

"Um, I didn't think you'd be back already. I was just going to leave a note on your desk. But if this isn't a good time, I can come back." Neil wasn't sure what he had just overheard. The way his uncle was acting was making him more uncomfortable by the moment.

"No, no, it's fine. Redd can just be rather high-strung about things. It's what happens when you have an Irish father and an Italian mother. He seems to have gotten both the best and worst of their temperaments. As I'm sure you've heard. We've got Marylin Monroe coming in to perform with you guys for one night in just a couple of weeks. He's just worried about security and all the fans that might invade the place, too."

Frank paused, picking up the drink from his desk, taking a sip and watching Neil's reaction over the rim of the glass. Setting it down, he continued, "Yeah, when I dropped you off, I decided I probably should come back in instead of taking care of the errands. So here I am. And as far as Marylin coming. Heck. For all you know, this will be the break you need to move up into the big time. She'll take one look at you, and between your good looks and playing, she'll whisk you off to Los Angeles. I'm sure someday you'll have girls chasing after you just like her fans chase after her. With those Batiste good looks and your talent, it will happen in no time."

Neil laughed at the thought of having hordes of screaming girls chasing after him. "Only in my dreams, Frank. I sure don't see that happening if I don't get out of this place."

"Hey now, don't knock it kid. Lots of big names got their start here. But that's not what you came here for now. Is it? What's up?"

Stopping to consider his next words, Neil was unsure of how to best phrase his concerns. Before he was able to answer, Redd came bursting back through the door. "Boss, we got a problem on the floor."

Shaking his head as he stood, he looked at Neil. "It's always something. We'll talk later, okay?"

"Yeah, sure. It was nothing important, anyway. Go. Take care of whatever it is you've got going on."

"Eh, just another disgruntled gambler, I'm sure." Frank said as he walked out the door. Neil stayed, still sitting in the chair, mulling over the view out the window and the information he had overheard before coming in.

Wondering what to do next, Redd interrupted his thoughts, sticking his head back in the door. "Hey man, you guys are getting ready to go back on. Think maybe you ought to get back down there?"

Chapter 19

Standing in the back of the club, Frank watched the patrons watching the band. When the band reached their half-way mark, Frank gave the signal to Redd and Michael it was time to go, trying to ignore his concerns that Neil could see them from where he was on the stage. Despite the fact they were trying to be inconspicuous, it was hard to miss the likes of Redd and Michael leaving anywhere. Glancing back, he noticed Vernon watching him. Turning his head, he saw Neil only had eyes on his music. "At least someone is paying attention to what they're supposed to be doing," Frank muttered to himself.

Exiting, Redd returned to the security office, while Michael went out to the main casino floor. Frank took the long way around. Making his way back to the security office. Checking the security cameras before nodding to Redd, they made their way out to the back service elevator. In order for this small heist to go off without a hitch, they had to be certain none of them were in the same place together. Not any longer than what would appear normal and necessary. Two of them in the service elevator made sense and raised no suspicions. But had it been all three, that had the potential to raise the eyebrows for the other guys in charge of watching the security cameras.

The cameras had been a recent addition. Nick being sure he was careful where he had them installed. He had been more concerned about catching gamblers on the floor trying to cheat at cards than he was about watching his staff. Due to increased pressure from local law enforcement, he made a show of putting a few in the back of house areas to in order to discourage any employee theft. Frank was well aware of the fact that one camera was always trained on the service elevator, having been involved with the installation.

When the elevator stopped one floor below their intended destination, Frank exited and turned right to make his way down the hall towards the main elevator. Redd remained advancing to the next floor, where he would meet up with Michael in the designated room. If all went according to plan, Frank would be back making his rounds on the main floor while Redd and Michael were finding their way out using separate back exits. They would then meet up back in Frank's office half an hour later.

Walking down the hall, Frank interrupted a couple who had obviously already had too much to drink for the evening. The woman was trying hard to guide her date to their room. Though Frank was guessing they weren't husband and wife. He kept hearing the man insisting he was going back to the gaming tables.

"Excuse me, can I help you with something?" He asked the couple.

"Nah," the man slurred. "I's jus telling the little lady

here that my luck is still runnin' high. I need to get back to the roulette wheel. I'm on a streak here."

The woman shook her head as if trying to signal to Frank that it was more of a losing streak without saying as much.

"I see. Well sir, I'm part of the staff here. Let me get word down to them that you're coming back in a bit, and they'll keep a chair available for you. But in the meantime, I think you ought to go rest. Even for just a few minutes. I think maybe your wife might want a moment to freshen up, too."

"Ha! That's a good one," the man hiccuped. "This here ain't my wife. But you will make sure they don't give away my lucky seat. Then alright. I guess it wouldn't hurt to take a brief moment in the room."

"Of course. I will see to it right away. Here, though. Let me help you with that door. These keys can be a bit tricky sometimes," Frank showed as he unlocked the door for the couple. "Have a good night now. And thanks for staying at the Crossroads."

Walking away, he could hear the guy crashing about in the room. Wondering how long it would take before he found his way to the bed and passed out. He was also hoping that this serendipitous delay was long enough to divert any suspicion from his involvement with what was taking place one floor up.

Arriving back down on the main floor, he made his way to the roulette table, checking in with the croupier regarding the gentleman who had just left. The croupier informed Frank the guy had only dropped a couple hundred dollars when the woman steered him away. "He appeared to be pretty drunk, though," the croupier said, pointing out who the waitress had been working at the table. Frank thanked him. Going over to the bar station to check and see how much the guy had had to drink.

"He must have ordered 5 or 6 martinis for himself and at least two cosmopolitans for his date in the span of an hour, but honestly, I never saw him actually drink them. His glass was empty every time I came back through, so I guess he must have been throwing them back pretty quick."

Hearing this gave Frank a moment of discomfort. He had known the cops to pull stunts like this before. They would come in, giving the impression that they were high-rollers, while making a show of flashing the cash and keeping everyone running for food and drinks. Yet somehow they would manage to pass off the drinks, always when no one was looking. Maybe they had someone else coming around with a bucket. Or something else that they would pour them into. All the while keeping their sobriety and wits about them. It was one of their ways of staking out the place. But why would they be here tonight? Maybe everyone was just on edge in anticipation of Marylin's visit. They were all well aware of the crowds it would bring out. The high rollers, the stars, and, of course, the crazy fans too. That must be the answer. Everyone was practicing tonight. He remained standing at the bar while hoping it wouldn't interfere with Redd and Michael and what they were up to at that exact moment.

Not five minutes after the thought passed through Frank's head, he spotted Redd walking towards him, a look of concern on his face.

"What's going on?" Frank asked as he met Redd halfway.

"They grabbed Leroy just as the band came off the stage."

"Who exactly grabbed Leroy?"

"The cops. Two of 'em waiting backstage when the band got done. I don't know what's going on man. But they got him in cuffs back there."

"Did they stop any of the others? Neil?"

"Nah, just Leroy. It's weird. They won't let anyone else in, they just kept saying they needed to ask him some questions. But I don't get it Frank. Why would they need to cuff him just to ask questions? And why here? Wouldn't they take him to the station? Something ain't right."

Frank thought for a minute before responding. "Okay, here's what you do. You go back to work act as though nothing's going on. Michael will be out soon, I'm sure. As long as you guys did what you were supposed to. Then no one is the wiser. In the meantime, I'll go back. See what this is all about. If the cops are harassing our band or employees, we should've been told they were coming. In the meantime, say nothing."

"Got it, boss." Redd said as he walked away, heading to the opposite side of the casino.

As he worked his way back to the band's dressing room, Frank kept running through the different possibilities of what the cops could be doing. Wondering if it was somehow connected to the scene at the roulette wheel. But what could they want with Leroy?

Coming around the corner, he found Clarence, Joe and Vernon standing in the hall. Duane, walking out of the men's room, almost ran into Frank. Much to his relief, Neil was nowhere to be found.

"What's going on, Clarence? I just heard the cops are back here with Leroy. Care to explain?"

"I don't know man. We came off stage. Your, er rather Neil, went out front to get a soda. The rest of us guys came back here. Only we found these two cops waiting. They grabbed Leroy before we could ask what they were doing and shoved him into the dressing room, locking us out. We been out here ever since."

"Alright, let me get to the bottom of this," Frank said as he removed his keys from his pocket. Unlocking the door, he heard Leroy saying, "yeah, Frank is the kid's uncle. But that's all I know man." Followed by an unintelligible mumble from one cop when he noticed Frank come into the room.

"We're a bit busy here. Come back later." One officer barked.

"No, I don't think I'll do that. You see, I'm Frank Barnes. I'm in charge of security around here. If there is a problem with one of my employees, I am to be notified. Definitely before you all come barging in and harassing him. Now. Would you kindly remove the cuffs from his wrists, then tell me in detail what is going on here?" Frank demanded, pushing his way further into the room.

"Mr. Barnes, we believe that Leroy here has some information that is vital to a case we're investigating. We didn't want to bother you with this. The chief thought we could get in and out quickly. We've asked him our questions, so we'll be on our way now." The second officer explained as he went about making a show of removing the cuffs and placing them back on his belt.

"Not so fast. Leroy, you go and join the rest of the guys. You still have another set to do. And don't worry about these two bothering you anymore. If they have anymore questions, I'm sure they'll go through the proper channels next time." Turning his attention back to the cops, he continued, "now, you two. Let's take a walk to my office. We can discuss what this is all about there. Or do I need to call the chief of police at home? Get him involved too?"

They followed Frank out of the room, realizing they'd not only get a chewing out but possibly a suspension as well if he made that call.

Coming off the stage, Neil made his way to the back end of the bar, finding an empty stool next to Duane's wife, Rosie.

"Um, Neil. You need to get back to the dressing room. Something's going on. And I think, well, yeah. You just need to get back there." Rosie said with worry in her voice.

Looking at Rosie and seeing the concern on her face, he asked. "What do you mean? I thought the guys just went back. What could have happened in the short amount of time it took me to walk from the stage to here?"

"I don't know. Clarence, Joe, Vernon, and Duane were all in the hall when I came out of the ladies' room. Leroy was nowhere to be found. But the look on Duane's face was not his normal calm and happy. I didn't ask, figuring it was best for me to get out. But I'm worried Neil."

"Yeah, I'll go see what's going on. If the bartender comes back, could you get me a soda?"

"Of course. I'll have someone set it up on your stand."

Nodding his thanks, Neil headed back towards the dressing room.

Arriving in the back hall, he saw Frank walking away with two police officers. 'That's weird,' he thought to himself. 'I wonder what's going on?'

"Neil, son, where you been?" Clarence asked.

"Out front getting a soda. Chatting with Rosie. Man, what's happening here? I just saw Frank walking out with two cops."

"Yeah man. They dragged Leroy into the dressing room just as we came off stage. Got no idea why. Leroy's at the bar trying to calm his nerves. Wouldn't say anything about what it was all about. The boy's wound up tighter than his drum."

"Huh. Well, I'll just have to ask Frank about it later, I guess."

"Right, I keep forgetting the man is your uncle. Yeah, maybe you can find out what's up with our boy. I hate to think I'm going to have to find a replacement for another guy so soon. Just after finding you. It's starting to feel like a revolving door going on here." Turning his attention to everyone else, Clarence called out, "Okay, Duane, you go fetch Leroy from the bar. Next set is just the usual. Let's put all this mess behind us and entertain these folks. Tips are depending on it."

COMING off stage at the end of the night, Neil packed up his guitar, then made a beeline straight for Frank's office. Still unable to shake the nagging thoughts he was having about why the cops were there. Leroy still wasn't telling anyone what they had questioned him about, either. When Neil asked one last time, Leroy snapped at him and told him, "leave it alone, man. Just leave it alone."

Navigating his way through the back halls, Neil was

almost to Frank's office. When he was stopped by the same two cops he had seen earlier.

"Neil Evans?"

"Yes, that's me."

"Come with us, please."

"Why? What's going on?"

"Sir. Please don't make this any harder than it has to be. Your uncle has asked us not to use the cuffs. But if we have to, we will."

"My uncle? What are you talking about? Am I under arrest or something? I haven't done anything."

Just then, Frank exited his office, looking downcast. "Neil, just go with them. I tried to tell them it was all just a misunderstanding, but they won't listen to me."

"But Frank," Neil started.

"Neil, look at me," Frank interrupted. "Go with them. Don't say anything. I've got a lawyer coming to meet you. We'll get this all sorted out."

Nodding his head, Neil handed his guitar to his uncle. "Alright, I'll come with you. No cuffs."

The officers looked at each other. Then back to Frank, before turning to Neil again. "Alright. Let's go out the back. We've got a car waiting. I'm sure we can get this all cleared up at the station."

Chapter 20

S itting in the interrogation room, Neil couldn't help but wonder what this was all about. The officers that brought him in said nothing the entire ride over. The desk sergeant that processed him was gruff. A man of few words as well.

Heeding his uncle's advice, he didn't say a word, other than "I'm waiting for my lawyer." Alone in the cold, grey room, he sat looking out the only window, a small square offering a limited view of the parking lot. A knock, followed by the door opening, interrupted his spiraling thoughts. "Neil Evans? I'm Patrick Leary, your lawyer. Have you said anything at all?"

Standing up to shake his hand, Neil replied, "No, sir. I kept my mouth shut. But I don't understand. Why am I here? I haven't done anything. Is this related to the bus ticket that the woman supposedly bought me? I thought that was all resolved and the bus company wasn't pressing charges."

"Please, Neil, have a seat. I'm sure we can get this

resolved fast," Patrick said, indicating the seat across the table. "Now. Let me take a look at the paperwork. See what we can figure out." Flipping through the few pages, hemming and hawing, Patrick finally looked back up at Neil. "Son, it appears that this Sharon Taylor is now saying that you were the one who instigated the trip. That it was your idea for her to present this fake voucher. She says you two started off in New Orleans, made a stop in Forrest City, Arkansas, and then were heading for Los Angeles."

"What?" Neil exclaimed. "No! None of that is true. Ask Fred back at the station in Forrest City. He knows me. I've lived in that town my entire life. I had nothing to do with this. I was just trying to help her out. I found myself caught up in this whole mess. How can she say all that now?" Running his hands down his face, Neil looked at the lawyer, dejected.

"Tell you what. We'll get the officers in here and see what else they'll tell us and we can get this straightened out. If what you say is true, we'll get you cleared of this mess."

"If what I say is true?" Incredulous, Neil just looked at Mr. Patrick Leary as if he had a second head growing out of his shoulders. "Where is my uncle? He can clear this up. I think he knows this Sharon woman. Get him down here, too. This is just ridiculous."

The door opened suddenly, interrupting their conversation. Two plainclothes officers walking in without waiting for acknowledgement. "Neil Evans, I'm detective Williams and this is my partner officer Simon. We'd like to ask you a few questions about your trip out here."

"Excuse me officer, before you go any further, I'd like to

know is my client being charged? Or is this just a fishing expedition?" Patrick demanded.

The two exchanged looks as detective Williams nodded before continuing. "Alright, cards on the table, so to speak. Sharon Taylor is pointing the finger at you. As you might remember when you first arrived, the fella's at the station back in Arkansas said you had nothing to do with it. And I'm inclined to believe that. But Miss Taylor is now spinning this tale that you two met in New Orleans and hatched this plan together. You went back to Arkansas ahead of her to set the whole thing up. She says she just went along with it. Hoping to get to Los Angeles and start a new life out there. Wanting to get away from you. And all the seedy characters you were associated with. She claims she was afraid for her life. Is any of this sounding plausible to you, sir?"

Taking a deep breath, clenching and unclenching his fists in an effort to control his anger, Neil looked at his lawyer, then back at the two detectives.

"No sir. None of that is true. Other than my being in Arkansas. I had never met her, seen her, had any idea of her existence before encountering her at the bus station that morning. My only plan that morning was to get a bus ticket. In order to get to Los Angeles while putting as much distance between me and that backwards town as I could. I wasn't thinking clearly. I had been up all night. Most of it spent walking into town. Before getting to the station, I stopped at the diner next door. You can even ask Bernie and Mabel. They both saw me and how tired I was. When I got to the bus station, I heard some commotion. I went over to see if there was anything I could help. When she offered to pay for my ticket, I took it as a sign and yeah, it was a rash decision that I made. I was about to give up. Just go home again. Thinking this dream I was chasing was fruitless. And well, on impulse I thought - why not? So yeah, here I am."

"But what about this connection to New Orleans that she claims you have?"

"My mother's family is from there. My uncle, who lives out here now, was originally from New Orleans. But I didn't even know that he was living here when I found myself stuck here. It was just a complete fluke that we ran into each other. Shoot, I haven't even been to New Orleans since I was twelve years old. So yeah. Her idea of me meeting her at all in that city, or working for whoever she says she's so afraid of, is just a bunch of horse hokey, too."

"So wait. Who exactly is your uncle, then?"

Before Neil could answer, Patrick interrupted. "What bearing does that have here, detective?"

"Well sir, if he's saying his uncle is his connection to New Orleans, then that's what bearing it has. Something is not adding up. We're just trying to get to the bottom of it."

Holding up his hand to pause any more discussion, Patrick replied, "Before we continue, I need a moment with my client, please."

The detectives excused themselves, leaving Neil and Patrick alone.

"Now listen to me, Neil. Be very careful what you say next. To me or to them. Your uncle called me to come down here and help you. There is only so much you can reveal about him. Do you understand what I'm telling you?"

Shaking his head, Neil said, "I think so. But I also feel like there is something else I'm not aware of. What aren't you telling me?"

"That's not for me to say. I'm sure Frank will tell you in

his own time. But please, just be careful. You can acknowledge that Frank is your uncle. But anything more than that. Just don't say anything else."

Patrick opened the door, allowing the detectives back in.

"Now then, Neil. What can you tell us about Frank Barnes?" detective Williams asked.

"You mean Frank Batiste. He's my uncle. My mother's brother. He lived in New Orleans all my life. That's what I thought until I ran into him one night at dinner with one of my bandmates. I know he works at the Crossroads. Head of security or something like that. But aside from that. I don't know much about him now. Or his life here."

The detectives exchanged a look between themselves, before officer Simon explained, "The man you call Frank Batiste goes by Frank Barnes here in Las Vegas. Yes, he is the head of security. But that security extends beyond just the casino and encompasses other duties for the Costa family. Do you know who that is?"

"No. Well, sort of. I know that Nick Costa owns the casino. But I've only seen him from a distance. I've never had a reason to meet him as I'm just a guitar player with Clarence and the Tru Tones. I don't have any other involvement in anything else going on in the casino. Uncle Frank, Barnes, Batiste, whatever you say he's calling himself, has given me no indication of anything else going on. Are you sure you have your information correct? I don't mean to question you officers, but I just don't see how what you're saying makes any sense."

Patrick shifted in his seat. "Detectives, my client has told all he knows. As you pointed out, the bus company and their agents back in Arkansas refused to press charges against my client. I'm not sure why he's here now other than you appear to be on a fishing expedition based on some tall tale this Sharon Taylor is telling you. If there is nothing else, I think we'll be taking our leave now. Unless you are bringing some other charges that I'm not aware of."

"Very well, Mr. Leary. Mr. Evans, you are free to go. For now. But don't leave town just yet. It's true, we are not going to press charges at the moment. But something here is not adding up. And believe me. We will get to the bottom of this. If you should think of anything else, please don't hesitate to let us know."

Returning home from the police station, Neil found himself wandering aimlessly around his apartment. How could this happen again? He wondered. Why would Sharon suddenly throw him under the bus like that? She knew he had absolutely nothing to do with anything she was involved in. And her connection to uncle Frank? What was that all about? Was she somehow connected to Mr. Costa? Was Frank involved with the mob back in New Orleans, too?

More frustrated with all the questions and not finding answers, Neil returned his attention back to what had brought him here in the first place. The empty stand in the corner where his guitar should be, reminding him of his dream of making it big in Los Angeles. Next to it sat the jar he'd been saving his extra change in. Counting out how much he had accumulated. Only to find it wasn't as much as he first thought. "Barely enough to get a bus ticket out of here," he grumbled.

Looking back at the stand, remembering that his uncle had the guitar safely locked away in his office, he thought of his mom, his grandpa Joe, and back to Frank again. They were the three biggest influences in his life, always encouraging him to pursue music and the dreams he had for stardom. Now he was unsure if he'd ever see those dreams become reality. Was this all he would ever achieve? Some background player in a two-bit casino band? Granted, the guys were all top-notch players, and he had fun playing with them. But none of them had a vision of being anything more than what they were. Just big fish in a small pond. And Frank, what was his story? There was something more going on that Neil wasn't being told.

He thought Frank had been content in New Orleans while living in the carriage house behind the family home in the Garden District. He had his business, his friends, family; they were all there. Frank Batiste had made a name for himself in New Orleans, and everyone thought he would stay until he died. But now, here he was in Las Vegas, the police calling him Frank Barnes? What was up with that? More pieces of this puzzle just weren't making sense.

Before he could focus on doing anything else, he needed to get out from under this bus con mess. He had to prove his innocence. Once that was done, he'd focus on saving up as much as possible as quickly as he could. He had to get out of this city before it swallowed him and his dream whole.

Tomorrow, well today, he thought, he'd get in touch with Frank and see what he could find out from him. He knew he had to get more definitive answers to some of these questions. Add to that, he would need to call the lawyer. He needed to find out what his next steps should be with the cops, too. He was not going to be left taking the blame for this.

Chapter 21

"Sharon!" Frank bellowed, storming into the apartment. "Where are you? What the hell did you do?"

"Frank, honey, what's wrong?" Sharon demurred, tying her robe as she came out of the bedroom.

"What's wrong? How can you ask me that? What did you tell the cops about Neil? I thought I told you to leave him out of this." Frank steamed into the living room, grabbing the whiskey bottle from the bar cart, pouring a double shot, downing it and pouring another one, before continuing. "The cops showed up at the Crossroads tonight. First, they questioned Leroy. Thinking he had something to do with. Oh hell! I don't know what. They always seem to assume he's up to something. But then, once they finished with him, they came out, telling me that Neil had to come with them to the station. Something about him being the mastermind of the bus ticket scam you pulled. Now tell me. Where could they have gotten an idea like that? Especially after the guy at the station in Arkansas clearly stated that Neil had nothing to do with it."

Sharon stopped in her tracks. Looking around, doing everything she could to not meet Frank's icy stare. She stuttered. "I… I, well…"

Striding over to her, Frank stopped inches from her face, his voice lowered to a growl. "You are going to fix this. You are going to tell me everything you told the cops. Then, Sharon, you are going to march your butt back down to the police station. You are going to give them a complete and true statement, absolving Neil of anything and everything. Do you understand me? Now, tell me, and don't leave out any detail, what it is you've done."

"Frank, it wasn't my idea. I didn't want to see him get into any trouble. You know that. I was abiding by what you said before and was keeping clear of him. I told all the girls not to mention me when he was around. But then Michael came to see me. And by see, well… you know how Michael can be." Sharon gulped.

Frank continued staring at her until she resumed. "Well, he told me that Nick had some concerns. He didn't say exactly what those concerns were. But he did make it clear that in no uncertain terms, I was told to go back down to the station. Talk to detective Williams. Give him a new statement saying what I told him in the first wasn't entirely true. I was to say I had met Neil in New Orleans, and we had hatched this plan. He went on ahead to Arkansas a few weeks before the trip out here. Back to the family home, to re-establish his credibility of the wandering musician. It's a small town Frank. You know that. I mean, they all knew he wants to be the next Elvis or something. So the story just evolved. I didn't give them many details, especially not about New Orleans. I said I had met him in the French Quarter. That way it couldn't be traced back to you at all. Telling them he was trying to find a way to Los Angeles in order to chase his dreams and that he had come up with this idea for a travel voucher. I guess the detective just filled in the blanks on his own. Honest Frank, I didn't mean to get him into any trouble."

"You didn't mean to get him into any trouble? What did you think was going to happen? And why didn't you come to me as soon as Michael came to you with this? You should have told me right away. This isn't making any sense."

Frank resumed pacing from the living room into the kitchen and back again. Stopping in front of the windows that faced out over the city, his back to Sharon, he declared, "I need to go see Nick. I refuse to believe this came from him. And I can't for the life of me figure out what Michael would get out of it, either."

Spinning on his heels, he turned and faced Sharon again. "Unless, hmm… is there something more you're not telling me, my dear Sharon?"

Seeing a dark calm cross Frank's face, Sharon gulped. "Uh, no. I think that's all of it. I don't know what you'd mean. Nothing else going on. Michael told me to go do this, that it was coming directly from Nick. Why would I question that? What would Michael get out of telling me to do this? Do you think he's trying to set you up? He also told me I wouldn't like the results if I didn't do what he was telling me to do. What was I supposed to do? You know Michael's tactics. I absolutely do not want to be on the receiving end of anything he has to offer."

"Right. Well, I'm going to return to the casino. I'll go have a talk with Nick. While I do that, I expect you to get your shit together. Head back down to the station and set things right. Fortunately, Neil is home now and cooling his heels for the night. He'll be back at work tomorrow as normal. By that time, his name had better be cleared. You understand?"

Sharon nodded. Not saying anything more to dig herself in any deeper, as Frank headed to the front door. "Don't be here when I get back," he called, slamming the door behind him.

$$\overline{\hspace{6cm}}$$

Chapter 22

$$\overline{\hspace{6cm}}$$

Pulling back into the casino, Frank wondered, 'was it really a good idea to go talk with Nick right now?' Still wound up from his fight with Sharon. 'How could she do that,' he thought to himself? 'Surely she's not that stupid. Trying to pull a stunt like this on her own? But why did Michael get involved? He only normally does what Nick tells him. Was this a direct order from Nick?'

Resolved, he knew he could only one find out one way. Frank strode across the gaming floor, heading straight for the penthouse elevator. Knowing Nick would still be up. The man never seemed to sleep. He was also aware Nick would see Frank was on his way up to his suite. Was he tipping his hand? Would Nick have an idea why he was coming before he even got to the door? Whatever the result, it was time for Frank to get answers.

Responding to his knocking on the penthouse door, a maid answered, pointing toward the living room. Walking across the marble floor, Frank found Nick sitting on the plush sofa, sipping a glass of red wine, while two showgirls walked around, modeling what looked like new costumes. Seeing Frank, Nick shooed the girls away. "Yeah, that's fine, girls. Tell Giorgio to make the changes I mentioned and we're good to go. Now go on, get out of here. Have a good night."

Frank admired that Nick always treated the girls with respect. Unlike some of the other casino bosses who thought the girls were available for their personal pleasures. Nick was always a gentleman. In an effort to clear his the mental distraction, Frank shook his head as he walked over to the sofa across from Nick. Standing until he was told to take a seat.

"Frankie boy. What brings you back so late tonight? No trouble? Right? I haven't heard anything from any of the guys."

"No Nick, no trouble. At least not here. I, well, I'm not sure how to ask you this. It's a bit of a sensitive matter, and well…"

"Stop beating around the bush, Frank. You know you can come to me. With anything. So if it's not something here, is it your nephew? Has he gotten into some sort of trouble?"

"No. Well, yes. Well, sort of. Sorry Nick, this is hard to explain. You know that he wound up here because of Sharon and her bag of tricks that she likes to sometimes play."

"Yeah, sure. But I thought she took the rap for that. And he was in the clear?"

"She did. But then the cops showed up tonight. They took Neil in for more questioning. Now they seem to think he was the mastermind behind that con of hers. Then I find out that she was told to go back to the cops and change her story."

Frank paused, trying to compose himself before throwing out his next accusation.

"I had it out with her when I got home tonight. The excuse she gave me, and I'm not trying to step out of line here, but her explanation was that it was Michael who told her to go change her tune. What I don't get, and please Nick, I mean no disrespect here, but why would Michael tell her that? I can't imagine he'd do something like that on his own. And for the life of me. I can't figure out why you might give an order like that, either. I mean, you know that I'm trying to keep Neil out of all this. Get him back on track to going to Los Angeles. Right?"

Nick sat, staring at Frank, no obvious expression on his face. Frank, looking back at Nick, thought, 'Wow. this guy has the poker face down to a T.'.

Clearing his throat, Nick leaned forward, resting his elbows on his knees. "Frank, Frank, Frankie... How long have we known each other now? No, wait, don't bother. It's been long enough. You know that I don't do things lightly. And you know I respect you, your family, your opinions. So hear me clearly. I had nothing to do with this. And I don't believe that Michael did either. He knows better than to go behind my back. Now Sharon, on the other hand. That little vixen of yours. She sometimes seems to have bigger ideas than that pretty little head of hers can handle. You know what I'm saying, right?"

Frank nodded, waiting to see where Nick was going to go next.

Standing, Nick crossed over to Frank, sitting down next to him before continuing. "Now, I know this was hard for you to bring to me. I understand that. And no hard feelings. Frank, you know, you're family here. And I want you to feel comfortable bringing anything to me at any time. But now this has me a bit worried. You know? Between this and your concerns with the upcoming plans. And the cops? We're going to have to do something about these guys. They seem to be harassing a lot of our guys lately. I know they were talking to Leroy tonight, too. You don't think that maybe he and Sharon are trying to pull something behind our backs, do you?"

"Nick, I, no. I can't imagine they would be that foolish to try something along those lines. But now that you mention it, I have seen Sharon hanging around him more lately. I keep telling her to stay away from the band. Especially now that Neil is here too -"

Holding a hand up to stop Frank from talking, Nick continued. "Okay, listen to me, Frank. This is what I want you to do. First off, Sharon is going to go back down to the station and sort this out. Once and for all. She's going to get Neil out of the pinch that he's in. I don't care what she has to do to convince the cops. But she is taking the blame for this. Second, I'm going to send Michael and Redd to have a chat with Leroy. If I find he's behind these shenanigans, I guess we'll need to be finding yet another new player for the band. I'm not liking all this turnover of late. But this next job is too important to be messing around with any sort of distractions. We have to keep things tight. No complications. And finally, as to your nephew, you have my word, nothing is going to happen to him. Not as long as you and I are on good terms. And I don't see anything changing that anytime soon. So tell him not to worry. He's in the clear. Just keep his head down, play his guitar, chase those dreams of his."

"Thanks Nick. That's a load off. At least where Neil is concerned. But what about Sharon? What do you want me to do about her?"

"This is going to be tough, Frank. But you make it clear to her, in no uncertain terms. If she doesn't do what we're telling her to do, she will not have her good looks to get her by any longer. And god knows, she doesn't have the brains to get very far either."

Chapter 23

As the sun came up, Sharon took her time, dressing in what she considered being her least flashy outfit, consisting of dark capris and a light blouse. All the while, trying to get her nerve to go back to the police station. Knowing she couldn't wait any longer, she made her way back downtown. Walking up to the desk sergeant's desk, she asked to speak to detective Williams. The sergeant, recognizing her from her last visit, told her to wait on the bench while he got the detective.

"Sir. That con woman from the bus station is back in the lobby," he told detective Williams. "I'm not sure why, but she's asking to speak with you."

"What does she want now? Oh fine, just send her back. This is not how I wanted to end my day. But let's just get this over with. Then I can get home to some peace and quiet," Williams grumbled.

The sergeant waved Sharon back as Detective Williams offering her a seat. "Miss Taylor. What brings you back to the station this morning? I thought we had settled all of our business," he grumbled.

"Yes, well, you see…" Sharon started, as she fidgeted in her seat. "Well, detective Williams, I um, I was mistaken on my last visit here."

"Mistaken? I don't understand. How could you be mistaken? You were so certain it was Neil Evans that was the mastermind behind your little bus trip. All the details you gave. And now suddenly you're saying you were mistaken." His voice rising to the point of almost shouting.

Sharon, cowering lower in her seat, meekly replied, "yes."

Scowling at her, detective Williams nodded for her to go on.

"You see, Neil had nothing to do with it, sir. Well, other than the fact he was in the wrong place at the wrong time. I'm aware you pulled him back in for questioning last night. And I feel just awful about that now. He's a good kid and doesn't deserve any of this hassle that he's getting. I was simply trying to save my own skin, because, well, I was afraid if I told you who was really behind it all, I'd get in worse trouble."

"Okay, let's take this from the beginning, shall we? So, Neil Evans. He was in the wrong place at the wrong time? And you want me to believe that someone else was behind this? I'm starting to think this was all your doing and no one else was involved. Isn't that the case, Miss Taylor?"

Detective Williams was shaking his head. Wondering how much more far out her story was going to go. "Look. It's already been a long night for me and I'm tired and want to get home. So let's cut to the end and you just tell me that you concocted this entire sham, district attorney Bilson will take care of the charges, you pay whatever fees and fines, serve your time and we'll all be on our merry way."

"But, sir, that's not what happened. Well, it sort of is. I wasn't the so-called mastermind behind all this. You have to believe me. I was just a pawn. And, well. The guy that cooked this all up in the first place is," Sharon stopped, twisting a tissue in her hands.

"Yes? Is who" the detective implored.

"Before I say, can we talk somewhere more private? I don't feel comfortable saying his name out here."

"And why is that?"

"Well, he's connected. You know," Sharon winked. "And I know he's got his spies. If he finds out I've been talking to the cops, well, I'm scared."

"Miss Taylor. I don't have time for this. Or for your games."

"Detective Williams, please. I'm not playing games. I'm frightened. And well, if we can't talk in private, then I guess my misfortune will be on your head."

"Now listen here, young lady. I will not be pushed into something. You have information? Fine. You can tell me here and now. Otherwise I will arrest you for obstruction, lying to the police and whatever else I can think of between here and processing. You got it?"

Taking a deep breath, Sharon realized she was getting even further in over her head. "Alright," she exhaled.

Lowering her voice, she began, "It's true I was in New Orleans. I had gone at the behest of Leroy Jones. He knew I had connections back there. He wanted me to pick up something. Before you ask, I don't know what it was. It was a small, wrapped package, about the size of a shoe box. I picked it up, got on the bus heading back for Las Vegas, and then mailed it to him when I got to Arkansas. So that's why it wasn't in my bag when you searched me after picking me up at the bus station. It was his idea that I should use the voucher scam to pay for the bus ticket. He had done it before. He said he never had any trouble. We both thought it would work just fine. I guess if I hadn't asked Neil to join me, maybe I would have made it back without incident. But I felt bad for the kid. He looked so lost and lonely. The poor guy was just trying to help a lady out. So, you see. He had nothing to do with it. I was only trying to get back here. I had to get back to work."

Setting down his pencil and paper, Detective Williams looked at Sharon. "You want me to believe that you went from here all the way to New Orleans? Just to pick up some package. Only then to mail it back here from some podunk town in Arkansas? You then finish your trip on the bus back here again? Why would you not just mail the thing from New Orleans in the first place? Or better yet. Why didn't the person who had the thing just mail it themselves? Lady, your story is getting more outrageous as you go. Are you sure this is what you want to stick with now?"

"Detective, I know it sounds far-fetched. And I know I have no credibility left with you now that I've given you three different versions of this story. But, I swear to you now. This is the truth. I feel bad that I got that kid in trouble. He doesn't deserve it. He was just in the wrong place at the wrong time. My conscience won't let me rest until I at least get him cleared of this. As to why I went and played a part in this scheme of Leroy's... Well, like I said. He's connected. Not just here. But in New Orleans too. Sir. I still have family back there. I don't want to see any harm come to them, either. I'm scared." Dabbing at her eyes, Sharon hung her head, playing the part of the innocent victim. "So please. Do what you will with me. I'm willing to accept whatever consequences I may face. Please just assure me that you'll clear Neil of any charges. Let the poor kid go on with his life."

"Ma'am. I'm going to have to have a conversation with the district attorney before I can give you any guarantees. But if, and that's a big if, what you say is true, then I guess the kid will be clear of any more suspicion. And, well, I won't speculate as to what your fate will be. Wait here."

Detective Williams rose from his seat, taking one last look at Sharon, shaking his head. Sharon pasted on a docile smile, in hopes it would make her appear humble and amenable. Once the detective was out of sight, she dropped her head as she thought to herself, 'at least Frank will be happy now that I've gotten his nephew off the hook. Hopefully, he'll forgive me as well. I can't say the same for Leroy. But he's expendable and the least of my worries at the moment.'

Chapter 24

"Frank, come in," Nick called from his desk. "Are Redd and Michael coming too?"

"Yes sir. They'll be here in just a minute. Michael was taking care of a guest. Redd is on his way from the security office."

As if on cue, Redd strolled in, nodding to both men. Silently taking a seat in one of the chairs to the side of the office.

"Alright, well, we can go ahead and get started. We'll catch Michael up once he gets here too," Nick said, rising from behind his desk and moving over to the sofa. This offered him a view of both the office and the strip below. One perk of being the casino owner, he had his pick of rooms when it came to deciding where he wanted his suite. First, he considered the one overlooking the pool and guests. But knew that would pose more of a distraction for not only him, but for anyone he had to have in for a conversation. And he didn't need that extra headache. This way, he could look out over the strip. See the competition. Who they had coming in for shows allowed him to weigh his successes and failures against what he saw on the other flashing neon lights and signs.

Turning his attention back to the men assembled, Nick paused, taking a sip of his scotch, and setting the crystal tumbler back on the table.

"Alright boys. Bring me up to speed. Do we have everything in place for when Marylin arrives?"

Redd looked at Frank. Deferring to him to fill in the boss on all the plans.

Frank replied. "Yes sir. We have the Mystique suite already cleaned and reserved exclusively for her. Also, three additional rooms on the floor for her staff and personal security. All of our security guys are up to speed. What to monitor and what to avoid. No one has asked any questions regarding that either. The only minor hiccup we still have is the local cops. They seem to have it in their head that we don't have enough security for her, and are insisting they post extra officers outside and even on the floor downstairs. I've been going back and forth with the chief at the station. I think I have him placated enough to just send a few guys over to be stationed outside. It's going to cost us a case of good whiskey, and a few extra dollars in donations to the police fund, but it's nothing we won't make back in a couple of hours."

"What the hell is wrong with that guy? Every single time we have some big name come through, we have to go through this bull with him. Frank, can't we can fix this before the next VIP comes to town?" Nick exclaimed. "Never mind. You know what? I'll get Michael to talk some sense into him. You've got enough on your plate, you don't need this too."

Running his fingers through his salt and pepper hair, Nick leaned back, looking out the window. "All these other guys running their casinos don't have these issues. The cops seem to leave them all alone. What bug do they have for me anyway?"

Redd sat stoically, as was his usual pose. Frank looked from Nick to the view and back to Nick again. "I don't think it's you, boss. This time I think it's because it's Marylin. You haven't been down to the station, but man, those guys, they've got pictures of her all over the place. They're trying to be discreet about it, nothing big or flashy. But you look at their desks, and especially under the desk sergeant's station. He's got magazines with her face all piled up. Everyone is just trying to get a glimpse. Thinking maybe they'd be the one to catch her eye and have a shot with her."

"Yeah, right. Like she's going to go for some two bit cop from this town. Give me a break. Alright, well then. What about the rest of the plan?"

"Right. Well, while she's doing her poolside stint, is when we'll take care of the necklace. I've got the duplicate already to go. Anyone who looks at it won't be any the wiser. No one will be checking it with a loupe or anything before she wears it. The jeweler inspected it back in New York before he let it out of his sight. And it's being delivered under lock and key straight to the vault. There's no reason for anyone to look at it again until it gets back to him. By that time, well. We've got that all covered."

"Yeah, how's that? You're being awfully tight lipped about your plan when it comes to that part, Frank. Something I need to know that you're not telling me?" Nick hissed. He didn't like it when people kept things from him.

Even Frank, who he trusted more than any of his other guys.

"Are you sure you want me to tell you, boss? I thought you wanted 'plausible deniability' and all that."

Redd shifted in his seat at that comment when the door opened and Michael strolled in.

"About time you rolled in here, Michael. What was the holdup?" Frank asked, turning his attention to the man that just walked in the door.

"Sorry Nick. Frank. That guest was more of a headache than I thought he was going to be. But he'll sleep it off and feel better when he wakes up. If he doesn't, well, then he'll be on his way home. And he knows those are his only two options." Michael replied, wiping his hands with his hand-kerchief, taking a seat in the chair next to Redd.

"Okay, so back to where we were. Frankie, you were telling me about this plausible deniability you think I want to have?"

"Yeah Nick. I know this is one of the biggest scores we've ever done. You typically don't want to know all the details. I guess I figured this time was no different. That way, if the cops come around later, you can say you knew nothing. And you won't be lying."

Thinking for a moment, Nick nodded, then shook his head. "Yeah, no. Not this time. I trust you, Frank, and the boys here, too. But this. This is just too big of a deal to not go over every single last detail. So I need to know everything."

Frank took in a deep breath. "Okay. Here's what's going to happen." He began explaining the details of how he'd replace the original with the duplicate. After that, Redd would be responsible for taking the original to the warehouse where it would be stored under lock and key. No additional security would be present. It would appear as though it was business as usual. Once the jeweler back in New York realized what had happened, he'd be raising all the alarms, and they didn't want to draw any unwanted attention. Once the heat died down, they would then transport the necklace to New Orleans. There, another jeweler would take it apart and sell it off in pieces, no one the wiser. At least, that was everyone's hope.

Nick nodded his head when Frank finished with his explanation. "Sounds like you got it all under control. Good man. Who is it again we have doing the work in New Orleans that's going to take care of it there?"

Not missing a beat, Frank replied, "Vince. I've used him in the past. He's good and discreet. While I'm sure he'll recognize the piece, because who wouldn't after seeing pictures of Marylin wearing it, he won't ask questions. As long as we pay him, he'll do the job."

"Right. Okay. I think we're done here then. Frank, you can go ahead and go. Redd, Michael, I need you two to stick around a minute."

"You sure, boss?" Frank asked, wondering why he was being abruptly dismissed. Was there something else going on that those two had to stick around for?

"Yup. All good Frankie. Just want to check in with these two knuckleheads. It's been a minute since I've talked with them."

"Alright boss. I'll be back in my office should you need anything."

Just as he was closing the door, Frank overheard Nick asking, "So this Sharon chick? What more can you tell me about her?"

Chapter 25

After trying to occupy his mind with songwriting most of the morning, Neil decided he couldn't sit around his apartment any longer. Going in to work earlier than normal, he was determined to find his uncle Frank. He had to find a way to get to the bottom of why the cops seemed to still think he was behind Sharon's con. He also wanted to know what connection she had to the Crossroads. And what else Frank wasn't telling him?

Walking into the showroom where the band performed, he found Marge sitting alone at the bar. Marge had been a showgirl during the Vaudeville days and found herself in Las Vegas after the traveling show circuit dried up. He could see the sparkle in her eyes, even with the house lights up. She had been stunningly beautiful back in her day. At night, though, when she came in all dressed up wearing her "trinkets" as she called them, it felt as though she was trying too hard. As if she was holding on with an ever loosening grasp to that one last glorious moment of her past.

Neil stopped, giving her a peck on the cheek. She had

become a surrogate mother, not just to him. But all the guys in the band, even Clarence. Heck, probably in the entire casino staff, if he had to guess.

"Marge, what are you doing here so early? Are you flirting with the bar backs again?" Neil teased.

"Oh honey. You know me too well. I was just telling, oh what's his name back there, about some of the things I saw back in the day. You young un's have no idea what sexy really is. We didn't have to show so much skin to get the customer all wound up. It was all in the presentation. Mystery, intrigue. Always leave them guessing and wanting more. That's what brings them back every time."

"I'm sure you had them eating out of the palm of your hand every time," Neil chuckled.

"Oh, don't you know it. Where do you think I got so many of my wonderful trinkets from? I didn't spend a dime of my own money on them. Oh no. These were all gifts from gentlemen. And well, some not so gentle. All across the country. In fact, these earrings I'm wearing now. They were from some fella back in your neck of the woods. Arkansas, or maybe it was Louisiana. Too recent to remember, my momma used to say." Marge paused to catch her breath, taking a sip of her umbrella adorned drink.

"But that's not why you're here so early, young man. My tales can wait for another time. I can see clear as day. You've got something on your mind. You need to talk about it?"

Maternal Marge always had an ear for whomever needed to talk. Or a shoulder to cry on when things got too bad. Usually, that was one of the showgirls, but her gentle tone touched something deep inside Neil. He wondered if he should confide in her now.

Shaking his head, he replied. "I'm looking for Frank.

Have you seen him around at all? We were having a conversation last night, but got side tracked with casino business and I told him I'd stop by today so we could finish. I didn't want to have to rush before tonight's performance, so I thought I'd come by early."

"No honey, I haven't seen your uncle around."

Looking surprised, Neil took a step back. "How…?"

"I know more than you think about what goes on around here. These old eyes are still pretty sharp. Not to mention my ears, too. But honey, I spotted the family resemblance between you two right away. Many others may not have even noticed, but I see it. And your secret is safe with me. Though I don't think it would matter much to anyone else. I'm sure those who *need* to know already do."

Smiling, Neil patted Marge on the hand. "You remind me of my mother."

"Oh, dear, that's sweet of you, but I'm just who I am. And your mother, rest her soul, will always be with you, in here," she said, tapping him on the chest. "Never forget that."

"Thank you. I won't. And thank you for your time. If you should see Frank around, could you tell him I'm looking for him? And oh. Don't you give these young guys too much to look at. You've got your reputation to think about," he said, as he gave her a peck on the cheek.

"Don't worry about me, honey. I got it all under control," Marge winked.

Leaving Marge at the bar, Neil went to check in with the security office, asking one of the guys when they last saw Frank. Steve said the last he knew, Frank was headed to Nick's office suite. Debating with himself whether he should try to find him there. He knew you didn't go to Nick's if you hadn't been invited. It was one of the few off-limits areas to staff. Now he found himself questioning why that was, too. What was Nick hiding? Neil was having more reservations about where he was finding himself now.

Lost in thought, he didn't hear someone calling his name. Looking up, he saw Frank approaching him from the other end of the hall.

"Man, what are you doing here? You didn't hear me calling at all," Frank said.

"Sorry. I was looking for you. Steve, down in the security office, said you were meeting with Nick. I didn't want to come to his office. Because, well. You know. But I guess I just got lost in my thoughts and wound up wandering the halls." Neil replied, his head hung down.

"Well, now you found me. I can see something is on your mind. Let's head down to the coffee shop and grab a bite. We can talk over a sandwich and some coffee, huh?" Frank said, steering Neil towards the elevators.

"Could we go talk somewhere more private? This isn't a conversation I think we should have with other people around."

Frank looked at Neil quizzically. "Sure kid. Let's go back to my office. No one will bother us. You sure everything is okay? You got me kind of worried now."

Neil shook his head. "It's this situation with the cops."

Frank nodded, saying nothing more until they reached his office and were behind closed doors.

"Okay Neil. Spill."

Neil started off explaining what had transpired at the police station. How the cops knew he wasn't the mastermind behind Sharon's con, but how they were pressuring him, trying to get information he just didn't have. Tiptoeing around what the cops had told him about uncle Frank, he blurted it out.

"They said you aren't who you say you are. Or rather, they think you are Frank Barnes, not Frank Batiste. And that Nick Costa has mob connections too. Here and in New Orleans. Does that mean you do too? How is Sharon involved in all of this? Aside from the bus trip? I'm so confused by all of this. The lawyer you sent to help me, Patrick, seemed to think that everything would work itself out and they still aren't pressing charges. But what the cops are telling me, and what I'm starting to see now, has got me wondering what I've gotten myself into here. And maybe I should just head home. Or to Los Angeles. It can't be any worse there than this mess now."

Frank furrowed his brow, trying to figure out how to best explain the situation to Neil without implicating himself or Neil in the process. The less Neil knew, the better. What was it, he had said to Nick earlier, 'plausible deniability' he thought. Taking a deep breath, he looked Neil in the eye and began.

"Neil, listen. The cops are not completely off base here. Yes, I am known as Frank Barnes here. The reasons why aren't important at the moment. Other than to say, I don't want some folks back in New Orleans finding out I'm here." Seeing Neil was about to interrupt, Frank held up a hand. "Let me explain everything before you start asking questions. You are just going to have to take my word on this."

Frank took a deep breath as he walked over to the

window. Looking out over the strip, he began. "It's true when Sharon was back in New Orleans she was pulling small cons on unsuspecting tourists, and quite frankly, she wasn't very good at it, either. When she got pinched by the cops at the bus station this time, I sent Redd down to bail her out. He told me the cops told him that she had some kid working with her. They were light on the details about who it was. I had no idea it was you. I only found out you were here when Clarence came to me, telling me they hired a new guitar player. You didn't see me, but I came in during one of your rehearsals and saw you playing, looking as happy as I've ever seen you. I was so proud seeing you up there, chasing this dream of yours. And I was also terrified. I was worried sick that you were going to get mixed up in the wrong crowd out here. It's easy to do. So I asked Duane to keep an eye on you. It didn't take much cajoling to get him to go along. He already liked you for you and felt bad for the situation you found yourself in. So, okay. That night at dinner wasn't a complete accident."

Neil started to interrupt, but Frank kept on talking over him.

"As to your questions about Nick, the mob, and any connection I may have. On that subject, I can't give you much information other than to say, don't ask questions. Yeah, I've done some things I'm not proud of. I don't want you getting wrapped up in any shady business. Stay out of anything that isn't related to your music. As for the cops, I spoke with Patrick earlier, and he assured me the cops have no charges pending against you. I'm guessing they are just trying to scare you into doing or saying something. Just keep telling them you don't know anything. Because in all honesty, you don't. Eventually, they'll give up and move on."

As he turned back to face Neil, Frank saw the look of disappointment all over his face. "I'm sorry, kid. I can't say more."

"Can't say or won't say more, uncle Frank?" Neil spit. "I looked up to you. All my life. All I wanted to do was grow up and be like you. Now I find out it's all a lie? You're tied into the mob, and what? What have you done, uncle? Why should I believe anything you tell me now? Has it always been a lie?"

Frank crossed the room, stopping inches away from Neil. Lowering his voice, he declared, "No. It's not all been a lie. Yes. I have been keeping things from you. To keep you safe. Kid, I don't want to see you hurt. Or worse. Keep your head down. This all goes away. Just keep playing until you make enough dough, then get on that bus and head straight for Los Angeles. You've got the talent. And if you stay here, it's just gonna get wasted."

Neil's face flushed. He took a step closer to his uncle. "I'm not buying any of this. Now I just don't know what to think. But I sure don't want any advice from you right now." Turning on his heel, he grabbed his guitar, storming to the door. Swinging it open, he walked out, letting it slam behind him, leaving Frank standing in the middle of his office.

Leaning against the wall, Neil tried to regain his composure but found he was still too upset to face anyone. Knowing he had time before the show, he decided to go down to the gaming floor. This would be his first time he would try his hand at the tables. If Frank was telling him to stay away, then he'd do the complete opposite. Nothing his uncle said had made any sense. So why should he start listening to what he told him now? He was his own man, he could make his own decisions. Suffer whatever consequences came his way. Maybe he'd luck out. Make enough that he could get out of this town sooner than he'd planned.

Chapter 26

Frustrated at the turn in his conversation with Neil, and what he had overhead leaving Nick's office, Frank grabbed a drink from his office bar. Slamming back a double shot of whiskey, he set the glass down hard before heading down to the security office.

When Frank barged in, the guys on duty took one look at his face and immediately turned back to their monitors. Without a word, Steve handed him the latest report on casino business. He knew if he said anything; he was liable to get his head chewed off. Or maybe even fired.

Glancing at the monitors, Frank noticed Neil at the blackjack table. "What the hell does he think he's doing?" He shouted at the screens.

"Sorry boss. Who are we talking about?" Steve asked.

"Neil. The guitar player with the band. He knows he's not supposed to be on the floor. If Nick sees this, it won't be a good night for him. Or the band. We can't afford any mistakes right now."

"Do you want me to go down and talk to him, sir?"

"No. I'll handle this. If you have to, and only if you should see Nick coming before I get to him, send someone to drag Neil away."

Steve nodded, turning his attention back to the monitor that showed Neil at the blackjack table. Throwing down the report, Frank muttered under his breath, "What is this kid thinking? He's gonna get himself fired, or worse, Nick is going to have Redd or Michael put the fear of god into him. That won't bode well for any of us if that happens."

Exiting through the hidden door onto the casino floor, he walked straight to the table where he had seen Neil. Not finding him there now, he asked the dealer what happened to him.

"Lost a couple hands. Then he just up and left. Thought he was gonna stick around and try to win back what he lost. But the kid seemed pretty down. And not just at losing the dough."

"Good."

"Sir?"

"Nothing. If he comes back, turn him away. He knows he's not supposed to be out here. He's with the band, and they all know the rules. Let your replacement know too. I'll take care of the rest of the staff." Frank directed as he began making his way back to the cashier's cages.

He was glad that Neil had lost some money. Maybe that would teach him the lesson to not bet against the house. The house always wins in the end. One way or another. But now, Frank had bigger problems to deal with. Between Sharon and her games. Marylin's upcoming show and what was to take place behind the scenes, too. He didn't have time for anything to go wrong, or anyone to even put one foot out of line.

Something Neil had said, though, was still nagging at him. Why hadn't the cops approached him before if they knew that he wasn't Frank Barnes? He was sure they had pulled his record if they had that information. It was only petty crimes he had in his file. Yet he knew the Las Vegas cops would use anything they could. In order to find out more information about what was going on behind the scenes of all the casinos. Granted, they had some cops on the payroll. But even those guys weren't privy to all the details, either. What went on behind all the glitz and glamour.

Guests were quick to part with their valuables, one way or another. Often times they cashed them in to supplement their money when funds ran low. There were also those who had lost them with no recollection as to how, chalking it up to a bad stroke of luck at the tables the night before, and accompanied by a nasty hangover the next day. Frank and the gang were always smart enough to not take everything. They would leave just enough money or a few pieces of jewelry behind, so it didn't appear obvious that the guest had anything stolen from them.

However, this next heist they had planned, well, that one was going to be more noticeable. He still had his reservations. But Nick kept reassuring him it would all work out in the end. Replacing the necklace with a high end replica, they'd leave the matching earrings, so no one would be any wiser to what had happened. Only if for some reason someone took a jeweler's loupe to the necklace before Marylin was going to wear it, then would they see it wasn't what it appeared to be.

Now, along with these concerns, he was now wondering if maybe he should go talk to the cops. Was it time to set his life straight? Get out of this racket? Head back to New Orleans. He had saved enough he could retire. For a while, at least. He could go home, clean up the family house, maybe finally open that bar he'd always been dreaming of. Reconnect with Remy, though he knew her mom wanted nothing more to do with him. She was happy enough to just cash the checks he sent every month. But still. He wanted to get to know his daughter, too.

Who was he kidding? He was in too deep here now. If Nick found out that he was even entertaining thoughts about what was going through his head. He would for sure find himself out in the middle of the desert. Most likely rotting away. Food for the creatures that called that desolate place home.

And what was with Nick asking Michael and Redd about Sharon? Nick had been well aware of the fact that she and Frank had a relationship. If you could call it that. But did he know something else about her that Frank wasn't privy to? Word had obviously gotten around about her little stunt with Neil. The fact she had been to the cops more than once now, too. Maybe that's all there was to it. Nick was more concerned than he first let on. She was a loose end. He wanted to make sure she was taken care of without having to get Frank involved. After all. It was harder to deal with someone you were personally involved with than it was for someone else who had no attachment. He hoped nothing would happen to her. At the same time, he couldn't waste any more emotional energy on her. She had gotten herself in too deep this time. She would have to find a way to get herself out.

Knowing he would have to go through with stealing the necklace, he was sure it was the only way he could see himself getting through this ordeal with his life intact. The first copy was almost done. He would keep it standing by in his safe. Ready to substitute for the real thing. That one would the one to be boxed up and shipped back to the jeweler in New York, no one the wiser. The challenge would be after the fact. Could he conceivably replace the original with yet another counterfeit copy? Would he be able to find someone to make the second copy in time? And without anyone realizing what he had done? He knew he couldn't use Marcus again since he worked too close with Nick and it would immediately raise questions.

He was glad that at least this necklace didn't have as many of the enormous stones as some of the other necklaces Marylin had worn in the past. This one had one enormous diamond at the bottom, surrounded by the highest quality small and medium diamonds. He would have to leave that stone to make it easier for him to be able to pass off another counterfeit copy to Nick when he asked for it. Knowing some of the other remaining stones would have to be set amongst the fakes in order for it to pass the glance test, he was sure Nick would put it through. This was one slight advantage Frank had in this case. He had time to keep it hidden away until the heat died down.

No. The biggest obstacle he would be left to face would be how he was going to get out of town. Taking with him what remained. Then not getting caught when Nick realized what he had done. He didn't want to abandon Neil. Now that they had reconnected again, he was hoping they would get back to a good place. Neil was upset with him right now, but surely, they could patch things up. But he didn't have much time. If it was going to happen, it would have to happen fast. He was going to have to make sure that Neil was protected. He couldn't live with himself if anything happened to that kid.

Chapter 27

Neil kept replaying the scene over and over in his head. Was everything Frank told him all these years just a lie? When did his involvement with these shady characters start? Was he connected with the mob even back when he was in New Orleans? Why did he leave New Orleans in the first place? He thought Frank had been happy there. Shoot. At one time, Frank had been talking about settling down and starting a family. Neil could have had cousins to hang out with. Share his love of music with. They would have gone to all the hidden gems of clubs that only the locals knew about. Now it felt like this dream was gone as well. Just like everything else in his life seemed to be going up in smoke.

But something else was under the surface of Frank's tone. His insistence on keeping Neil safe and out of trouble. Neil couldn't help but wonder, had Frank done something that Nick or someone else was holding over him, and that's why he was going along with whatever was planned? Not of his own free will. But because of a secret? Maybe he was being too quick to pass judgement against Frank. Perhaps he didn't have all the puzzle pieces. But yet, why didn't Frank feel like he could confide in Neil? After all. They used to tell each other everything. Or so he thought. At least he had always told Frank everything.

Stopping in his tracks, he started to turn, thinking perhaps he should go back and try to talk to Frank again. Try to patch things up. He didn't like being estranged from him. Did he have a chance of talking him out doing whatever it was Frank felt like he had to do? Was it possible? Could he convince Frank to go to the cops and spill his secrets to them? What would the consequences be? He wondered. Would he wind up in jail? No, it would probably be worse. Especially if Nick and his associates got word of what Frank did. Sure as anything. Frank would wind up dead in the desert. Somewhere no one could find him. But between the two of them? Could they find some way to get him out of this untenable situation and back to New Orleans, where they both belonged?

Neil was finding himself stuck between a rock and a hard place. Staring out the doors that overlooked the strip, he kept muttering to himself. "There's only one thing to do. I have to go back to Frank. I have to convince him to go talk to the cops. Or something. He's the only family I've got left now and I can't lose him, too."

Determined in his decision, he headed back to the dressing room, dropping off his guitar and suit for the show later, before heading back out to Frank's place.

Walking through the lobby, he kept looking around, making sure he wasn't being followed. Though he didn't think he had given anyone reason to, all the thoughts running through his head kept making him nervous. So much so that he wasn't watching where he was going and plowed straight into Audrey.

"Neil, slow down there, fella. You're about to barrel everyone over," she laughed. "Where you off to in such a hurry?"

"Oh, Audrey. Sorry. I guess I wasn't paying attention. As usual. My head is just full of all sorts of thoughts."

Rest a hand on his forearm, Audrey leaned in closer. "Something you need to talk about? You know I'm a good listener."

"No, well, maybe. I don't know. I don't want to pull you into the middle of anything. I know you have your own stuff to deal with."

"Neil, come on. Come over here a minute. Let's talk."

Walking over to a quieter corner, away from the tables, Audrey leaned her shoulder against the wall, waiting for Neil to start talking.

"Audrey. What do you know about who runs this place?"

"Neil, we've had this conversation before. I mean. As far as I know, Mr. Costa is the one that runs the place. I'm guessing he owns it, too. At least that's who I've always been told owns the place. Of course, I don't see him all that often. Aside from when he's in the audience for a show. Usually it's one of the guys, Michael or Redd, or someone else who comes and gives messages or instructions to us girls. Why? Have you heard something otherwise?"

"But what do you know about him? Can you give me specifics?"

"I'm not sure I know what you're getting at. And I'm

not sure I want to know either. If I were you, I wouldn't be asking so many questions. You've kept your nose clean all this time. Don't go sticking it in where it doesn't belong. You do know these walls have eyes and ears everywhere, right?"

"Yeah… I know. I'm just worried about Frank. Something's going on with him and he's not telling me. We always talk about everything. Well, I guess I always talk about everything. Now that I think about it, he hasn't said much. About, well, anything. And this Sharon person. She keeps showing up in the strangest of places, too. I just feel like it's not a coincidence anymore that I ran into her at the bus station."

"Listen Neil. I don't know what's happening. And it's not my place to pry, either. If you think Frank is in trouble, why don't you go talk to him? Or maybe Redd. He'll be straight with you. But whatever you do, don't go asking Michael any questions. I don't trust him. As for Sharon, she used to be one of us. A lot of us girls are still friends with her and she comes back to visit. I think maybe she and Frank went out a couple of times. But it was nothing serious between them. I think she has some connection with Leroy. And I know he was from somewhere back in your neck of the woods. So while it seems farfetched, I still believe it was all just a coincidence."

"Maybe you're right. Maybe I'm just in my head. Everything has happened so fast since I've been here. And of course. I had no intention of even winding up here. I guess life just has other plans for me right now. Thanks for setting me straight."

"Of course, honey. Now I have to get back. A couple of us girls are putting in a few extra hours today. But come find me later. If you have a chance. Maybe we'll grab a bite to eat before the show."

Neil gave her a quick hug as they parted ways, making his way to the front door and the taxi stand. He still had to go to Frank's and ask him some questions.

Chapter 28

Detective Williams returned to the holding room, finding Sharon impatiently waiting. Accompanying him was the district attorney and a stenographer.

"Ma'am, I'm Peter Bilson, the district attorney. Of course, you already know Detective Williams, and this is Miss Sanders, who will take notes of our meeting. Are you comfortable with that?"

"Yes. As I was telling the detective here, I know I've given you all three different stories now, but this one is the truth. And yes, there is more to it that I haven't gotten to yet. I think you are going to want to hear the entire tale, before you start asking any questions."

Raising an eyebrow, DA Bilson sighed. "Yes. I'm aware of your many different versions and I reserve the right to pass judgement until after I've heard what you have to say. But bear in mind. While you are not under arrest at the moment, anything you tell me can be used in a case against you as well. If I deem that to be feasible."

"I understand. I also would like to request protection when this is done. Once I tell you what information I have, I do fear for my life. But, as you said, it's up to you what you decide to do. All I can do now is tell the truth."

Detective Williams grunted, and DA Bilson just glanced at him, shutting down any other remarks before they could be made.

"Alright, start at the beginning then."

"As I told the detective here. I did go to New Orleans to pick up a package for Leroy. However, what I didn't tell him before was that Leroy was taking his orders from Nick Costa. From what I can tell, Leroy has a friend back there who is a first class counterfeiter when it comes to gemstones. He also deals in the real thing. I gleaned from the bits and pieces I heard or was told that I was picking up loose stones for someone here to use in making a duplicate necklace. I don't know who the original necklace belongs to. Or what it looks like. The package I picked up was wrapped so I couldn't see its contents. I'm guessing, and this is only a guess because I know that she's coming to the Crossroads soon. The necklace in question is going to be a duplicate of one that Marylin Monroe will be wearing at her big event. Because of the value of the piece, it will be stored in the casino's safe until she's ready to wear it. That will make it easy enough for Nick or his guys, rather, to swap out a counterfeit copy for the real thing. No one will be the wiser. This isn't the first time they've done something like that. And if you don't stop them, it certainly won't be the last either." Pausing to clear her throat, Detective Williams interjected.

"So you mean to tell us? No wait, you want us to believe that this million dollar necklace is going to be stolen right under her nose? Surely they couldn't be that stupid. Thinking they'd get away with it. As soon as it's returned to the jeweler, he'll figure it out. We'll be all over that place in a heartbeat."

"Yes. Well. That's the part of the plan I don't know anything about. My guess is that they have somewhere to keep it until things quiet down. You know you won't find anything in the casino. And you'll have no way of proving it happened there. They definitely aren't stupid, detective."

Turning to detective Williams, DA Bilson interrupts the conversation to ask, "Why did you not find these stones when she was picked up at the bus station?"

"Well, sir. We took her possessions into custody as well. But because it was a ticket scam, we didn't have any reason to do anything more than a cursory search of them. They sat in the corner of the office until she was released."

Shaking his head, DA Bilson turned his attention back to Sharon. "Alright. Here's what's going to happen. You are going to go back to the casino. You are going to act as if none of this conversation ever took place. If you don't want additional charges brought against you, then you will cooperate and continue to bring back more information. I don't care how you go about getting it. But you will find out. Then you will tell detective Williams here when exactly this is going down, where the necklace will be hidden and who all is involved. Once you do that and we are satisfied with what you tell us, then we'll see what to do next."

"You're crazy. You know that, right?" Sharon deadpanned, looking at both men. "I'll get myself killed if I try to do that. Nick. His guys, none of them are never going to tell me what they're up to."

"Look honey, you got this much information already.

I'm sure you can use your feminine charms or something to get what we need." He leered. "Otherwise, you'll be spending the next ten years at least behind bars. Then where will your looks get you once you're out of here? Provided you still have those looks after all that time."

Shaking her head, Sharon laughed. "And why haven't you been able to convict them of anything before this? You're just as bad as the rest of them. You don't give Nick and his crew enough credit. They have been pulling off stuff like this for years. You think they're going to tell me anything about this plan? I can't even show my face there right now."

"You have 24 hours to consider this offer. If you don't accept, then I'll see you in court. Decide to accept. Then contact the detective here and he'll work out all the remaining details with me. Once we've apprehended them, then we'll take care of you. I'm sure you won't have any trouble starting a new life somewhere else, right?"

Rising from his seat signaling an end to the conversation, DA Bilson hears Sharon mumble, "fine."

"Fine, what?"

Looking defiantly at him, she repeats, "Fine, I'll do it. I don't know how, but I'll get you the information. But I want your word. Once that's done, I'm out of here. No charges, and a new life."

With his hand on the doorknob, DA Bilson nods. Looking at the detective, then back to Sharon before exiting the room.

Detective Williams turns his attention back to Sharon. "Now then, when you have information for me, I want you to call the desk sergeant and leave him a message. You won't need to come back to the station. We'll meet somewhere else. Just let whoever is on duty know where I can reach you. I'll be in touch. Don't take too long, either. The clock is ticking."

"Am I free to leave now?" Sharon demanded.

Waving his hand at the door, the detective barely offered a glance at her as she gathered her purse and scarf, departing in a huff.

Returning home from the police station, even more agitated than before, Sharon marched across her apartment to the bedroom. She knew she was facing the choice of whether to tell Frank anything, or just play dumb, skip town, and try to start over somewhere else. Or should she do as the district attorney asked? Make every attempt to get as much information as she can? All of these questions racing were pushing her to the edge.

Yanking a suitcase out of the closet. "If nothing else, I can be prepared to leave at a moment's notice," she whined.

Throwing in clothes, jewelry, and a few sentimental keepsakes, a pounding on the door startled her, disrupting her thoughts and packing. Not expecting any visitors, she slowly approached the door when she heard shouting coming from the other side.

"Sharon, damnit, open this door. I know you're in there."

'Shit, it's Leroy. What could he want?' She wondered.

More banging, which she knows will soon alert her nosy neighbor, Mrs. Zanger, if she doesn't answer.

"I'm coming," she called cheerily, hoping to appease Leroy and his incessant noisy barrage.

Opening the door, she's met by the angry face of Leroy as he shoves his way in. "What took you so long?" He demanded.

"I was in the bedroom. Not that it's any of your business. What are you even doing here?"

Shoving her further into the living room, Leroy growled. "Who you been talking to, Sharon?"

"What do you mean? Who have I been talking to? Man! You come barging in here. All bent out of shape. I don't even know why you're here, Leroy. And I think you need to leave." Sharon replied, trying to find a way of escape.

Stopping dead in his tracks, Leroy leans forward and grabs Sharon's arm, twisting it as he continues to berate her. "I know you were at the police station again. I know the district attorney was there, too. So I'm going to ask you one more time. Who were you talking to and what were you telling them?"

Mouth agape, Sharon stuttered. "What? How? I don't know what you mean…"

"Yeah, I think you do and I think you're going to tell me, or this pain you're feeling in your arm is going to be the least of your worries."

Wincing, Sharon tries to take a deep breath to compose herself. Hoping to come up with a decent enough lie that would appease him. At least long enough for her to get out of the apartment.

"Fine. Let me go. Let's sit down and I'll explain. It's not what you think."

"We can have this conversation right here. No need to sit."

"Leroy, please. It's been a long day. I need to get ready for work. Just let go of me so I can think straight. Then I'll tell you what's going on."

Dropping her arm, Leroy shrugs. "You got one minute. Explain."

"Okay. Well, I talked to Frank, and he wanted me to go back down and clear his nephew's name. That's the short of it. Look. Neil didn't have anything to do with this. It was a wrong place at the wrong time situation. I used him as a means to an end. So, yeah. I went back down to the station. I told the detective and, yes, the district attorney. That's all. Nothing else. I didn't mention your name, or why I was in New Orleans, or anything. You have to believe me Leroy, they don't know anything more than the bus con."

"Yeah. Well, if that's the case, why do I see an open suitcase back there on your bed? You planning a trip somewhere? You think you can get away that easily?"

"What? No. Well, yes. I mean, I am planning a trip. With Frank. That was the other thing he and I discussed. He thought it might be good for us if we got away. Just for a few days. After, well, you know, after all this."

"Uh huh. Yeah, I don't think so. Frank wouldn't take off like that. Not when he knows how much heat is going to be around the place after this."

"It's true. You can ask him yourself. We're just planning on getting away for a few days. Nothing much. But this has been in the works for a while now. I think he's using it as some sort of cover. But what do I know? I'm just the dumb girlfriend, right?" Sharon sneered. She could see the wheels turning in Leroy's head. Hoping this was her chance to get away from him. Now she knew she would have to go see Frank one more time. Before Leroy had a chance to get to him first.

"Fine. I'll believe you. For now. But if I find out you're lying to me, you know what's going to happen."

"Yes, Leroy, I know. Now, if you don't mind. I need to finish.. I have to work tonight and I'm already short on time." She gave him a slight shove, inclining her head toward the door.

"Alright. Alright, I'm going." Leroy grumbled, reaching the door.

Finally with him gone, Sharon finished her hurried packing job, grabbing her purse and suitcase, then headed down to her car. The decision having been made for her. Her next stop had to be Frank's place.

Chapter 30

Pulling up to Frank's building, Sharon took a deep breath to steel herself. Still not knowing what she was going to say or do. She just knew something had to happen. Stepping out of the car, she saw a shadow pass by his front window. 'At least he's home,' she thought to herself.

Walking through the lobby, she took the elevator straight to his floor, timidly tapping on the door, knowing better than to use her key right now. Walking in on Frank when he was in one of his moods was not something she wanted to add to the list of grievances he was holding against her. Not sure if it was loud enough for her to be heard, she knocked again. Harder this time.

"Coming. Geez, I heard you the first time," she heard Frank call from inside.

"Sharon, what brings you back here again? I thought I told you to go back to the cops?" Frank demanded, glaring at her.

"I did. That's why I'm here. But can we discuss this inside, please?"

"Fine, come in. But this can't take long. I've got things to get done."

"Of course. I won't take up much of your time," Sharon murmured, as she thought to herself, 'I hope.'

"So what is it? I would have thought they would have kept you at the station if you did what I told you to do. And admit to what you did."

"Frank, please listen to me and hear me out before you interrupt. First off, Neil is in the clear. They know he had nothing to do with my escapades on the bus. He was a patsy I used on the spur of the moment. No charges will be filed against him. He can go home. Or go wherever it is he wants to now." Sensing that Frank was about to say something, Sharon barreled on.

"But this is where things get sticky. The district attorney was there. Apparently, they know that something is going to go down at the casino. He was being coy with the details. He kept trying to trip me up, get me to say something or point the finger at someone. All I told them was that I had gone back to New Orleans to pick up a package for Leroy. I didn't know of any other plans. I left you and Nick out of the conversation. Yet somehow, they seem to think that I know more than I'm telling them. They are trying to make me an offer of protection if I give them any information that will lead to Nick's downfall. Look. I sort of know what you've got going on. But I don't want to know anything more. And I don't want any other involvement. I just wanted to let you know what was coming. That being said. If you can tell me something else. Anything I can take back to the cops and the DA, then please tell me. I'll go back to them and then I'll disappear. You'll never hear from or see me again. I promise." Stopping to catch her breath, she could see a vein bulging in Frank's forehead.

"What the hell Sharon? What have you done?"

"Frank, look, I told you. I didn't involve you at all. You know they've been after Nick for well, forever now. They would have to be stupid not to think that something is going to happen. With Marylin coming to town that always brings chaos. It's the perfect cover. Someone, somewhere, is going to take advantage. And if it's not Nick, then it will be someone else. But you know. The cops will have an extra eye on the Crossroads, regardless."

Frank stood up, sat down again, taking a couple of deep breaths, trying to settle back into the couch. "Start from the beginning. Tell me exactly what went down. Who said what. Then I'll decide what to do next."

Sharon recounted her time at the police station, retelling the story once again. Once Frank was satisfied she had told him everything, he shook his head.

"Alright. I believe you. I also believe you want out of here. Don't even think about going back to New Orleans, either. That city is now off limits to you, you hear me?"

"Of course. I know I can't show my face anywhere near there. Honestly, I don't know where I'll go, but I promise it will be somewhere no one will know me."

"So here's what you do. Go back to the cops. Tell them word for word what I'm about to tell you and then leave. If you're smart, you won't take them up on any offers they're making. They'll only try to drag you back in again when things don't go their way."

Frank outlined in detail what Sharon was to tell the cops, then offered her a drink. "I don't think so, but thank you, I think it's best I go now. I'm sorry Frank, I didn't mean for any of this to happen," Sharon sniffed, holding back the tears she knew were coming.

Walking her to the elevator, Frank escorted her back down to the lobby. "For what it's worth. We did have a good thing for a while. I'm sorry it has to end this way. But I do wish you all the best in wherever life takes you next."

Exiting into the foyer, Sharon turned back to Frank just as he saw a taxi pull up. He grimaced when he saw who it was. Sharon, seeing the look on his face, glanced over her shoulder. Mumbling an "oh," as she wiped away the tears that were now trailing down her face.

Chapter 31

As the taxi was pulling up alongside the curb at Frank's building, Neil saw Frank in the lobby with someone. "Shoot, looks like he's got company. Now what?" Before he could answer his own question or even open the car door, he saw Frank and company step out of the front door. Unsure of what to do next, he ducked down in an attempt to not be spotted.

Peering over the edge of the seat, he saw a woman turning back to face Frank just as he held the door open. From what he could tell from her posture, this didn't look like a cheerful parting of the ways. Her silhouette looked familiar, but he wasn't sure who it was. When she turned back around, he got a good look at her face. Realizing it was Sharon. But why was she crying?

Before he had a chance to tell the driver to take him back, he saw Frank look over Sharon's head, directly at him. Now it was too late to do anything else. He slowly exited the taxi before making his way up the path to where they were both standing.

"Neil, before you say anything, please let me explain," Frank implored.

Sharon, keeping her head down, didn't offer any explanation.

"Yeah, uncle Frank, I've definitely got some questions. Even more now than when I first pulled up." Turning his attention to Sharon, he stopped and took a deep breath before continuing. "And you. Do you have any idea what I've been through since your little stunt? Seriously! What were you thinking? And why did you have to get me involved?"

Sharon looked at Neil, then at Frank, and started to open her mouth in reply. Before she could get any words out, Frank interjected. "Neil, why don't you come inside? Sharon, I think it's best if you leave now. I'll talk to you later once I've had a chance to think over what we discussed. Under no circumstances are you to come back here. You understand?"

Nodding her head, Sharon started moving towards her car. Frank stood, watching as she got in and drove off, before turning his attention back to Neil.

"Yeah, we've got a lot to discuss. Get inside kid, and I'll answer all your questions this time. You deserve to know what's going on."

Walking into the living room, Neil looked for any indication as to what may have just taken place. Not seeing anything out of the ordinary, he stopped at the bookcase containing Frank's extensive record collection and family photos.

"Drink kid?" Frank asked.

"No. Thanks." Neil replied, too soft to be heard.

Hearing the clink of ice hitting the bottom of the glass, Neil turned around to face his uncle.

"So, should I start? Or do you want to explain? No wait, I think I better start. At least that way I can ask the questions first. Before you can make up some other tall tale."

"Neil, listen, it's not what you're thinking."

"Oh no, tell me, what am I thinking, uncle Frank? How could you possibly have any idea of what it going through my head at this exact moment?"

"Based on the look of hurt on your face. I can well imagine. But alright, I'll let you ask your questions first."

Frank, gesturing at the sofa with his drink, sat down as Neil began.

"Honestly, Frank, I'm not sure where to begin. I guess with the obvious. Did you send Sharon to get me out here?"

"What? No! I swear to you Neil. Like I told you before. That was a complete fluke. I had no idea she was stopping in Forrest City. I knew she had gone back to New Orleans. But her running into you and all that happened after that, no kid, I had no hand in any of that. Sharon can be a bit of a wild card, if you get my meaning."

Looking at his uncle, Neil sensed what he was telling him was the truth. But he also knew Frank was still holding back.

"Okay, say I believe you. I still think there is more that's going on. That there's more you are keeping from me. I know you said Nick is connected. That much I get. But how deep are you in Frank? Do I need to be worried that I'm going to lose you next? I don't think I could deal with that too."

Shifting forward on his seat, Frank looks at Neil, taking a long sip of his drink before answering. "Alright, here's the story, kid. I am in deeper than I let on. It has to do with something I did a few years back. I'm not going to give you all the finer details. This is for your safety. As well as mine. This is my penance, if you will. Plans are in the works for something and it's happening soon. It's my last hurrah and then I'm out. If all goes well, I'll leave this place behind. I'll be out of the business. For good. Now. Before you go asking any more questions, know that I will be out of touch for a while. No. I'm not going to tell you all the details right now. Just know when it's time. I'll be in touch and let you know where I am and that all is well. I'm trusting you, Neil, to know what's best. Keep your head down. Play your gigs. Get out of dodge as soon as you can."

"But -"

"No, no buts. If you need cash to get out of town now, tell me. I'll give it to you right now. Or is it a girl that's keeping you here? Have you gotten involved with Audrey or one of the other showgirls? Is something more happening between you two that you're not letting on?"

"I, what? No! No, that's not what's keeping me here. You're here, Frank. You're the only family I've got left. And I guess that's a big part of why I'm still here. If I go home, you know daddy is just going to yell at me. Tell me what a failure I am. I guess I've got enough saved to get me to California now, but I've got no prospects there either. So, yeah. Maybe it is easier for me to stay here at the moment."

Shaking his head, Frank looked directly at Neil. "I am not your only family. This is probably going to come as a surprise. But you do have other family. Back in New Orleans. You've got a cousin there. Remy. She's just a little girl right now. But some day she's going to grow up. I need you to promise me you'll look out for her when the time comes."

"Wait? What? Who -,"

"It's all in the letter. And before you ask, you'll get that when it's the right time. I know I'm still not answering most of your questions, but it's for your own good. I don't want anything to happen to you. I love you like a son, Neil. You are my sister's flesh and blood and when I look at you, I still see her. I promised her I'd look after you and that's what I'm trying to do. So. Here's what I can tell you."

Frank continued his explanation, telling Neil what he had found himself involved in while living in New Orleans. How this resulted in him working for the Costa family in Las Vegas. Not giving any details of the upcoming heist he was going to be involved in, Neil came to the conclusion on his own that he had a pretty good idea of when it was going to happen. Finishing his explanation, Frank stood up and stretched.

"Now. You are going to head to work. Just go about your normal routine. Nothing is any different, you understand? Am I clear?"

"Yeah, but I'm still worried about you, Frank. Are you sure you're going to be okay? I mean, the cops seemed pretty interested in talking to you. Why can't you go and tell them what's going on? I'm sure they could get you out of town. Or something."

"I'll think it over. But for now, I don't want you concerning yourself with any of that. You got me?"

Shaking his head, Neil agreed. What else could he do? Having just learned he had a cousin he didn't even know yet. He wanted to be sure to be around to meet her at some point. He had to trust that his uncle knew what he was doing.

"Alright. I guess I'll head on over to the Crossroads now." Standing, he walked over to his uncle and put his arms around him. Giving him a big squeeze, he muttered into his shoulder, "stay safe, uncle Frank. Please. For me and for my little cousin Remy."

Chapter 32

After Neil left, Frank sat back down, reviewing his plans once again. The first copy of the necklace was complete, currently sitting in his desk here at home. He'd have to take it into work soon, since that one would be the one being sent back to the jeweler. The second one he hadn't even had started yet. He needed to get his hands on the original in order to have some of the actual stones from that one set into it. He had given a picture to his Jimmy to have him start whatever preliminary work he could. But now. With all the chaos Sharon had brought, he was rethinking his time line. Placing a quick call to Jimmy, he asked how long it would take for him to finish the job. Once he had the original necklace in hand. Jimmy replied. "A day for me to take out all the stones. Another day and a half to reset it into the new piece. One more day after that to make sure all the diamonds are fully set and give it a final polish."

Breathing a sigh of relief, Frank leaned back in his chair,

disconnecting the call. Taking the next few moments to consider all that he and Neil had discussed.

Maybe he should go to the cops? But what could he tell them? How could he keep himself out of jail? Or better yet, alive, while still getting away with the remaining stones? He knew it would be risky going back to New Orleans once the investigation was finished. The Costa family had reach all the way back there, too. Yet he knew he had to return. He had family there and he needed to make amends to his daughter and take the necessary time, while he had it, to get to know her. To start a new life.

Next, he thought about what other information he could give Sharon that she could feed to the cops? He decided he couldn't go to the cops himself. This was going to have to be his way out. He could give her just enough details that would enable the police to arrest Nick and the guys after the fact. Hopefully, then they would have enough evidence. Enough to put them all away for years. If not for life. He would just have to make sure she was clear on the timing when this information was to be shared.

This was the biggest risk he was facing. Being sure that Nick, not to mention all the other guys who could come after him for retribution, would be securely locked away. Otherwise, chances were good he wouldn't make it out of the state. Much less the city. No, he'd for certain wind up dead, and likely the same fate would befall Neil as well. Despite the kid not having anything to do with what he was involved with, the Costa family was not known for forgiveness. Or understanding. If there was collateral damage of other members of your family or friends being killed, well, too bad for you. It was the message they were known for sending.

Oh, how he was longing for the simpler days back in New Orleans. To return to the house in the Garden District, with its wrap around porches, old live oak trees, and its prime location for celebrating all the events the city had to offer. With easy access to all his favorite haunts, even though sadly some, like the Gibson, had recently closed their doors, he could still go out and enjoy the music and the food the city presented at any given time. Even the storms that would blow through. Yes, even those he missed. One thing he could say for certain about Las Vegas, despite its sun and year round warm temperatures, it was just too dry and dusty for his liking.

But enough wallowing. Now it's time to focus on what's next. He told himself. Satisfied with what he had conceived to tell Sharon, he turned his attention to getting ready for work. He would find her after finishing his shift. Give her specific details and the timeline of when to deliver the information. He'd hoped she was being smart enough to stay away from the club tonight, and that she was prepared with her bags packed for a quick getaway. Otherwise, she'd likely find herself out in the middle of a dark, deserted highway, late at night, with no means of getting home.

Arriving at the casino, Frank checked in with the security office, making sure everything was in order before proceeding to his office.

Finding Redd and Michael outside his door, he pulled them inside to discuss the final details for Marylin's upcoming visit.

"Okay guys, we have three days left to prepare. At this point, we shouldn't have anything else that needs to be done. But I want you to go over it with me. One more time."

Michael, taking the lead, explained all the details. "Upon Marylin's arrival, the necklace will be transferred to the casino safe. Once the courier is assured of its safety, they'll leave. It's their understanding that the casino security would take care of delivering it to Marylin when she calls for it. After she finishes her appearance, Redd will be the one to retrieve the necklace from Marylin's suite. He'll take it to the safe and make the switch at that point." Redd interrupted, asking if Frank had the copy ready.

"Yeah, I've got it locked up at home at the moment. I'll bring it in tomorrow before anyone gets here. I didn't think it wise to leave it lying around in here."

"Of course, boss. Just crossing all my t's and such."

Michael continued on with his explanation, detailing how Redd would then take the original necklace to the safe house. Returning to the casino, he'd give Frank the only key. "The fewer people we have involved, the better Nick feels about it all." Michael said, finishing his detailed explanation.

"Sure. Sure, I get that," Frank nodded. "I've got it all lined up for it to be taken apart once it's quiet again. I'm guessing it will be a few weeks, at least before that happens. Once the jeweler discovers what they have ain't the real thing. You know both the locals and the feds will get involved. So you guys need to make sure you are on your best behavior. You understand me?"

"Yes, boss," they said in unison.

"Alright, good. Now. Go get out of here. Get back out on the floor. And oh, I had a talk with Neil. He shouldn't be causing any more trouble at the tables. Poor kid was just having a bad day. Seems the cops around here just can't seem to leave him and this whole bus escapade alone. I think that's all cleared up now, too. In case Nick or anyone else should happen to ask."

Nodding, Michael stood, walking to the door while Redd remained seated.

"Something I can do for you, Redd," Frank asked.

"Yeah boss. I was just wondering, well, Sharon. I noticed she hasn't been around much lately. Well, I know she was mixed up in that whole thing with your nephew and all. Do we need to be worried about her?"

Taking a moment to consider what Redd asked, Frank shook his head. "No," he replied. "She's not going to be any more trouble. I've had a talk with her and she's gone back to the cops to clear it all up. I'm guessing she's going to have to do some time. Maybe pay a fine. Who knows? But no, she won't be any problem. Now, if there's nothing else?"

"No, Frank, nothing more. Thanks for clearing that up," Redd said as he rose, leaving Frank to his duties.

Watching the door close, Frank asked himself, "what was that all about?" It was out of character for Redd to ask those sorts of questions. Had Michael asked, he wouldn't have given it a second thought. Now he found himself wondering, was something more going on that he wasn't privy to? And more importantly, should he be concerned?

Picking up his phone, he placed a call to Sharon, telling her to meet him in the coffee shop in an hour. That would afford him enough time to make sure the band was playing. This way, she wouldn't inadvertently run into Neil or anyone else again.

Chapter 33

After having met with Frank the night before, Sharon now had all the details she needed to share with the police and district attorney. Nervous about what this could mean for her life. Opening the door to the police station, she swallowed the lump in her throat. Approaching the desk sergeant, she asked to speak to detective Williams. Seeing the look of recognition crossed his face, she paced while he walked back into the squad room.

"Williams. That woman is here to see you again. You sure you two don't have something going on?" He joked.

"Sergeant. Get your head out of the gutter. She's a confidential informant. Hopefully, this means she has some valuable information to share with us. If this pans out, it could be the big break we've all been looking for. Imagine Nick Costa and his crew behind bars. Do you know what that would do? For all of us here? Not to mention the city itself?"

"Sure." He drawled. "And I'm Marylin Monroe's date

for that big appearance she's got coming up at his place too."

Pushing past the sergeant, detective Williams strode out the waiting room where Sharon was still wearing a path across the linoleum floor.

"Ms. Taylor, please, if you'd follow me." He said waving at a door leading back to a small conference room.

Once they were settled into the chairs, detective Williams pulled out a tape recorder, starting the recording process with the date, time and names of attendees.

"Since we don't have a stenographer here right now, this will have to be our official record of the conversation. Keep in mind. Until you have a signed deal with the district attorney, this information can and will be used against you as well. Are you sure you wish to proceed?"

"Yes, I'm sure. Though I would like you to call the district attorney and record his side of the conversation as well, having him state what he's offering me. I'm putting my life on the line here and I prefer to be able to continue living it, regardless of where I may end up."

After calling the DA and getting his consent, detective Williams turned back to Sharon and began his questioning.

"Alright. So you stated in your last interview that you picked up the counterfeit stones in New Orleans and brought them back here. What else do you know?"

Clearing her throat, Sharon began giving the details Frank had shared with her regarding what was going to happen next.

"Once Marylin arrives at the casino, the necklace will immediately go into the vault. She will be shown to the VIP suite where she will first get ready for her appearance at the pool. Then she'll come back to room to get ready for her performance with Clarence and the Tru Tones later in the evening. When she's dressed for the big event, the necklace will be delivered to her room under armed guard. She'll come downstairs to make an appearance on the casino floor where they will have a red carpet rolled out. The press and photographers will be stationed on one side, the public on the other. She'll do her usual. Wave to the crowd. Pose for the pictures. Nick Costa will then join her, serving as her escort into the showroom. She does a couple of songs. A few more pictures, then is whisked off stage and back up to her VIP suite. Hotel security will escort her too. Taking the necklace and returning to the safe. That's where it will stay until the following morning. It will be picked up by another security courier. He has been hand-picked by the jeweler to transport the necklace back to New York. I don't know at what point they are going to make the switch. I would guess while the necklace is in the safe. It's my under-standing that either Redd Doyle or Michael Leon will be the one to do this. I know they have somewhere they will take it off site and keep it there until they deem it safe to break it down and start selling off the gems. And before you ask. I don't know where that is. If I had to guess, it's a warehouse somewhere. Then again, for all I know, it could be a resi-dence too. That's one thing Nick is good at. He has plenty of hiding places and no one but him knows where they all are. I know Frank Barnes knows of a few. But I also know he's not involved in this. Redd and Michael, I'm sure they both know of some too. I think the only person that knows all the likely hiding places is Mr. Costa himself."

As she paused to drink the water they had provided for her, Sharon watched as detective Williams' pen scratches over the paper in his notebook.

"So you're telling me that they have an exact duplicate already made, then?"

"I guess. I'm not one hundred percent sure of that. The package I brought back was supposed to contain the stones they were going to use. At least that's what Leroy told me the other night."

"Hang on a minute. When you did you talk to Leroy? And why are we just now hearing this too?"

"It was just in passing. He had been drinking after the band finished their set and I guess I just caught him at a chatty moment, telling me a lot of what I just told you. Saying he was also glad the package wasn't discovered when I first got back. Otherwise, he would have been in some serious trouble."

"Okay then. So what about Frank Barnes? What can you tell me about his involvement in this plan?"

"Frank? Um..." Sharon paused, trying to remember what it was he had told her to tell them. "Well. I mean, he's head of security, but as I said, he doesn't have any involvement in this that I'm aware of. I suppose he's guilty by association, but I've never heard his name mentioned in any of the discussions I've been privy to. And that's not been many, by the way. I've pretty much told you all I know."

"Surely he's got some knowledge of this. After all, as you said before. He is head of security."

"Well, I guess. I mean, I know he's heading up all the details for Marylin's visit. Then again, I think he's so busy with that. Maybe Nick is keeping him out of it for just that reason?" Sharon said, knowing it was off script, but unsure of how else to answer. This had not been one of the scenarios that Frank spelled out for her. "I mean, he wouldn't need the distraction of something like this. Not when he's going to have his hands full with press, photographers, and crazy fans, right?"

Detective Williams looked at her, eyebrow raised in question, before making another note on his pad.

"Is there anything else you can think of? Any other detail you may have left out? Someone else you are trying to protect? Neil Evans perhaps?"

"No." Sharon shouted. "How many times do I have to tell you people? Neil has nothing to do with any of this. He was just in the wrong place at the wrong time. He just got roped into my little scheme. Yes, he's Frank's nephew, but that is it. He doesn't know anything about this. Please, just leave the kid alone."

"Okay, okay. Just calm down. I had to ask. From what we've been able to find out, the kid is clean. No trouble back in Arkansas, and none here either. But if I should find out otherwise, be sure he will face the consequences. Just like everyone else."

Taking in a deep breath, Sharon exhaled slowly. "Thank you. I truly do feel awful for all the trouble he's already had because of me and I don't want to see him mixed up in anything else. There's nothing else I can tell you now other than what I've already said. Right now. I'm just tired and just want to go home. Or well, somewhere I guess."

"Home is a good idea. For now," detective Williams said. "Try to go about your normal routine as best you can. Don't give anyone any reason to question what you are up to. If we have any further questions, we'll reach out. Discreetly, of course. As District Attorney Bilson said, if all of this checks out, then you'll be in the clear. He'll drop the other charges and as long as you stay out of any future trouble, you won't be seeing either of us anymore. At least not until we need you to testify."

Sharon stood up, stretching and shaking her head. "I don't know about that. I mean once I do that. Testify that is. If I do that, then my life is over. Regardless of if Nick is behind bars. Personally, I'd rather just get out of town. Never see this place again."

"One step at a time. For now just go about your life and we'll be in touch."

Knowing any argument or further discussion wouldn't get her any further with the detective, Sharon left the station, heading for her car, hoping she made the right decision.

Chapter 34

Over the next three days, the casino buzzed with a flurry of activity. Everyone working overtime in preparation for Marylin Monroe's appearance. Knowing the press and paparazzi would swarm her upon her arrival. Fans would also come, hoping to catch even a fleeting glimpse of the blonde bombshell. Frank brought in the duplicate necklace, making sure it was safely stored in his office where no one else would have access to it. Doubt still niggling at him after his conversation with Michael and Redd, he couldn't shake the feeling of someone holding back on important details he ought to know. Unsure if it was one of them. Or if it was just the multitude of plans and arrangements, that he was responsible for overseeing. This sense of agitation grew in his stomach.

The only sense of relief he found was in knowing at least Sharon had done what she was told. Frank knew the district attorney was trying to make a name for himself, making an attempt to move up the political food chain. He was certain with the information Sharon had supplied to him, this could be what he needed to accomplish that task. But that had to be the least of Frank's worries right now. No. Right now, he had to focus on the matters at hand. In less than 2 hours' time, the woman that everyone man fantasized about, and every woman wanted to be, would arrive. Chaos would ensue. Starting at that moment on, everything needed to go according to plan. He would keep his head on a swivel. No detail overlooked.

Walking down to the clubroom, Clarence and the Tru Tones were starting an early set. Frank taking note of all the players there. Just as they should be. He was still worried that something would happen to the Neil, but had to bury that concern for now. As soon as this night was over, he could focus his attention on getting him out of town. The sooner that was done, the better he'd feel. After that, it would just be a matter of him making his getaway. In just a few short weeks, which he was sure would feel like the longest of his life, he would be on his way home to New Orleans.

Walking back out across the casino floor, he could feel the excitement permeating the air. Patrons and staff alike were on high alert for Marylin's arrival. The men were clean shaven, hair slicked back, wearing tuxedos or their Sunday finest, with their ties sitting straight under their chins, all standing tall. The women on their arms, knowing they couldn't hold a candle to Ms. Monroe, still went above and beyond, decked out in their best, dripping with jewels, furs, and gowns.

All the showgirls and servers were sparkling in their VIP costumes. The staff who had been working behind the scenes in the costume department had been busy for weeks leading up to this night. Thankfully, all the security guys dressed to blend in with the patrons. Just as they had been instructed to do on occasions like this. No one would be the wiser as to who was who. The press was set up in their gauntlet out front, each jostling for a prime position with the hope of capturing the million dollar shot.

Patrolling the main floor, Frank observed where all of his security guards were stationed. Everyone was in the position where they were supposed to be. He was relieved not to see a single police officer anywhere in the building. 'Good,' he thought. 'They are staying outside like they're supposed to. At least that's one thing going right so far.'

Moving toward the cashier's vault, he could see heads turning as the excitement built outside. Glancing at his watch, he realized it was time. Marylin Monroe should be pulling up now, and then the real chaos would begin.

As if the universe read his thoughts, flashbulbs began exploding. Screams of adoring fans filling the air, almost drowning out the chimes and bells of the slot machines and shouts from gamblers at the tables. Making his way towards the main entrance, Frank arrived on schedule to greet Ms. Monroe and her security team.

"Ma'am, welcome to the Crossroads. I'm Frank Barnes, head of security. Anything you or your team needs, please don't hesitate to call on me. If I may, I'll take the case to the vault now. When you are ready for it, just call down and I'll have it personally delivered to your room. We want to make sure everything is secure. Up until the absolute last moment, it's needed."

"Thank you, Mr. Barnes. I'm Jones, one of the couriers

Mr. Rueben hired to transport the necklace here. If you don't mind, I'd like to accompany you to the vault. You understand, of course."

"Yes, of course. I'd expect nothing less. Please follow me." Frank replied, leading Jones to the vault, while Marylin stayed behind, swamped by fans and press alike.

So far, everything was going according to plan, just as Frank expected it would. He would have been surprised if the courier had not wanted to accompany him in. Opening the vault door, he moved into the room, retrieved a key for a safe deposit box, and held it open while the guard removed the necklace from the lock box and placed it on a stand inside.

"Quite a stunning piece, isn't it?" Jones said while taking off the gloves he had been wearing to handle the necklace.

"Quite. Then again, so is the neck that will be showcasing it later. The rest of her isn't too bad either." Frank laughed.

Jones grinned in return as Frank escorted him out and back to the main floor.

"If you just stop by the front desk, they'll give you your room keys and take care of anything else you may need. As I said before. Just call me direct when you are ready for me to deliver the necklace to the room. Until then."

Jones nodded as he walked off towards the desk. Not bothering to look back to see where Frank might be heading next.

'Numbskull,' he thought to himself. 'The guy hands over a million dollar necklace and doesn't give it a second look. I supposed he'll be out of a job soon enough.'

Returning to the security office, Frank found Redd, Michael, Nick and the rest of the on duty staff milling around the window that afforded a view of the entire casino floor.

"Why is no one watching the monitors?" Frank shouted. "You think now is the time not to be paying attention?"

The guys that were supposed to be watching returned to their seats, mumbling apologies as they went. "Sorry boss." "Got distracted by that beauty sashaying across the carpet." A few of the excuses Frank overheard before he turned his attention to Nick and the others.

"Mr. Costa. Sir. Guys, why don't you follow me into my office, please." Frank said. Stopping to pour everyone a drink, he made sure the door was closed before settling into his chair behind his desk.

"Okay, step one has now been taken care of. The courier didn't even bat an eye. Nor did he bother to look back at me after he was out of the vault. Now that Ms. Monroe is heading to the pool, and the rest of her staff has checked into their rooms, we wait. They'll call for the necklace this evening, as planned. Once she's finished with tonight's performance, Redd and Michael, you know what you have to do."

"I'm going to suggest instead of Redd retrieving the necklace and going off site, you take care of it, Frank," Nick interjected. Though it was not a suggestion based on his tone of voice.

"Sir?" Frank questioned. "I thought we didn't want to do this on property. That we wanted to get it out as quickly as possible. Also, if I leave, that may draw unwanted attention."

"Yes, well, at first I thought that. But after additional consideration, I decided I don't want to take any unnecessary chances. Once you have the original necklace to return to the safe, make the switch. You'll then make your way back to the club as though you're just doing your normal check on things. No one will leave early and no one will be the wiser. When you get done with your shift tonight, you make the drop on your way home. Everything looks normal."

"Sure boss. If you think that's best." Frank said, throwing his drink back. "Now, if you gentlemen will excuse me. I've got some other work I need to finish up."

As soon as Nick and the guys left the room, Frank reached into his desk drawer, pulling out the counterfeit copy. Jimmy had done extraordinary work. Identical in design and style, the only difference being lesser quality stones. To the casual observer, they would think it was the real thing. Even the security guard would be none the wiser if he even bothered to open the box again when he retrieved it. If all went according to plan tonight, the switch wouldn't be found out before the necklace left Las Vegas. Not until the necklace reached the jeweler back in New York. At which time, Frank would have the original necklace well hidden. Yet another copy being made.

"Marylin! Over here!"

"Ms. Monroe, can you turn this way, please?"

"Oh my, would you look at that necklace! Stunning!"

When Marylin Monroe made her appearance that evening, these were just a few of the many calls Frank overheard as he walked through the casino. The necklace was as stunning as everyone expected it to be. The lights playing off it as though it had been designed for just this moment.

Of course, most eyes were focused on not only the necklace, but the rest of her as well. How could you not? It was Marylin Monroe, after all.

Approaching Nick, Frank stopped next to him while surveying the crowd.

"Looks like a great night, boss. All these people here, spending their money. We should sponsor more events like this," Frank joked.

"Ha ha, funny Frankie boy. You know I don't mind that we do it every once in a while. But too much attention on the place? Nah, not my style. I'll stick with the good game we got going. Everything else going according to plan?"

"Yup. No problems. Everything is all good."

"Good. Good. Once this is all over, make sure to give Redd and Michael a few days off. I think they earned it. You too Frank. You need to spend some quality time with that nephew of yours."

"Sure, boss. That sounds like a good idea. I heard him during that last set and he's doing well. Maybe I'll take him over to LA for a few days. Try to make some contacts for him. I think the kid has a future with his music."

Nick nodded, watching the parade Marylin was leading, dozens following in her wake.

"That's my cue to step into the limelight. You make sure everyone else is taken care of while I take care of our star. We want Ms. Monroe to enjoy the rest of her stay."

"Of course Mr. Costa. I'll take care of everything." Frank said, watching Nick walk over to Marylin, taking her arm and escorting her to the stage.

Frank hadn't expected Nick to suggest that he take a few days off. That came as a surprise. But a welcome one, it was. Now he had a way to help get Neil out of town. And before any of the details of what was about to happen came out. Then he could more easily go into hiding himself.

Making his way into the fray of the crowd surrounding Marylin, he found her lead bodyguard, asking as they moved with the crowd, "everything still good on your end?"

Nodding, the guard, "all good. Ms. Monroe is just finishing up here. She'll go into the club next and do her part. Once she's done with that crowd, we'll go back up to the room through the back hall as planned. She's hoping to get out of town without too much fuss."

"Of course," Frank said. "We'll have it all clear. Just ring me up when she's done, and I'll take care of everything. I'm guessing the plan is still to pick up the necklace in the morning?"

"Yes, that's the plan. Another courier will be by first thing in the morning."

With a handshake, Frank excused himself before heading back toward the club room to make sure Clarence and the band were prepared for the chaos that was about to descend.

Finding Neil at a table with some VIP guests, Frank stopped and whispered in his ear, "meet me at my place tonight after you're done. We need to talk."

Neil looked at his uncle with a question in his eyes, replying, "Sure, I'll see you then."

Moving towards the side of the stage, Frank nodded to the rest of the band, letting them know it was show time. As the band took the stage, Marylin entered the room, a path opening in front of her, leading her directly to the stage.

In what seemed like the blink of an eye, Marylin

performed her numbers before being whisked away. As she was being escorted back to her room through the back halls of the casino, Frank took an elevator to her floor. Meeting her security team there, he retrieved the necklace. All the while assuring them he would place it back in the safe where it would stay until morning.

Chapter 35

Placing the box containing the necklace in his jacket pocket, Frank took the service elevator back down to the main floor, giving all appearances to anyone watching that he was taking a more secure route as he headed towards the cashier's cages and, ultimately, the safe.

Exiting the elevator, he moved through the back halls, avoiding some, but not all, security cameras. He had to make it appear as though he was heading for the safe. Knowing full well that once the subterfuge was discovered, the police would review and track everyone's moves.

Patting the left jacket pocket containing the box with the original necklace and the right holding the counterfeit necklace, he knew these next few minutes would change the trajectory of his life and he had to be sure nothing got in the way.

Entering the vault, he tipped his head to the cashiers who were busy at work dealing with customers. He wanted to make sure it appeared business as normal and that he was observed going through the motions of placing the necklace back in its assigned box, where it would stay until morning. Even with the last minute change in plans, there was no way Nick would let this go down without tracking each and every movement of every person involved.

Keeping his back to the cameras, he was about to deftly make the swap when one of the new cashiers entered the room. Turning to see who came in while he was in there, he quickly removing his hand from his pocket, admonishing them that the house rule was only one person in the vault at a time. The cashier nodded in acknowledgment as they left, leaving Frank on his own again. Once he was certain no one else was entering, he turned back to the task at hand. To anyone who may be watching the monitors, it would appear as though all was doing was reaching into his pocket and pulling out the necklace before placing it back on its stand. Once it the security box was closed and double locked, he turned back to the direction of the door, knowing the cameras would catch his face. Brushing off his hands in order to hide their shaking, he was thankful the camera couldn't detect his heart racing. This was the do or die moment. From here on out, he had to be sure everything else went according to his plan.

Coming down the back hall, he slowed his stride before approaching the dressing room, bending down as if to check his shoelace. Not hearing anyone coming from either direction, he stuck his hand in his pocket, feeling the velvet box, when he heard whistling behind him.

Looking back over his shoulder, he saw Leroy coming down the hall.

"Hey Frank, my man. What's going on?" Leroy called.

Clearing his throat in an effort to steady his voice before

answering, Frank replied, "Leroy. Not too much. Are you guys done with your set already? I thought you had another 15 minutes left in the show?"

"Yeah, we do. But Clarence decided to do a couple of acoustic numbers. Feature that nephew of yours. I have to say, the kid surprised me, man. I didn't think he'd last. But he's still here. So it's all good man. What are you doing back here? We rarely see you around these parts?"

"Just checking in on all the places. You know how it is. We got Marylin in the house. All hands on deck, making sure nothing goes wrong. Can't be too safe. Especially with those stones she had hanging around that gorgeous neck of hers."

"Yeah, she's a beauty. But me, I'm more partial to the darker-haired girls. You know, like Natalie Wood or Sophia Loren."

Frank laughed, "Why does that not surprise me Leroy? Well, listen. I got to get back to it, man. Stay out of trouble."

Leroy nodded and headed off towards the dressing room. Frank let out a long breath, considering his options. With the last minute change of plans Nick had thrown at him, the unsettled feeling he had been having just intensified. Even though he was no longer meeting Redd in the dressing room, no one else was supposed to be back there either. Leroy showing up only added to his apprehension. Maybe it was just a fluke. He had nothing to be worried about. Continuing on down the hall, he turned the corner and found Redd standing outside the dressing room, shaking his head.

"Redd, what's going on?" Frank asked.

"What was Leroy doing back here?" Redd questioned.

Explaining what Leroy had told him, Frank led Redd

back down the hall. Keeping his hands at his side to avoid patting his pocket, he continued, "Even though we're in a blind spot of the cameras here, just keep walking as though nothing is out of the ordinary. You go let Nick know everything has gone according to plan. I'll finish my rounds. Then I'll go back up to my office before I close out for the night."

"You got it, boss." Redd replied as he headed out back onto the main floor of the casino. Frank followed behind. Head held high, glancing around as he always did when he was on the floor. Not wanting to draw any further attention to himself, he headed back to the club room. Staying to listen to the last few minutes of the acoustic portion of the set Leroy had been telling him about. Leroy was right. Neil was fantastic. His playing had improved significantly since arriving here. Now Frank knew if the kid could just get out of this town, he could make a name for himself and have that career he always dreamed of.

But first things first. Frank had more pressing matters at hand.

Chapter 36

Arriving home, Frank rushed into his bedroom. Grabbing a small suitcase off the top shelf of the closet, he stashed the stolen necklace in a hidden pocket. Racing around, not paying attention to what he was pulling from the drawers, he randomly threw clothes in on top of it. Time is short, he kept reminding himself. Plus, he still needed to find the time to drop off his bag in the designated hiding place.

Hearing a knock at the door, Frank opened it to find Neil, guitar slung over his shoulder and suit bag in hand.

"Hey uncle Frank. What's so important you wanted to meet so late? We could have gotten breakfast tomorrow or something."

"Neil, quick, come inside." Frank insisted, looking over Neil's shoulder at the same time.

"Hey uncle, what's going on? You're acting spooked, like someone is gonna jump out of the bushes or something."

Closing the door, locking it and sliding the security chain in place, Frank gave a nervous laugh.

"Sorry kid. Just coming down from the adrenaline rush of today. That's all. Every time we have one of these big names come through, it puts everyone on edge. But that's something else I wanted to talk to you about. Come in. Take a seat. Let me get you a drink."

"Just a soda. If you don't mind. I haven't acquired much of a taste for anything else."

"Of course. So how was it from your end this evening? Did you have fun? Did you get to meet Ms. Monroe?"

"It was great. And nah. The closest I got to her was seeing her from behind on stage. Which, of course, wasn't a terrible view to be looking at either. She was in and out so quick. It seemed like as soon as she got on the stage, they whisked her off. Other than Clarence greeting her. None of us had a chance to do anything more but play."

Frank nodded in Neil's direction while pouring the drinks.

"But I did see you talking to some attractive young lady at the VIP table. Is there something going on I need to know about? You two weren't making plans to run off to one of the wedding chapels now, were you?"

Laughing, Neil shook his head. "No, uncle Frank. She was just someone we were told to schmooze. You know how it is with these VIPs. My music is what's coming first right now. As you've reminded me on more than one occasion."

"I'm glad to hear that. Because that's actually one of the things I wanted to talk to you about," Frank replied, handing Neil his soda. Taking a seat across from him, he settled back into the sofa. Taking a deep breath, he continued.

"So. Now that we've made it through the chaos of this event, Nick suggested I take a few days off. I know the band is taking off for the next few days as well. So you have some time. What I'm suggesting is. What would think of going over to Los Angeles during this time? I've got some contacts in the industry I'd like to introduce you to. Make some connections. Maybe even take a tour of a studio or two."

Dumbfounded, Neil sat, mouth agape, before regaining his ability to speak.

"Wow. Uncle Frank. I don't know what to say."

"Just say yes, kid."

"Yes. Absolutely yes. Wow! This is not at all what I was expecting when I came here. I had all these different, awful scenarios playing out in my head. But this one never even crossed my mind. I thought for sure you were going to tell me it was time to go home. Or something like that. I've been saving up as much as I can. My goal of getting to Los Angeles is still always in front of me. I'm more determined now than ever to make something of this dream."

Frank looked at Neil for a moment, considering both of their futures before responding.

"Nothing could be farther from that idea. Now listen. Go home and pack a bag. Couple casual outfits and a suit for the evening should be enough. And of course, bring your guitar too. I'll swing by and pick you up first thing in the morning. We can get over there by early afternoon. We'll have the rest of the day to bum around the city. I'll show you the sights. The day after, we'll take some meetings with some folks I know. You've got what it takes, kid.

That much I'm sure of. It's just a matter of getting you in with the right people. But if you have any doubts or reservations, now is the time to tell me. If you are thinking of staying here and putting down roots…" Frank trailed off.

"No. I'm ready. Let's go! Meet with whomever you've got in mind to set appointments with. I just hope I can sleep when I get home. Because now I'm even more wired than I was earlier this evening."

Frank laughed, "oh to be so young again. You'll be out as soon as your head hits that pillow. So go on, get out of here. I'll see you in a few hours."

Neil got up, Frank walking him to the door. Pausing just long enough to give him a big hug.

As Neil pulled back, surprised by the emotion he saw in Frank's eyes, he asked, "What was that for?"

"I'm just proud of you, Neil. You've had some tough times growing up. Yet somehow you've managed to come out unscathed. On the other side of things. I'm believing this trip will be the next step in chasing those dreams of yours. You deserve it all."

Neil blushed. Nodding as he picked up his gear, he headed back out. "See you in the morning, uncle Frank."

"Yeah kid. See you in the morning."

Chapter 37

Tossing and turning all night, Neil lay in his bed, considering all of what his uncle had suggested. Was this his chance to finally make it to Los Angeles? What piece of his soul would he have to sell off to get a record deal? Now that he knew of his uncle's involvement with the mob. Could he be sure these people they were going to meet were legitimate in the industry?

With all these questions running through his head, it was going to be hard to fall asleep. Frank would be here soon. At best, he wouldn't get more than a few hours.

When the clanging of the alarm clock woke him, Neil rolled over, rubbing the sleep from his eyes. Seeing the time, he was struck by the thought, 'It's now or never.' Having no idea what the outcome of this trip would be. He knew what he had to do. Frank was right, Las Vegas was no place for him. This was simply a stopover on this journey he found himself on. He would hate to leave the guys in the band in a lurch if he did find success in Los Angeles. They had settled into a great groove for themselves. Even Leroy had finally agreed that Neil was one of the band. But he was getting ahead of himself.

"First things first." He said to the room. "This may not even amount to anything. But I have to give it a try."

A knock at the door interrupted his thoughts. Opening it, he found his uncle leaning in the doorframe, casual as could be. Sunglasses perched on his nose, a t-shirt and jeans. And what were those? His uncle was even wearing tennis shoes? It had been years since he had seen his uncle this casual and relaxed. Maybe this trip was something they both needed after all.

"Hey uncle Frank. Let me grab my bag and I'm ready to go."

"Don't forget your guitar as well. These guys we're meeting. They are going to want to hear what you've got before anything." Frank reminded him.

Neil laughed, "oh yeah, I haven't forgotten that. And if I didn't say it before. Thanks again for this."

Frank smiled, "Kid, you're doing me a favor. Now come on. We've got miles to cover, sights to see, and dreams to chase."

Everywhere they went, it seemed like uncle Frank knew someone. Whether it was executives at Capitol, or the busboy at The Brown Derby, Frank was busy talking up Neil's talent, making appointments, or at a minimum, putting the idea of his talent into people's heads.

Los Angeles was bright and beautiful, in a completely different way from Las Vegas, and most certainly from Forrest City, too. Everywhere you looked, people were heading places. Looks of determination, confidence, and beauty shining on everyone's faces. Girls holding folders containing headshots, guys doing their best James Dean or Elvis impression. Sunset Strip, the Hollywood Hills, and even the hotel; all the places they went, both Frank and Neil turned heads. Just about as much as theirs were turning, too.

After a day and a half of sightseeing, back to back scheduled meetings, casual run-ins, even some impromptu walk-ins, Neil was feeling the effects of continuously being on the go.

"Frank, I don't know how much longer I can keep up this pace. I thought Las Vegas ran me ragged. But man, I can't remember the last time I took a breath."

Frank laughed and raised an eyebrow. "Aw, kid, you have no idea. Sin city is all flash and neon lights with little else to show behind that facade. Here, though. This is where the hard work happens. Sure, you've got the talent. But if you want to make it in the business, you have to have the endurance. Not to mention the drive to keep going. Even when all you want to do is give in. Are you telling me that's not what you want now? Because if so, we can drive back. You can pick up right where you left off with the band and just be content to be a lounge player. If that's what you really want."

"No. It just feels like my head is just spinning with excitement right now. We've met so many amazing people and you just seem to know everyone. I mean, if all of this is available to you, what are you doing in Las Vegas?"

Frank paused, pushing his sunglasses up on his head before turning to face Neil. "Listen, I've tried to explain as much as I can to you, and I know you still have questions that I haven't answered. I get it. It's frustrating. It is for me too. But, in time, I promise it will all make sense. For now, do you trust me?"

"Of course."

"Good. Here's what we're going to do. Nothing is on the schedule tonight. Let's go back to the hotel, take a little time to rest. Maybe go out to the pool. Soak up some of this sun. Have a drink, a bite to eat. Tonight we'll go back down to Sunset. Leave the guitar here. No trying to sit in with the bands. Nor do you need to be trying to make any kind of impression. Just watch. See what it's all about. See if you can picture yourself here. Working the hustle. Doing what has to be done. If after tonight you don't think it's for you, no big deal. We'll head back and that's the last you'll hear me speak of it. But... and this is big. If you decide this is what you want, then you make that decision. There's no turning back. Tomorrow has the potential to be the first day of the rest of your journey here. Make or break. I'll do what I can to help you out. But kid. It's your talent that will take you the rest of the way. I can only open so many doors. The rest is up to you."

Bowing his head in thought, Neil gave serious consideration to what his uncle had just said. This had been his dream since he was a kid. Ever since he heard that first song, held his first guitar, he knew music was his future. Even though there had been plenty of times, he never even thought he'd get here. Now he was here. He couldn't squander this amazing opportunity that was in front of him.

"Yes." He said.

"Yes?" Frank quizzed.

"Yes, okay. Let's go back to the hotel. A little downtime

will do me good. And I won't make any decisions until after tonight."

Frank settled his sunglasses back on his nose, put the car back in drive, and pulled out from the curb, smiling to himself. He knew this was only the first step for Neil. And maybe it would turn out to be his salvation, too.

Chapter 38

While standing at the bar, waiting on their drinks, Frank caught sight of one of Nick's other associates, Dave, sitting on a stool at the other end. 'What is he doing here in Los Angeles?' Frank thought to himself. 'He can't be here looking for me?'

As if reading his mind, Dave saunters over, clapping Frank on the back. "Frank, man, what are you doing here in LA?" he bellowed over the music.

"Just showing my nephew around the town, Dave. What brings you to the land of sunshine, beaches, and babes?" Frank answered as jovially as he could, while trying to mask his underlying concern.

"You know. Just running an errand for Nick. And yeah, he mentioned you were taking a few days off. He didn't say you'd be here too. Had I known, I would have just given you the package, man."

"Nah, as Nick said, I'm taking a few days off. Things have been crazy back at the Crossroads. Everything leading up to and just after that Marylin event. So I'm just taking it easy and enjoying myself. No work for me while I'm here with my nephew, you know what I mean?" Frank smiled.

Dave shrugged, saying, "yeah, I get ya. Guess you were up to the eyeballs with all the shenanigans. Everyone deserves a little down time now and then. Glad you and your nephew are getting to spend some time together. He's the one that's playing with the Tru Tones, right?"

"Yeah, that's him. Good kid. Great guitar player. I'm trying to introduce him to some folks here while we're in town. Maybe get the kid a break here. Get him out of the sin city. He's still green under the collar, coming from Arkansas. No sense in him getting in over his head. If that's not his scene."

Dave smirked. "Not everyone's cut out to be like us, are they, Frank?"

"No. And that's probably a good thing, too. But it was good seeing you. Hope all goes well. If you're back before me, tell Nick I'll be back soon. Though he should already know. But you know how overwhelmed he can get sometimes."

"You got it, man. See you on the flip side." Dave called over his shoulder as he turned to check out the blonde that had just walked in and taken a seat on the stool next to his.

Walking back to the table, Frank thought to himself 'that was close'. Worrying that Dave might have been sent to find him. Because maybe somehow, Nick had already found out about what he had done with the necklace. As far as he could tell, Dave gave him no indication of anything being wrong. Frank to let out the breath he found he had been holding. Concluding he was still in the clear, he decided it would be best to take a couple of extra days here in Los Angeles. Focus on getting Neil on track and out of the scene in Las Vegas more quickly than he first planned. Then he would return home. The one obstacle he foresaw with this plan would be the delay of getting back and clearing out again before anyone noticed he was gone. This, he knew, was where it was going to get to be the most difficult for him. And difficult was putting it mildly.

Seeing Neil engrossed in the music, he stayed a step away, watching his nephew for a minute. A couple of the people they had met earlier in the day had already left messages at the hotel. They were interested in hearing more from Neil. Not wanting to tell him or say yes to any of these opportunities just yet, he knew there was one more appointment set up for tomorrow. Having been in contact with an A&R guy at Capitol records, it was his hope this would be the golden ticket Neil was in search of. If that didn't pan out, then he knew he could call one of these others he had standing by in the wings. A contract with them would be enough to get the kid out of Las Vegas. Out from under the influence of anyone or anything in that gritty city.

Chapter 39

Knocking on Nick's door, Michael stood shifting from one foot to the other, waiting to hear it was okay to come in.

"Yeah," Nick hollered from behind the door.

Taking that as his cue, he walked in, stopping in front of Nick's desk, waiting and fidgeting.

Seeing the look of consternation on Michael's face, Nick's mood immediately shifted.

"What's going on Michael? You look like everything is about to fall apart?"

"Boss, I, well, I'm not sure where to start."

"How about the beginning? I don't have all day for you to beat around the bush."

"Right. Yeah. Okay, well, you remember how I told you I was concerned about Frank's girl, Sharon?"

"Yes. Go on."

"Well. I got word that someone saw her coming out of the police station again. I'm just a little more than concerned about how much time she's been spending there. It seems like she's been back and forth an awful lot, and well, I'm wondering if she knows something more, or she's squealing on someone. And if that someone is Frank? How is that going to reflect on us, boss?"

Standing up, Nick took a deep breath before posing his next question. "Who saw her? And is it possible that is just related to the mess she created with Frank's nephew? After all. She made quite a bungle of all that."

"One of the cops we've got on our payroll saw her talking to that detective again. Also, the district attorney was in the room this time. Maybe it is about Neil. But boss. I just don't have a good feeling about this. It seems like this should have already been resolved. And Leroy has been acting all squirrelly too. I've got someone keeping tabs on him as well. It seems he went over and had some sort of confrontation with her. They couldn't hear what was going on after he went inside when she closed the door. But he was pretty steamed when he left her place. Muttering under his breath that she was going to mess everything up. I know. I'm not privy to all the details of what you've got going on -"

"You're right, you're not!" Nick interjected.

"I know, sorry, boss. I'm not trying to step out of line here, but I'm just trying to watch out for you. This has been one of our biggest deals yet. And well, I'd be lying if I didn't say everyone else is a little worried."

Pausing, Michael looked at Nick. Trying to judge if he had said too much or how Nick was going to react.

"Listen Michael. Sharon went back to New Orleans to retrieve something. Leroy was the go between. That's all you need to know about their involvement. Other details are being handled by other parties. Meaning the less you know, the less you have to share if, for some reason, someone comes asking. And believe me. Now the necklace is back in New York, and someone is already asking. As you also noted, I am the boss. You'd do well to remember that. I understand your concern. I've already discussed this with Frank and he's assured me she's doing the right thing. She's cleared Neil. She's taking her punishment for her little con, and that's that."

Taking a sip of his drink before continuing, "Now, as you know, Frank is gone for a few days. From what I've heard, he and Neil are over in Los Angeles doing their thing. Trying to get that golden ticket for the kid. I have no reason to suspect anything more is going on with him. That being said, I want you to keep an eye on Frank's place. Make sure no one that shouldn't be is coming in or going out. That includes Sharon. I also want to know as soon as Frank gets back."

"Sure boss. I understand. Do you want me to send someone to Los Angeles, too?"

"No, I've already got that taken care of. That's how I know what they are doing already. And I don't see that changing. I don't think Frank would be stupid enough to involve his nephew. Not in any of the plans we've got going on. He wants to keep the kid out of our business. Now. If you've got nothing else? I've got a casino to run and you've got work to do as well, yeah?"

Michael nodded, excusing himself from the room. Making his way back down to the security office, he'd have to recruit a couple of guys to help monitor Frank's place. He was going to have to be sure they would be loyal to

Nick. Not go squealing to Frank. It would mean keeping Redd in the dark on this, too. Not that he thought Redd was in cahoots with Frank. He just knew Redd didn't have the stomach for what might need to be done if Nick found out that Frank was indeed double crossing them.

Chapter 40

"Okay, kid. Today is the most important day of this week. We've got the scheduled meeting with Alan Foster at Capitol records. Then, if we find we've got time left, there are two other guys from yesterday want to have follow-up meetings with you, too. So, remember what I told you. Confidence is key. You've got the talent. Now you just need to make them see it and leave them wanting you. More than you want them."

"Are you sure, Frank?" Neil asked, twisting his hands around the handle of his guitar case. He was sure his nerves were evident to anyone looking at him. He was even more nervous now. More so now than when he first showed up in Las Vegas and faced the biggest uncertainty of his life. "I mean, this is Los Angeles. Everywhere I turn, I see and hear so much talent on these streets. Who's to say that I'm going to be that one in a million lucky breakout star you seem to think they're looking for?"

"Yeah, I'm sure. Neil, you doubt yourself too much. And I

get it. Every performer I know goes through that. Heck, even the showgirls complain that they think they're not pretty enough. Or their legs aren't long enough. Or any other dozen of complaints that none of them should be making. So trust me and listen. You've got more talent in your fingers than most others I've seen. If this guy at Capitol doesn't see that, then it's his loss and he'll be sorry he didn't jump at the chance early on when he sees you make it big. I'll be there. Make the introduction. Then excuse myself from the room. It's sink or swim time and I know you. You're going to swim."

Neil shook his head at his uncle's bravado and belief in him. But he would take as much encouragement as he could to help bolster his ego. Especially before walking through those famous doors. This was the opportunity he had been dreaming of since he was a kid. Though he never thought he'd actually make it out here, here he was. Standing on the brink of having what could turn out to be the biggest meeting of his life.

Frank announced themselves to the receptionist and told her they had an appointment with Alan Foster in the A&R department.

"Of course, sir, he's expecting you. He'll be down in just a moment. If you'd like to wait over there," she said. Pointing at the grouping of sofas and chairs.

Nodding, Frank ushered Neil over, giving him one last encouraging pat on the back, when Alan Foster emerged from the elevators.

"Frank, great to see you, man. And this must be Neil. Good to meet you too, son. I've heard so much about you. Come, come. Let's go up to my office. We can have a chat." Alan said, ushering them back into the elevator.

"Yes sir," was all Neil say as Alan continued dominating the conversation as the elevator rose.

"So I hear you've been playing with Clarence and the Tru Tones at the Crossroads for the past few months. That's great. An outstanding way to hone your chops. Have you written any of your own material too? Because you know, we're always looking for that original materiel, the next big hit as it were."

"Yes sir. I've written a few things. Not as much as I'd like. Playing six nights a week. And with rehearsals every day doesn't leave much time for anything else."

Alan laughed, "yeah kid, I get that. But keep in mind, once you strike out on your own like this, you'll be doing just that. And more. You need to make sure you've some time scheduled in your day for writing, too. Because without more material coming from you, the record company, regardless of who it is, won't wait long before they move on to the next guy or gal who comes along. It's a dog eat dog business and if you think Las Vegas doesn't sleep, you've seen nothing yet."

Swallowing down the rock in his throat, Neil knew it was going to be hard work. But hearing this coming directly from someone involved in the business gave him another pause. Seeing the hesitation in Neil's eyes, Frank jumped in to the conversation.

"Alan, listen, he's ready. And he knows what it is to work hard. This kid has been playing guitar since he was knee high to me. Shoot, I bought him his first guitar and he's been going at it ever since. There are no distractions in his life right now. No serious girlfriend and absolutely no gambling, either. Despite living where he does, this kid has kept his focus solely on the music. When we get to your office, you show me a place where I can go make a couple of calls and then the two of you can spend some time together. You can hear the talents he's bringing to you and then make your call."

Alan looked at Frank, then back to Neil before turning back to Frank again. "Yeah, yeah, alright. I'll have my gal get you set up." Looking back to Neil, he nodded, "and it looks like you've got some big shoes to fill based on your uncle's praise here. So let's go hear what you've got."

After an hour of playing some of the standards along with a couple of his own songs, and much discussion mostly on Alan's part, Alan and Neil walked out of his office. While Alan had a big smile on his face, Neil was looking overwhelmed. Rising from his chair, Frank looked between the two men. "All good then?" He asked nonchalantly.

"All good!" Alan exclaimed. "Man, you weren't kidding. This kid has got it. The looks! The chops! Heck, even the voice. He just needs a little more coaching. He's the package deal, Frank. Why have you been keeping him hidden from me for so long?"

Frank laughed and shook Alan's hand. "Alright then. I'm glad to hear you heard what I've been telling you. Now, before you start whipping out any paperwork or booking world tours, we've got a couple more people we need to meet with. So I tell you what, you write up your proposal, drop it by the hotel later, and we'll get back to you in a couple of days. Sound like a deal?"

Alan shook his head. "You drive a hard bargain, sir. But yes, I respect that. I'll get the paperwork drawn up. Be sure you don't wait too long to get back to me. You know what it's like. All I have to do is open the front door to find a dozen more just waiting in the wings."

After shaking hands all around, Neil and Frank rode the elevator back down to the lobby. Walking out onto the sun coated streets. Neil turning to his uncle, shaking his head in bewilderment. "Did that really just happen?"

"Yeah kid, it did. I told you it would." Frank said with a grin.

"I... I... I just can't believe it."

"Ha ha, believe it Neil. And now, start believing in yourself, too. This is just the first step. You've got so many opportunities ahead, I can't wait to see what happens next."

———————————

Chapter 41

———————————

Strolling into the lobby of the hotel, Frank spotted the night manager behind the front desk. He was anxiously looking around. Seeing them come in, he hurried out to greet them.

"Mr. Evan. Mr. Barnes. You both had deliveries this afternoon. Sir, Mr. Evans, this arrived by courier for you. Said it was of utmost importance that I place it directly into your hands." He said rather reverently, handing over a large envelope with the Capitol Records label prominent on the front.

"Wow, that was fast. Alan wasn't kidding when he said they wanted me to make a decision," Neil declared.

Looking at the manager, Frank inquired, "and you have something else for me?"

"Oh, yes, sir. Mr. Barnes. A gentleman left a message." Glancing down at the paper, the manager continued stuttering his way through. "It is imperative that you return to Las Vegas at once. Something is wrong and Nick must speak with you." Looking up, he wiped the sweat beginning to bead on his brow. "Sir, I don't mean to overstep, but the tone of the message was not very, shall we say, cordial? Do I need to contact someone for you, the police, perhaps?"

Not taking any time to decipher the message, Frank replied in an attempt to assuage the manager. "No, thank you. I believe it was just one of my work associates. He's a rather gruff fellow. Comes across more aggressive than he actually is. I'm sure it's nothing."

"Very well, sir. Well, if there's anything else I can do to be of any assistance, please just ask."

Nodding, Frank turned to find Neil with his head already buried in the papers he had withdrawn from the envelope. "Wow. Oh. My. Wow." Was all Frank heard coming from his nephew as he they strode to the elevator. As the doors opened, Frank let Neil walk in first, then paused.

"Hey kid. Listen. I'm going to make a couple of calls. Why don't you head on up to the room? Go through that contract with a fine-tooth comb. But do not. I repeat, do not sign anything yet. I've got a lawyer I know here in town. I want to let him take a look at it first."

"Sure thing, uncle Frank. Just, wow. I just never imagined I'd be holding a contract like this in my hands. I'm just flabbergasted."

Laughing, Frank patted him on the shoulder, "like I've been saying, kid, you deserve it. Now, get. I'll be up shortly."

As the doors closed, Frank turned back to the lobby, searching for a phone. Selecting the one furthest away from any activity, he placed a call to the Crossroads. Once connected to Michael on the other end, he cut to the chase.

"Michael. What's with this message I just got at the hotel? What's going on?"

"Frank. Thanks for calling back so quick. I know you are taking a few days off in Los Angeles. And you're there with Neil. But something ain't right here. Nick is acting all fidgety and won't tell anyone what's going on. He wants you to get back here quick, man. Says he'll only discuss this with you. You don't think something's gone wrong already with the job, do you?"

"I don't know. Like you said. I've been out of the loop for a couple of days. Listen, connect me to Nick if you can. Let me try to talk to him. I've still got a couple more things I need to take care of here before I can come back. Maybe I can talk him down a bit. See what's going on. I'm sure it's nothing, and you should be able to handle it until I can return."

"Hang on a second. Let me see if he's in his office."

While Frank was on hold, a dozen scenarios played out through his head. Surely Nick hadn't discovered anything already. The necklace was still with him. Definitely not where Nick thought he was going to stash it. But he also wouldn't have a reason to go looking for it either. They had built into the plan to leave it hidden for at least a month until things quieted down. Figuring even the jeweler would have made the discovery by now. But with that, it still shouldn't be raising any abnormal red flags on their end yet.

"Frankie. Hey glad you were able to find the time to call back so quick. When can I expect you back here?" He heard Nick say, interrupting his train of thought.

"Nick, hey. Um, things are going good here. Neil just got an offer from Capitol records. I'm hoping to take another day or two. Help him to get it all wrapped up. I want to make sure he meets with a lawyer. Get them to read over all the fine print. But I should be able to be back the day after tomorrow. If that's soon enough. Michael was pretty short on details. So now I'm not sure what's going on. Or why you need me back so quick."

"I don't want to say too much over the phone. Ya know? Apparently, the necklace that Ms. Monroe had been wearing was not what was returned to the jeweler. The cops have been here asking questions. Which is to be expected in something like this. For now, we seem to be in the clear. They know our security system and all. But Frank, this jeweler is being a real pain. Calling me at all hours says he knows we've got something to do with it. Said his couriers are the most trustworthy guys he's got. How he never thought they could do something like this. He can't fathom how in the world this could have possibly happened. He's threatening to involve the feds, too. Demanding to speak to you since you are the head of security. I've tried putting him off as long as I can, short of having someone in New York go and talk to him."

"No, yeah, I don't think that's necessary. Give me the guy's number and I'll give him a call tomorrow and smooth things over. And who is to say that the necklace didn't go missing along the way somewhere else in the process? As long as Neil's appointments go well, we should have everything wrapped up here by lunchtime. I can be back tomorrow night."

"That's my boy. See Frank. This is why you are in charge of these things. I know you'll calm him down. But listen. Once you are back, we need to make sure to go over everything. Be absolutely certain we didn't miss any detail. You get my meaning?"

Frank could hear the underlying message, even without seeing Nick's face. He knew Nick was having thoughts something else might be going on. Though he couldn't figure out what that could be. He was going to have to tread carefully once he returned.

"Of course. I'll sit down with everyone that was involved with the event. We'll do a complete review of everything that led up to Ms. Monroe's arrival, all the way through to when she and her team departed the hotel. I have complete confidence that everything is exactly as it should be. We'll review all the video footage as well. And of course, we will make sure to turn over copies of all that to the authorities, too."

"Alright then. You tell that nephew of yours congratulations and I'll see you when you get back. Just drop by the apartment when you get back in. We'll chat about the trip. Then set up a time to meet with everyone else the following day."

Agreeing, Frank hung up the phone, feeling the acid in his stomach burning. This was not how he expected things to be playing out. He certainly didn't want to take Neil back with him. Afraid if he did, he'd be putting him in harm's way. But could he just leave him here in Los Angeles on his own? Maybe this contract was just the thing. Perhaps he could enlist one of Alan's gophers to help out. See to it that Neil got settled some place for a week or two. Until Frank could get the remainder of his things moved. Then Frank would have time to get his affairs in order as well.

Pacing back and forth, Frank was trying to decide what to do next. "First things first. I need to call Ron Harding and get Neil set up with him. Once that's done, I know he'll be in expert hands and that's one less thing I'll have to worry about," he mumbled to himself. Returning to the phone bank, he put in a call to Ron, setting up an appointment for the next morning.

When Frank returned to the room, he found Neil surrounded by the contract documents spread out across the bed.

"Hey kid, I was joking when I said to go over them with a fine-tooth comb. I got an appointment scheduled for you tomorrow morning with Ron Harding. He's an outstanding attorney here in Los Angeles. He will make sure everything is on the up and up."

Neil grinned, looking up at Frank with a deer in the headlights look. "Thanks Frank. I can't make heads or tails of all this legal mumbo jumbo. I swear they make it way more complicated than it needs to be."

"Yeah, that's why the lawyers charge the big bucks. They use one hand to explain all those fancy words and catch phrases, hoping you don't notice the other hand slipping around to pick your pocket. But trust me. Ron's a good guy and he'll make sure you're taken care of."

Shifting from foot to foot, Frank paused for a moment before continuing. "But listen, I need to tell you something else. I just got off the phone with Mr. Costa. It looks like I need to go back earlier than expected. I need to take care of something."

"Of course. Do we need to leave now?" Neil interrupted, as he started to get up from his seat.

"No kid. This matter is something I need to handle. You need to stay here. Remember, your appointment is all set for tomorrow morning. I've already arranged with the front desk for a car to pick you up and take you wherever you need to go for the next few days, and the room is already paid for. Ron knows all this, too. If he says everything is good with the contract, he'll get you squared away with all the other details that will follow. Between him and Alan's gophers, they'll help find a place for you to move into. They can help start to get you settled, and then we'll figure out what to do about getting the rest of your stuff sent over. Now, I'm going to drive back tonight," holding his hand up before Neil could interrupt again he continued. "It's late, but I'll be fine. I've made this drive dozens of times. I could do it with my eyes closed."

"But -"

"No buts. Look Neil. This is your dream. I'm not going to let my work issues get in the way of it. So you stay here, charge whatever you need to the room and I'll see that it's taken care of. Once I'm done with this little thing at work, I'll return here. Then we'll go out and celebrate in style. I promise we'll stay in touch the entire time. Trust me. This is no big deal. Nothing is going to happen to me."

Neil stared at his uncle, knowing that underneath all his reassurances, a kernel of concern was simmering. Yet he also knew well enough that Frank wasn't going to tell him anything more outright. It would be fruitless to ask any more questions.

"Okay. But Frank, be careful. I feel like we've just gotten back to each other. I don't want to see anything happen to you too. I've lost too many people in my life already."

Walking over to him, Frank grabbed Neil in a bear hug. "I'll be fine, kid. You'll see. I always manage to find a way to come out smelling like a rose."

Chapter 42

Watching the sun setting in his rearview mirror, Frank made the drive back to Las Vegas that night. Arriving earlier than expected would give him the time needed to set the last steps of his plan in motion. Knowing both of his phones at work and his apartment would be under surveillance, he'd have to be careful making any calls. He hated leaving Neil by himself, but he had to trust that Ron would look out for him until Frank could return.

Once he finished here, he would talk to Ron about what his options were. Maybe now was the time to talk to someone in charge. Whether that was the feds or local law enforcement, he wasn't sure who would be his best option. Whoever that turned out to be, his first priority was making sure Neil would be safe. That no harm would come to him. Neil had lost too many people in his life already, as had Frank. And he wasn't about to add one more name to that list.

Pulling into town well after dark, he drove past Neil's

place. Doing so to make sure no one was waiting for him there. He wouldn't put it past Nick. Even Michael, at this point, could have lookouts stationed here and at his place. Even though it appeared to be clear, he drove back to his place, taking a circuitous route. He circled the block twice to make sure no one had followed him and there were no unwanted guests waiting at his building, either. Seeing nothing out of the ordinary, he chose to be cautious, parking down the block before causally strolling back to his building. He knew they'd expect him to park in his usual spot in the garage. He would do anything he could do to delay anyone finding out he was back.

Approaching the apartment building, he steeled himself for the possibility of finding someone outside his door. Seeing no one in the lobby, he rode the elevator up; the doors sliding open with its usual chime announcing its arrival. This would surely alert anyone that someone was coming. Peering out, he saw the coast was clear.

Perhaps he was reading too much into Nick's call. He supposed it was just the jeweler being a pain. Still, he wouldn't take any unnecessary chances. He crept quietly down the hall, put his key in the lock, and cautiously opened the door. Not turning on any lights, he slipped off his shoes, tip-toeing into the living room. The curtains had remained open just as he had left them. They allowed in just enough light for him to see if anyone else was in the room. As far as he could tell, everything stood in its proper place. There was also no indication that someone had been there since he left. No one was hiding around a corner.

Walking into the bedroom, he looked around, finding nothing amiss there. He moved on to check the closet and the bathroom. No signs of anyone snooping in here either.

Breathing a sigh of relief, he went back to the closet and grabbed an overnight bag. Throwing in enough clothes to last him a couple of days, he returned to the kitchen. It was then he noticed the envelope laying on his counter. 'How did I miss that?' He chastised himself.

Immediately recognizing Sharon's handwriting, he knew it wasn't going to be anything good. Hadn't he told her to stay away from him and his apartment? What had she been doing here? Did she say something else to someone she shouldn't have? Was that why Nick was so concerned now? He couldn't take his time to read the letter now. The sooner he got out, the better. Stuffing it down into his pocket, he made his way back to the door. He slipped his shoes back on, leaving the same way he came in. Pausing in the lobby, he looked up and down the street. Making sure the coast was still clear. He hadn't given Michael or Nick any reason to believe he'd be back sooner, so there shouldn't be anyone watching. 'Then again...' he thought, 'anything is possible.'

Once clear of his place, he duplicated his route back to Neil's. Parking down the block and around the corner, he hurried back, letting himself in with the spare key. Glancing around, he noticed Neil wouldn't have much that needed to be shipped over if he did indeed stay in Los Angeles. Who was he kidding? He would make sure the kid stayed. It would be the safest, well, one of the safest places for him. Anywhere away from this chaos would be better than coming back here.

Dropping his bag on the chair in the bedroom, he flopped down on the bed. Exhaustion from the day setting in. "Just a few hours," he muttered as sleep over took him.

Chapter 43

Waking to the desert sun streaming through the window, Frank realized he had slept more than a few hours. It had to be close to noon based on how bright it was outside. Rubbing the sleep from his eyes, he rolled over. Looking at the clock on the nightstand, he read the display. 1:14. Realizing it was even later than he expected it to be, he sprang from bed, rushing into the bathroom.

Splashing water on his face, he hurriedly brushed his teeth and got dressed, jeans and a t-shirt today, wanting to blend in as much as he could. He knew it would be hard considering how many people would recognize him and his car in this town.

Opening the front door to the hallway, he turned to the left, then the right. Seeing no one coming down the hall from either direction, he headed towards the back stairs. Granted, it would take him a longer going this way. But he didn't want to give any indication that he was back in town yet. Taking the front stairs down into the lobby would be too obvious. Going down to the garage and out the back, he navigated his way back to his car without risk of being seen. He was sure by now Nick would have someone stationed at least at his apartment and possibly even out here in front of Neil's as well, to see if he returned there first. One thing was for certain. Nick was not a patient man when it came to keeping appointments. If you said you were going to be somewhere at a certain time, you better be there on time. Or early. Or be prepared to pay the cost if you weren't.

Not seeing anyone around back, Frank dodged his way up and down driveways, behind other buildings and businesses until he arrived at his car. Reaching in the glove box, he pulled out a single key and stuck it in his front pocket. Deciding his car would attract too much attention, he walked another block down to the bus stop and waited. Trying his best to hide behind the small group standing there, he saw a car driving by with Redd at the wheel. Michael, in the passenger seat, was scanning both sides of the street. Watching the car stop on the next block, close to where he had parked, he cursed under his breath. "Damn."

Now he was certain they were setting up surveillance to watch for his return. He would have to work even faster if he was going to hide the necklace again and still show up in time for his meeting with Nick. Boarding the bus, he rode through two stops before disembarking and hailing a cab.

Being extra cautious, he had the cab drop him off two blocks from his first destination. He hadn't picked up on anyone tailing him since boarding the bus. But he was also well aware it wouldn't take long for Redd and Michael to figure out he was using some other means of transportation around town when they saw where he had parked his car.

Fortunately for him, no one else knew of this hiding spot he had acquired years ago when he had needed a place to stash items he brought with him from New Orleans. He returned here only twice more over the years he had been living in Las Vegas, always keeping it as a last resort. Knowing that this last job would be, well, his last. It was only fitting that he used it one final time.

Sliding his hand into his pocket to find the key, his fingers brushed over the envelope he had stuffed in there earlier. He was sure of it being Sharon's way of trying to weasel her way back into his life again. It was typical of her. Do something to make him mad. Then give him a little time to cool off. She would then come back and apologize, saying she'd never do it again. But she always did. She always managed to do something stupid, which left him running the risk of being found out. He was glad he hadn't told her about this place. This had been his one insurance policy. Slipping the key into the lock, he entered the dark building, finding his way to the back corner based on memory alone.

Spinning the dial on the safe, Frank yanked it open, setting the necklace inside. Picking up a small bag that held loose diamonds he had from a job years ago in New Orleans, he considered the contents. Maybe he should use some of these in the duplicate necklace? Unsure of what he should do, he placed the bag in his jacket pocket.

Despite his reservations of being spotted, he knew his next stop was going to have to be at Jimmy's. Jimmy had no connection with the Costa family. He was the one person Frank trusted right now to make another duplicate. He also knew Jimmy wouldn't be happy that the time frame had moved up and drastically shortened. But he had no control over that at this point.

Grabbing cash he had ready for emergency situations, he figured he could use it to sweeten the deal a little. Shoving that in his pocket, he tucked the necklace back in. Then closed up the safe. In and out of the building in under five minutes, he began the next phase of his journey to meet with Jimmy.

Making sure he still hadn't picked up a tail, he arrived at Jimmy's. Noting the surprise on Jimmy's face when he answered Frank's knock, Frank shook his head, not saying anything until he was safely inside.

"Dude. What are you doing here already? I thought you said we had at least a month before I had to do anything?" Jimmy asked as they moved back into the workshop.

"I'm sorry. The time line has shortened dramatically. If I could have waited longer, believe me, I would have. But I'm afraid I'm going to have to ask you to work fast. How long will it take you to get the stones out of their settings?" Frank asked, pulling the necklace out of his pocket.

Whistling, Jimmy took it to his workstation, laying it out on a clean cloth before inspecting it with a loupe. "This is some stunning work. You sure you want to break this down? Right, no. I can answer my own question. Of course, you need to break it down. This is entirely too recognizable. I can break it down easily enough in a day. Resetting it. That's going to take some time."

"Okay, here's what I want you to do." Frank explained. Instructing Jimmy to take out some of the medium stones and all the smaller ones, then place them in a bag. "I'll come back for those tomorrow morning." He said as he handed him the bag of lesser quality diamonds. "Leave the big ones intact and set in these others to fill out the rest. Those are going to be the ones that someone will be sure to look at first. As long as they see those are genuine, they won't gonna care about the rest."

Jimmy nodded in agreement. "Sure man. I can do that. But I thought you said the plan was to reset the other stones into other pieces. In order to hide them in plain sight? Not just duplicate the same necklace."

"Man. I don't want to get you in any deeper than you already are. So I'm not going to give you any other details. Other than to say, the necklace needs to stay as close to original as possible. I can give you a week to take care of the resetting. I wish I could give you more time. But that's going to have to be enough time." Frank said, as he handed Jimmy a stack of bills.

Pocketing the money without looking, Jimmy nodded. "Yeah, I get that. Thanks for watching out for me, man. I'll get to work now."

Slapping Jimmy on the back, they agreed on a time for Frank to pick up the loose stones the next day.

Once he had the smaller stones in hand, he would split them down into even smaller packages. In order to hide them where no one would find them. He would leave a few in one of Neil's drawers. It would be small enough, tucked away into an old sock. No one would notice or even think of looking there. The remaining stones, though they wouldn't be that big and recognizable. He would leave them in the safe deposit box at the bank. With all the scrutiny sure to follow, there was not going to be a way to offload those any time soon. Years down the road, maybe. But right now, they would remain safe, tucked away, out of the hands of the Costa family and the law.

Finishing his other stops, he arrived back at Neil's. He had just enough time to shower and change before having to leave to go meet with Nick. Rehearsing again what he was going to say, he was deliberate in how he dressed. In addition to what he had on his person. Remembering the letter from Sharon was still in his other pants and knowing he wouldn't have time to deal with it after this meeting, he decided it was time he read it and dealt with whatever last drama she was trying to stir up.

Chapter 44

Dear Frank. By the time you read this letter, I'll be gone. I don't know where and please, whatever you do, don't try to find me. Oh, who am I kidding? I know you won't. You told me as much already. I'm sorry. I wanted to try and stay for you. I thought maybe we could try to work things out one last time. When I heard you went to Los Angeles, well, I knew. This was the end. I guess that was the answer to my questions.

Sorry for being so vague. Let me get to the point. If you're reading this, then you must be back in Las Vegas. And that means the local cops and probably the feds are now looking for you, too. I can't tell you again how sorry I am. But I had to tell them. I couldn't spend any more time in jail. And the deal they were offering me was just too good to pass up. I didn't tell them everything; I promise. Just enough that they'll want to talk to you. But hopefully not charge you.

Really Frank, I am so, so sorry. I know that these are just words on paper. You probably hate me now. You possibly even want to kill me. And I don't blame you. I've not always used my head. As you told me on so many occasions. But I'm hoping that this one time I did. I told them exactly what you wanted me to. I hope I gave you enough cover as well. In order to get out of this mess and hopefully get your life back. I've enclosed the business card of the district attorney I've been talking to. He is expecting your call, Frank. Please, if not for me, then for your nephew. Call him. Get yourself out of this situation. Back to the life you had before.

With all my love, Sharon.

Crumpling the letter in his hands, Frank shouted, "what the hell Sharon? Could you even be any more vague?" Rereading the second paragraph again, Frank was trying to decipher what she meant by what she told them. How much did she tell them? What exactly had she told them? What other details did she go into? Pacing back and forth, he tried to breathe deep and calm himself down. Now, not only did he have to worry about Nick and what he knew, but did Nick also know about Sharon and her visits with law enforcement? Besides looking for Michael and Redd on his tail, he also had to worry about looking over his other shoulder to see if the feds were behind him, too? Today was getting worse and worse by the minute.

Stopping mid stride, he shook his head to clear it. He knew he had to make life-changing decisions right this minute. Should he show up for the meeting with Nick? Or should he take his chances and hightail it back to Los Angeles? Try to lose himself in the crowd of that city. At least there it wouldn't be as easy to find him as it was here. Here, he was a sitting duck. No, he knew they'd catch up to him just as easily in Los Angeles, too. Going back right now would also put a target on Neil's head. And he couldn't have that on his conscience.

Grabbing his bag, he stuffed the letter down as deep as it would go and made his way down to his car. Opening the door, he determined the best course of action would be to pull directly up to the front entrance of the Crossroads. He would use it to his advantage if Redd and Michael saw him. Maybe they'd spot a fed tail if there was one. He could use that as a distraction. He knew he had to face Nick. If he didn't, he'd never be able to stop running.

Rehearsing his speech in his head, playing out all the scenarios he could imagine, he pulled up to the valet station. "Mr. Barnes, great to see you back, sir." The valet greeted him.

Tossing the keys to the kid, Frank nodded and marched confidently into the lobby. Feeling the chill of the air conditioning brush over his exposed skin, he knew the cold he felt in the pit of his stomach had nothing to do with the temperature in the air. It was time to face the music.

Walking into Nick's office, Frank was surprised to see it was only Nick sitting at his desk. Having not seen Redd or Michael when he first entered the casino, he thought for certain they would have been in attendance too. Maybe luck was on his side. Maybe Nick was just only concerned about the jeweler and still had no idea about anything else Frank had going on.

"Frank, welcome back from Los Angeles. I thought maybe we lost both you and the kid to the land of sunshine and movie stars."

Shaking Nick's hand, Frank laughed. "Nick, no. You know you can't keep me away from here for too long. Too much sunshine and I start to turn into ash. I need the neon lights, bells and whistles of the slots, and the showgirls. Give me the nightlife of Las Vegas over daytime anywhere else."

Keeping his guard up, Frank saw the look Nick was giving him. Maybe it lasted a little longer than Frank thought was necessary. He couldn't get a clear read about what was coming next.

"So, Nick, what's going on? You sounded pretty concerned on the phone? Is the jeweler now thinking we had something to do with this?"

"No, I think I've talked him down from that idea. At least, for now. The cops, while they keep sticking their noses in, they seem to think it was someone outside of here, too. Since the courier has disappeared, they are looking for him too. Figuring he had some involvement. But still. It's got me nervous, Frank. You've got the necklace stashed somewhere safe, right?"

"Of course. As we agreed, I checked on them as soon as I got back. They are still right where I left them and no one else knows where they are. They'll stay put there, as planned, until all this heat dies down and we can then safely move them without drawing any more attention."

Nick leaned back in his chair and sighed. "Ah good. That's what I needed to hear. It takes a load off my mind. Honestly Frank. This all went down almost too easy. Then this guy started calling. He kept saying the necklace he got back wasn't the same as what he sent out here. Telling me how he's always trusted this courier. He didn't think it could possibly be him. And you were gone. I know, I know. I told you to be the good uncle and help your nephew out. And before you say anything. I don't think you had anything to do with anything. You've been with me longer than any of these other guys. It's just this is our biggest haul yet. And the proceeds of this? Well. Let's just say I won't have to worry about the nickel games much longer. And then there's Michael. Well, he's been raising some questions. You know what I mean?"

"Um, no Nick, I don't. What has Michael been saying?"

Watching as Nick turned his chair around, facing the window, Frank heard him take in a deep breath before turning back again.

"He seems to think things haven't been quite right. Ever since your nephew got to town." Holding his hand up to stop any protests from Frank, he continues. "I'm not saying it's Neil, Frank. No, Michael was bringing up concerns about Sharon and how when she returned, she brought all that heat on herself and, subsequently, your nephew. I know you've known her for years. And you wouldn't be involved with her if you didn't think you could trust her. But the concerns Michael raised had me worried for a minute."

Not expecting fingers to be pointed at Sharon, Frank bites his tongue while trying to maintain his composure.

"Sharon? She doesn't know anything Nick. Sure, she's pulled a few of her own cons. That thing with the bus, that went horribly wrong and she knows it. That's why she hasn't been around lately. The cops were charging her and at first she tried putting the blame on Neil. Thankfully, it didn't take them very long to figure out he couldn't have been the 'mastermind' behind it all. As far as I know, they've got her now, and it looks like she's going to serve her sentence. I mean, I haven't heard from her since before I left. But that's the last I knew of the situation."

Frank could feel the sweat beading on the back of his

neck. He couldn't stop to wipe it, knowing Nick would see it as a sign that he was holding something back.

"You've only been gone a few days. As you know, in a few days a lot can happen in this town. I'm hearing stories that she's no longer serving that sentence you speak of, Frank. No, what I'm hearing is that she's not only talked to the locals, but she's also spilled what she knows to the feds and that they are offering her a deal. So. Based on that, do you want to reconsider what you just told me?" Nick said, straightening up in his chair, staring directly at Frank.

Jumping out of his seat, Frank placed his hands on Nick's desk and leaned over. "Nick, I know nothing about this. As you said, I've been gone for a few days. When I left, Sharon was trying to save her own bacon while clearing up any accusations against Neil. I briefly spoke to her before I left town to tell her she was on her own. I want nothing more to do with her. Especially after the hell she put Neil through. That was the last straw for me. She doesn't know anything about anything. So whatever it is she thinks she can give the feds is petty and I don't see how it's going to help her or, more importantly, hurt you. Or any of us."

Rising from his seat, Nick leaned in close to Frank's face. "Take it easy now, Frank. Do you forget who you're talking to here?"

Taking a step back, Frank replied, "no sir."

"Alright then. Why don't you sit back down. Let me get you a drink. Then let's discuss what our next steps are going to be."

Chapter 45

As Nick filled Frank in on the details of the calls he had been receiving from the jeweler, Frank knew his concerns about his deception were unfounded. The necklace was still safely hidden away as far as Nick was concerned. Not wanting to show his relief, Frank plastered a frown on his face.

"How are we going to handle this, Mr. Ruben? Even if he believes it was the courier? It seems like he's not going to let up on us, either. Eventually, he or his insurance company is going to get the feds involved. If they aren't already. We can't have that happening. Not if what you say about Sharon talking to law enforcement is true as well."

"I've got someone lined up in New York who is going to take care of him. How is not your concern. What I want you to focus on now is what are we going to do with the necklace? It seems it's going to take longer for the heat to die down. But I don't have time to sit on this for an extended period either. I do have other parties who have a stake in what we've done. They aren't going to be happy with more delays. I'd like to get it broken down and start moving some of the smaller stones, at least. So you see my conundrum?"

"Yeah boss, I see it. And I think I may have a solution. I've got a guy who can break down the necklace. He can cut down some of the bigger stones to a smaller, more manageable size. Let me get in touch with him. See what he can do. The smaller stones we may have to sit on a while longer, though. I can't see how we could possibly do anything else with those. Unless, of course, you want to set them in another piece and try to sell that. Hide them in plain sight, as it were."

"And that's why you are the head of security, Frank. I like the way you think. Get in touch with whoever it is you need. Get the ball rolling on this. The sooner we can be done with this, the better I'll feel."

Rising from his chair, Frank nodded. "I'll let you know by end of day tomorrow what our next steps will be."

Nick nodded as he rose from his chair. "Good. Now I've got to go show my face downstairs for a few minutes. Looks like we've got a few new high rollers who may or may not pose a problem."

"Anyone I need to be aware of, boss?"

"No. I've got Redd keeping an eye on them. Between him and a couple of the girls I've got hanging on their arms, I think we've got it covered. You just worry about what's on your plate for now. And hey, tell that nephew of yours 'good job'. I knew the kid had talent. But for him to score a deal so quick like that is no easy feat."

Parting ways at the elevator, Frank motioned he'd take the stairs. "Too much good food and drinks the past few days. Gotta watch my figure, ya know." He joked.

As he descended each flight of stairs, Frank could feel the knot in his stomach begin to dissolve. After processing all that had just transpired, his thoughts turned to what he needed to do next. He didn't want to have to give up any of the smaller stones he was holding back. But maybe having the large ones cut down would keep Nick appeased. Thinking nothing was out of the ordinary. He would have to talk this over with Jimmy and see what he could come up with.

Arriving at the security office, he acknowledged the guys monitoring cameras, purposefully avoiding any other interactions while making his way to his office. Knowing he couldn't make any important calls from his office phone, even if the feds weren't monitoring him yet, he knew Nick had surveillance and listening devices throughout the building. He didn't want to run the risk of finding out the hard way if any had recently been installed in his office.

Spending the next hour going over paperwork that had piled up while he was gone, he returned a few inconsequential phone messages before letting his secretary know he'd be gone for a couple of hours. Making a promise that he would be back before the nighttime rush advanced too far. "Just in case anyone comes looking for me," he said.

Leaving the casino, he drove his normal route that would make it appear as though he was heading towards his apartment. Using this time, he was trying to spot if he had anyone following him. Once he was certain no one was, he turned and made his way to back to Jimmy's to discuss next steps.

Having more time to give it additional thought, he decided he would forfeit some of the medium stones. They would have to be cut down to a smaller size as well. But this would still leave him with a majority of the small stones. And it would be plenty to fund his retirement. Along with the cash he saved over the past years. Unlike Nick, he was in no hurry to get rid of his stash and knew he could keep it hidden as long as necessary. The hardest step would come after delivering the pieces back to Nick. Disappearing and staying below the family's radar was something few had ever succeeded in doing.

Chapter 46

Arriving at Jimmy's, Frank found him working on the necklace, so lost in concentration, he didn't hear the door open and close.

"Man, what the hell? You don't go sneaking up on someone like that!" Jimmy exclaimed.

"Sorry, man. I knocked, but I guess you didn't hear me. Why would you go leaving the door unlocked like that?"

"No one bothers me here at this time of night. I don't even think anyone knows I'm here. No lights are visible from the front of the place. And I do my best work when I'm not interrupted."

"Yeah, alright. My bad." Frank apologized, looking at the worktable. "Looks like you've made good progress already."

"Yup. Got all the small ones out already. Just a few more of these medium ones to go. But you weren't supposed to be here till tomorrow morning. So why are you here now? Something I need to worry about?"

"Not exactly. No one is aware of what I've got you doing. It's just a slight modification, if you will. You'll still have the week to finish. Instead of resetting them into a duplicate necklace, I need you to create a couple of new pieces. Go ahead and take out all the stones, cut down the large one, as well as the medium ones, too. Whatever you decide needs to be done. It's your own design. Necklace, bracelet, earrings, I don't care. Along with the extra cash I paid you earlier, I'll arrange for a little more when the job is done. Provided you can still finish in the shortened time frame." Hoping this would be enough motivation that it wouldn't be a problem, Frank looked at Jimmy, waiting for his answer.

"You sure about this man? You'd get more for them if you leave them intact."

"I'm sure. I can't say any more. As long as you can have that done in the same time frame. Then I think everything will be good."

"Yeah sure. I'm up for this challenge. I even have a few ideas in mind for pieces I can make."

"I knew I could count on you. Thanks for doing this."

Jimmy nodded, waving his hands at the loose stones.

"Those are ready. If you want to take them now. The rest, I'll set aside for you to pick up at the end of the week."

Agreeing to that, Frank scooped up the small stones, placing them in three different bags. Thanking Jimmy again for his willingness to be flexible with all the changes and his discretion.

"Any problems man, you let me know right away. Otherwise, you won't hear from me until I'm ready to come back and pick them up."

Jimmy turned back to the project on his workbench, grunting his goodbye.

Leaving out the back door, Frank took his time making his way back to the car. Still suspicious that Nick was having him followed, he knew he had to be careful going back to his apartment. Aware he was quickly running out of time before he had to be back to work, he packed one last bag and put in a call to Neil.

"Neil, glad I caught you. How are things going? Did you meet with Ron Harding yet?"

"Uncle Frank. Yes, and man, things are going great. I don't know how I can ever repay you for this. Mr. Harding looked over the contract. After making a couple of changes, he sent it back to Alan over at Capitol. Much to my surprise, they agreed to it all. You are talking to the newest artist on the Capitol label now."

"Aw kid, that's fantastic. This is what you've always dreamed of. That is all the thanks I need. Well, that and for you to put in the work and make this a success. I expect to see you playing the big gigs soon. Maybe even back in New Orleans, headlining at a club on Bourbon Street sometime soon."

Neil laughed, "only if you're going to be there, uncle Frank. Who would have thought that an unplanned bus ride, and getting conned by a stranger, would be my path to this?"

Chuckling, Frank shook his head. "Who woulda thought? But on a more serious note, I need you to do me a favor."

Hearing the change in the tone of his uncle's voice, Neil expressed his concern. "What is it Frank? Are you in trouble?"

"No. I'm fine. It would seem that Sharon has been talking to the cops again. She may have gotten the feds involved, too. Now it's got a few people concerned. Nothing for you to worry about. You are still in the clear. There shouldn't be any more complications. Nor visits from the cops for you. If, for some reason, they come around hassling you, have them call Ron or even Patrick back here, and one, or both of them, will set everything straight again."

"Are you sure -" Neil started.

"Listen Neil. Finish up what you need to. Hop on a bus and come back here in the next day or two. I'll arrange to have a couple of the maintenance guys help get your place packed up. They can get you moved back to Los Angeles before you can say jackpot. But you owe it to Clarence and the guys to give them a proper notice too. I know they're going to hate to lose you, kid. But honestly, those guys are never going to leave the Crossroads. They've been here a long time and have gotten too comfortable in this gig."

"I know. I feel bad about leaving them in this situation again. We finally got to a good place and a tight groove. I only wish I could find a way to take them with me."

"Don't worry about them. They'll be fine. Who knows, maybe you can poach Duane once you've got your feet under you. But like I said, you take care of you. Do what you have to. If you can, try to get back here tomorrow. I'll be around. Working most of the day. Come find me when you get back. Got it?"

"Sure thing. I've only got one more meeting later this morning and then I'll catch the late afternoon bus. I'll meet you first thing tomorrow. Breakfast at the diner?"

"Sounds like a good idea, kid. I'll see you then."

Knowing Neil was getting settled, at least for the most part, Frank set out to tackle the next part of his plan. Hiding the remaining stones somewhere in Neil's belongings where no one, not even Neil, would find them.

Chapter 47

Stepping off the bus in Las Vegas, the bells and whistles of the penny slot machines immediately assaulted Neil's ears. Throwing his bag over his shoulder, he mused to himself that he wouldn't miss all this cacophony. It was one of things that made writing music that much harder here in Las Vegas. The constant twenty-four-hour noise didn't give a person much chance for quiet, and that's when he worked best.

During the past days spent on his own in Los Angeles and even on the bus ride back, he started writing two new songs. It was a major stipulation in his new contract. He had to come with his own original material. Even though he would have access to other songwriters he could work with, he was determined to record most of his own music. Knowing full well he was going to have to put in the work if he wanted to make his dream come true and make a name for himself, he was no stranger to hard work. In fact, if he was being honest with himself, he was looking forward to staying busy, excited to learn new skills and all the different tasks he knew would be involved with in this endeavor.

Opening the door to his apartment, he found it just the way he had left it. Spying an envelope on the counter that he knew hadn't been there before, he immediately recognized his uncle's handwriting. Picking it up he turned it over. Seeing Frank's handwriting scrawled on the back flap. "Do Not Open".

'Do not open?' He wondered. Why leave this here then if he didn't want me to open it? Shrugging, he dropped it back on the counter and proceeded into his bedroom. He considered unpacking his bags, but what would be the point? It wasn't as though he was going here much longer. A week at the most, he was guessing. 'Man. Clarence and the guys are really not going to be happy,' he thought. Oh, they'd be thrilled for him, too. But lately it seemed they had a hard time holding on to guitar players. Looking at the clock on his nightstand, he saw that if he hurried, he could make the last set at The Crossroads. Better to rip off the bandage now. Get it out of the way. At least then tomorrow, when he met with Frank for breakfast, he could let him know what his timeline would be.

Walking into the club, Neil heard them starting their last set of the night. Discovering they had found a guy to fill in on guitar, Neil could hear he was pretty good. Could this player was the answer to the question hanging over his head? Maybe it would make for an easier transition than he thought.

Catching Duane's eye, he nodded in greeting as he wound his way through the crowd to a table in the back corner. This was the first time he could take in all the nuances he never noticed before. How crowded together the tables were in the back section. The middle of the room reserved for the four VIP booths. Each of which you could fit half a dozen people comfortably. The front tables had more room around them. Though they weren't as plush as the VIP tables, you were closer to the action. It felt strange to him being on the other side and seeing things from the audience's point of view. When it dawned on him, this would probably be the last time he got the chance to be just a spectator he felt overwhelmed by what was to come. Waving down a waitress, he ordered a soda and tried to settle back to watch the show.

After the encore, he saw Clarence and Duane making their way to his table. He knew they would get stopped by fans along the way, he used this extra time once more to rehearse the words he was going to say.

"Neil, my man. My rock star!" Clarence bellowed. "I see Los Angeles couldn't hold you for long. Please, tell me you're back."

Looking down at his drink and then back up again, Neil shrugged.

"Uh oh." Duane cut in. "I know that look. I've seen it on my kid's face. It's not good news, Clarence. Well. At least not good news for us."

Clarence turned to Duane, looked back at Neil, and stood tapping his foot. Just waiting for Neil to speak. Seeing that the ball was in his court, Neil cleared his throat and began rapid fire recounting all the events, meetings, and sights he saw. He told them about everything that had taken place over the last few days. Finishing with the new of signing a contract, he apologized to Clarence, saying, "I truly, honestly, did not think this was going to happen. I figured I'd just go on a lark. I was only intending on having a good time for a few days. See the sights. Get to spend some time with my uncle and then be back here with you guys. If there was a way I could, I would take all of you with me in a heartbeat. Being the new kid, I don't have that kind of pull. At least not yet. But, and I mean this sincerely, as soon as I can, man. I want to get any and or all of you over with me."

Shaking his head, Clarence looked Neil dead in the eye before breaking into a huge grin. "Kid, I am so thrilled for you. And whether you expected it or not, I did. We all did, in fact. You know you're not supposed to be here. Hell, Las Vegas wasn't even on your radar when you so abruptly landed here. So yeah, none of us could say we didn't see this coming. Did I wish it had taken a little longer? That you had stuck around a while? Sure. But this here is a once in a lifetime opportunity. You'd be a fool to pass up. As to taking us with you, nah. You know we belong here. Shoot, I'll probably be buried right here. Just shove me in a box under the stage."

Duane looked at Clarence and laughed. "Speak for yourself, man." Turning to Neil, he took on a more serious tone. "You know we've got your back. Regardless of what happens. You'll always have a place here. But you better be sure to come over to the house for one last meal. Otherwise you'll have the wrath of Rosie to deal with. Having been on the receiving end of that, I wouldn't wish that on anyone else."

Neil smiled, taking in both Clarence and Duane and his surroundings. "You got it. And Clarence, if it's all the same to you, I'd like to finish out this week if I can. I feel like I owe it to you and the guys. That is, if you haven't already replaced me with the new guy you've got playing now."

Slapping him on the back, Clarence declared, "You got a deal. In fact, we'll have the both of you playing. You can take lead. Show this new kid the ropes. By the end of the week, maybe he can start to fill one of your shoes. Now. Come on backstage and let's tell the rest of the guys. I'm sure they'll want to raise a toast to your new adventure as well."

Chapter 48

Walking into the diner the next morning, Frank spots Neil in their usual back corner booth. Visible from across the room, he can see Neil's leg bouncing up and down in anticipation of their meeting. Or maybe it's just nervous energy he's yet to burn off after all that's happened in Los Angeles. Whatever it is, he quickly makes his way to the table hoping to settle him down and not drawing any unwanted attention.

"Neil, you're here early. Did you sleep at all?"

"Good morning Frank. Yeah, I did. Best nights sleep I've had in a while. I even managed to stop by the club last night. I talked with Clarence and the guys. And much to my relief, they were all so happy for me. Sad to see me go, of course, but it looks like they've already got my replacement lined up. So after this week, I guess I'm on my way back to Los Angeles." Neil replied, the words racing out of his mouth.

"Just how many cups of coffee have you had this morning?" Frank laughed. "You're talking so fast I can barely keep up."

"Sorry. I'm just excited. I mean, when I first got to town, well, you know everything that happened. The last thing I want to do is go home with my tail between my legs. Daddy would never let me hear the end of it. Now this is the chance that I've been dreaming of for years. And well. I just don't want anything to mess it up."

"No worries. It's sunshine and blue skies for you from here on out. You've gotten past the first gatekeeper. And I know you're going to do whatever it takes to make it to the next level." Frank paused, taking in a deep breath. "But there is something else we need to get out of the way this morning. And I want you to listen, no questions until I tell you everything. Got it?"

Neil nodded, looking at Frank with a million questions already in his eyes.

"Okay. First off, the letter. I'm guessing you found it when you got home last night?"

Neil dipped his head in reply as Frank continued.

"That letter is not to be opened. Well, not to be opened for a while, anyway. You may hear some things over the next few weeks. Some of those things will be true. Some won't. Don't try to figure out what's what. I need you to trust me and trust your gut."

Frank stopped as the waitress came by to fill their coffee and take breakfast orders. Once she was out of earshot, he continued. "Turns out Sharon has gone back to not only the local cops. But sources of mine have confirmed that she's involved the feds as well. She has spilled all she knows. Now get that look off your face. You're fine and nothing is going to happen to you. I've already made sure of that.

What I don't know right now is what exactly or how much she's told them. That's my next stop after we finish breakfast. As you know, some people I work with are obviously not happy about this turn of events. They have no reason to think I'm involved with what she's done at this point. I'm going to make sure it remains that way. My goal right now is to find out what the feds know. Who they are after. Then I'll deal with the next problem at hand."

Lowering his voice, Frank explained about the theft of the necklace and the questions the jeweler has been relentlessly asking. Intentionally leaving out the details of his ongoing deception of Nick and that he had hidden some of the actual stones amongst Neil's things and in a safe deposit box. The fewer details Neil knew, the better off he'd be.

"This was my last job, Neil. I'm done. I'm tired and I want to go home. Home to New Orleans. I've got money set aside. The Garden District house is still in good enough shape for me to come back to. Even though I don't need that much space. In fact, I may move back into the carriage house and rent out the main house. But my biggest concern right now is that you are being taken care of. Patrick knows some of this. At least he knows the details of what's important to you and your situation here. So if something comes up here, he'll take care of it. Anything that comes up in Los Angeles, you've got Ron on your side. He can work with Alan. Alan can also handle any other Capitol executives that try to insert their two cents. I see that look in your eyes, and I know you're worried. Don't. I've got a multitude of plans and contingencies in place. I'm going to be fine. All that being said, there is a good chance you will hear that I'm dead. This is where the letter comes in to play. If you should hear news of that, the first thing I want you to do is wait two weeks."

Neil started to interrupt, but stops when Frank holds up a hand. "No questions yet. Remember. You need to wait two weeks. Some time during those two weeks, you should receive a postcard from Tupelo Mississippi. As long as you receive that, that is the signal to let you know I'm okay. If you don't get the postcard by the end of the two weeks, then, and only then, are you to open the letter. Everything you need to know will be spelled out in full detail. Including the next steps you can take. What you decide to do after you get through reading that. Well, that is up to you to determine."

Taking a sip of coffee, Frank could see the worry and fear on Neil's face. "As to what I have left to do today. Here's what you need to know."

Laying out his plans, Frank explained he would be making stops at the police station, the federal building, and back at his apartment before going in to work. "From here I need you to go back home. This afternoon you show up at work as if everything is normal. Meet up with guys, rehearse, play your show tonight. You probably won't see me. Don't go out of your way to look for or ask about me either. If I have the chance, I'll drop by the club, but I'll stick to the back like I typically do. This week life has to appear as normal as possible. This is of the utmost importance. Before. You're in the clear with the cops. I will confirm that fact again with the feds, too. At the end of the week, Mickey and Danny will come help you load up your stuff and drive the truck over. You and I will take my car to drive back over to Los Angeles and get you settled. I've already told Nick I'm taking a few days to help you again, and he's fine with that. In fact, he's sent his congratulations too. I'm sure he'll put in an appearance before you go, too. That's all there is to it. Now, what are your questions? Based on the look on your face I can see you've got some."

Neil, sitting back in the booth, looked over at Frank. A hundred questions and scenarios stampeding through his head. Trying to rein them all in, he sighed. "I guess, really, I only have one. Are you sure you're okay? Is there something you're not telling me? Is this the last time I'll ever see you?"

Frank smiled. "That was three, by my count. But here's the short answer. Yes. Yes. And no. I know your life hasn't been an easy one, kid, and I'm not making it any easier on you right now, either. But trust me, I know what I'm doing and what you need to focus on now is your music. With that, I need to go." Frank stood, pulling Neil up out of the booth. Hugging him close, he whispered in his ear, "I have always believed in you. Your momma did too. She's watching over you right now. Everything will work out in the end. I love you, Neil. One of these days, most likely later on in the future, I'll try to answer all of your other questions, too."

Neil hugged Frank back hard before letting go. Swallowing down the lump in his throat, he looked at his uncle. Before he could say anything more, Frank turned, heading toward the door.

Chapter 49

Hating the way he was leaving Neil, Frank reminded himself it was for the best. 'The kid is going places,' he thought. 'I'm not going to be the one that stands in the way of his success.'

Pulling up in front of the federal building, he checked once more to make sure he still wasn't being followed. With what he was going to do next, he had to be sure. If he parked out front, his car would be easily recognized. Instead, he drove further down, turning the corner where he found an out of the way parking spot. In no particular hurry, he ambled back to the building, observing the hustle and bustle of the downtown street. All these people walking around, minding their own business. They have no idea what goes on behind the scenes of all these places they simply take for granted. If only they knew. Would they readily be so accepting and welcoming to the casinos and their owners? Those that are already here. And all the new ones being built. The city was changing every day. Not necessarily for the better. Maybe what he was about to do next would help bring about that change. If even just for a little while.

Walking in the front door, the smell of burnt coffee and the whine of the air conditioning immediately struck Frank. Thinking to himself, 'they certainly have it cold enough in here. Perhaps that's just one of their many interrogation techniques.'

Approaching the desk, he asked to speak with the agent in charge of casino related crimes. The officer on duty placed a call and instructed Frank to wait. Someone would be out for him shortly. Glancing around, Frank didn't notice anyone he recognized, but kept his head down all the same. When a tall, lanky gentleman approached him, hand outstretched, he knew there was no turning back. "Mr. Barnes? I'm agent Jones. I understand you wish to speak to me?"

"Yes. Is there someplace more private we can talk? I have some information I think you are going to find valuable. But it's not for public ears, if you understand."

"Of course, follow me, please." Jones said as he led him down a hallway. Opening a door to an interrogation room, he gestured for Frank to enter. "So, what is it you have to tell me, Mr. Barnes?"

Settling down into the hard metal chair as best he could, Frank took stock of the man across from him. He was about to trust him with more information than this guy ever anticipated getting in his career.

"Before I begin, I have a question that needs answered. Once you tell me what I need to know, then I will give you all the information you need on Nick Costa."

Agent Jones raised an eyebrow at the mention of the name. Clearing his throat, he stammered. "I, um, I see. Well, I guess what is your specific question and I'll see if I can answer it."

"I need to know precisely what Sharon Taylor has told you. Yes, I know she's been communicating with the district attorney, but I don't know if she's also been talking with you and I don't have a lot of time. And I really don't want to have to repeat anything you may already know. Once I know what she's told you, I'll fill in all the other details. And oh, by the way. Neil Evans, he has nothing to do with anything. If I so much as get a whisper that you are trying to involve him in any of what I'm about to share, I will not continue to cooperate."

Turning in his seat, Agent Jones stood. "Just a moment, please, Mr. Barnes. I don't have all of that information in front of me. Let me go see what I can find. While you wait, can I get you something to drink?"

"No. Again, I don't have much time. Go get whatever or whoever it is you need to. Let's get this over with."

Drumming his fingers on the table, waiting for someone to return, Frank began having second thoughts about what he was doing here. Was this the right decision? He was about to turn a corner. He knew there was no coming back from this once he did. About to rise from his seat, he startled when the door flew open. The second gentleman accompanying agent Jones walked into the room while talking rapidly before Frank had a chance to register what was taking place.

"Mr. Barnes. Or should I say Mr. Batiste? Yes, we know who you are. But I will say I am rather surprised to find you sitting in here. What is it that you think is going on?

And yes, yes. I know you don't have much time. Well, neither do I. So let's get down to it, shall we?"

Stunned, Frank stared at him, asking, "And you are?"

"I'm special agent in charge, George Wendell. I've been in touch with the district attorney, and I understand you have some questions about a Sharon Taylor and Neil Evans?"

"Mr. Wendell. First off, I have questions about Ms. Taylor. What she may or may not have told you. As to Mr. Evans, no, I don't have any questions about him. My instructions were quite clear to agent Jones here. He has nothing to do with any of this. Never has, never will. He is to be left out of it. Completely. If you can not guarantee me that you will leave him alone, then I will take my leave now. You'll be sitting here wondering what it was that I came in here to tell you."

Glaring at Frank, agent Wendell paused as if it pained him to utter his next words.

"Very well. You have my word, we won't bother Mr. Evans again. Though I still have my doubts about him. And you vouching for him doesn't necessarily give any credence to his character."

Feeling unsettled, Frank hesitated, digesting what special agent Wendell said. Choosing to ignore his insinuations about Neil, he began.

"First, I need to know what Sharon Taylor has told you. About me, and more importantly, about Nick Costa."

Special agent Wendell opened a folder, placed in front of Frank and said, "here is her statement that she gave to the local police and the district attorney. We are still transcribing her official statement to us, but it matches up with what she told them. You can read it for yourself. She, too, exonerated Mr. Evans. Said he was an unwitting bystander who got roped into her scheme. But because he's related to you, Mr. Batiste, he still remains a person of interest."

Reading over the document, Frank came to understand Sharon knew more than he had first thought. She wasn't as dumb as she pretended to be. Over the time they had been together she had gleaned quite a bit of information.

"Very well. I see the holes that I can fill in for you. And once you have my information, that's it. We're done. I don't want any sort of protection. I simply want to be left alone. I will not testify. There will be no other follow up. No other questions. And again, nothing is to happen to Neil Evans. And this time I want it in writing that you will leave him alone. Those are my conditions. If you are agreeable, then we have a deal and you can prepare for one of the biggest busts that I'm sure will close many case files for you."

Shaking his head, agent Wendell grumbled. "I can't give you those guarantees. Especially you not testifying. How do you expect us to corroborate the information? Then prove it in court if you're not there to back it up?"

"These are my terms. Take them or leave them. If you choose to leave them, then I'll be on my way. I'm a busy man and I'm quickly running out of time and patience." Frank stood, pushing his chair back.

Sensing he was between a rock and a hard place, Agent Wendell knew he had little leverage if he wanted the information Frank claimed he was about to offer.

"Very well." Agent Wendell replied. Turning his attention to agent Jones, he instructed him to bring in the tape recorder and then type up the documentation regarding Neil's exoneration and Frank's other demands.

Frank spent an hour and a half to detail all he could

about the inner workings of the Costa family and the Cross-roads casino. After answering Agent Wendells remaining questions, it was well after lunch by the time Frank was on his way out of the federal building. Feeling like he just stepped off a cliff instead of the stairs, he didn't see Michael approaching.

"Boss, strange to see you here," Michael stated, snapping Frank out of his stupor.

"Michael. I could say the same," Frank replied, trying to keep his voice steady. "What business do you have here?"

"Just trying to track down a few missing details. Mr. Costa asked me to look into something for him."

Trying to be casual and hide his apprehension, Frank slid his sunglasses on while looking straight at Michael. "Right. Of course. Nick mentioned that to me. Did you find what you were looking for?"

Shuffling back and forth, Michael looked at Frank, then looked over his shoulder. "Yeah boss. I think so. But still, what were you doing here? Everything okay?"

Frank could tell Michael was holding something back. Biding his time before responding. "Sure. Things are all good. I was also following up on something for Nick as well. I got what I needed as well. So I guess now I'm headed back to the casino. You need a ride?"

"Nah, I'm good. My car's parked right over there. But I don't see yours anywhere."

"Oh, I had to park around the corner. No spots out here when I arrived. Guess a lot of people had business here today."

"Right. Okay. Well, I guess I'll see you back at the Cross-roads then. You sure you're okay, boss?"

"All good Michael. Just tired. Been a busy week, and it's

not slowing down. See you back at the office." He called as he turned to make his way back to his car.

Glancing back, he saw Michael turn back towards his car without ever setting foot in the building. His guard back up on high, Frank knew he had to be even more careful now.

Chapter 50

Remaining alert the rest of the week, Frank went about performing his normal duties at the casino in hopes of not raising any more suspicions. Fortunately for him and the rest of the staff, at least from a security standpoint, it was proving to be a relatively quiet week. There were none of the normal big gamers scheduled to come through. No stars and their frenzy of fans and photographers would be there, either. Why couldn't all weeks be like this Frank thought, sliding his sunglasses on.

Stepping outside, Frank surreptitiously glanced around, once again making sure he wasn't being followed. On too many occasions this past week, he was certain he spotted a tail. Whether it was Michael or law enforcement, he couldn't be sure. The last thing he wanted to do was alert anyone to Jimmy's existence. He was a valued connection he had kept to himself all these years. Now he hoped he wasn't about to expose him.

Pulling up to Jimmy's, he walked straight in, not bothering to knock this time. Inspecting the loose stones first, Frank was amazed at the work Jimmy had already done cutting the medium size stones down into smaller ones. He couldn't tell that they had been set into anything else before.

Turning his attention to the newly crafted pieces, he took his time admiring the work. Jimmy was an artist. He had done an outstanding job of creating three new originals. A necklace, bracelet, and ring made a complete set. Anyone with the means would be more than willing to pay a small fortune to own one, if not all three. The lucky lady on the receiving end would be the envy of all.

Paying Jimmy the balance due and a bonus, Frank began saying his goodbyes. While thanking him for all the work he had done for him over the years, he took a moment to admonish him. "No one knows of your existence. Try to keep it that way and take care of yourself, man."

With one last stop to make before returning to work, Frank drove to the bank in Indian Springs. This would be his most important one of the day and once having done that, he knew he reached the point of no return.

Returning to work, he immediately launched into his nightly rounds on the main floor. Finding everything in order, he made his way back to his office to check for messages. He was sure there would be at least one more from the jeweler in New York. The man had called him so many times over the past two weeks, and the last call had been especially hostile. Not finding any additional messages he was surprised. He started to wonder what may have happened before thinking better of it, knowing he shouldn't question why. That could only lead to more trouble. And he certainly didn't want to know any of the details regarding how Nick had taken care of the guy. Whether he had paid him off, or took a more permanent approach, was not his concern. The less he knew in this case, the better. His deal with law enforcement was tenuous enough, as it was. He didn't want to give them anything else that had the potential to ruin his deal or bring more trouble to his doorstep. The feds had more than enough information from both him and Sharon to put Nick away for years. If not for the rest of his life. One more charge wouldn't make a difference.

Finding everything else in order, Frank decided it was time to head back to the club to hear Neil playing with Clarence and the Tru Tones one last time. Standing in the back, taking it all in, Frank just listened, letting the music wash over him. He would miss being able to do this on a regular basis. Not only hearing the big names that came through, but how much Neil had grown in his skills as well. It reminded him of what he was doing this all for.

Bringing his attention back to the room in front of him, he noticed Nick's table in the middle had the reserved sign in place. Set up with a champagne bucket, glasses, and water carafe, the table was ready, waiting for him and his guests to arrive. Frank knew Nick's guests would get there first. Nick always had to be the one to make an entrance. He would put in his appearance later. After all, this was Neil's last night. And Nick told Frank he wanted to send the kid out with a bang. Hopefully, only a proverbial bang and not one from the wrong end of a gun. Frank couldn't entertain that thought. If anything happened to Neil, he wouldn't forgive himself. Let alone be the one responsible for what he would do in retaliation.

Placing his hands in his pockets, he felt the bag

containing the new set of jewelry Jimmy had made. 'It's now or never,' he thought as he made his way out to the back hall and into an uncertain fate.

Chapter 51

Brushing his hand discreetly over his pocket one last time, knowing he was being watched, Frank knocked on Nick's door. Hearing a muffled "come in" from inside, he tentatively opened the door.

"Nick, you in here?" Frank called out, stepping through the doorway.

As Nick walked out from the adjoining room, Frank caught his breath, knowing it was the room where Nick had his own bank of security cameras that recorded everything for his later review. It had been the one wild card Frank had no control over in this entire situation. Knowing that Nick would watch and rewatch the tapes frequently had the potential to be his downfall.

"Frank. Hey you made it. Got the package?" Nick inquired.

No preamble, no chatting. This was unlike Nick. Taking another step into the room, Frank squared his shoulders, replying, "All here, boss. As requested."

"Good. Good. Just set it on the desk. I want you to come back here and take a look at something."

"Sure Nick. What's going on?"

"Come in here and I'll show you."

Frank didn't care for the ominous tone of Nick's voice. He couldn't be sure if it was being directed at him. Or perhaps something else had Nick so on edge. Placing the velvet bag containing the jewelry on the desk, he started walking into the next room when he saw a monitor with a freeze frame of Clarence and Leroy on the screen. Unsure of where this could be headed next, he kept his mouth shut until Nick started the conversation.

"Something strange is going on with the band. I've had my eye on Leroy now for the past few weeks and I think he's up to something. Or maybe it's involving all of them. I'm not sure yet. Now I know your nephew has only been with them for a short time. Before you start defending him, no, I don't think he's involved in whatever is going on. But I also think he may know something. Or have inadvertently seen or heard something. I need you to find out what that might be. Even if he doesn't know what it is, you will. Especially before he goes back off to Los Angeles."

Shaking his head in an effort to try to wrangle his thoughts, Frank continued looking at the screen before responding.

"I don't understand. What is it that you think Leroy or any of the other guys have been getting up to? I mean, I know that he's had a few run-ins with the local cops over the past couple of years, but from what I understand, it hasn't been anything more than drunk and disorderly sort of stuff. And before you ask, yes, he's also been spoken to about his involvement with Sharon and their escapades."

"I'm not sure. It's just ever since, well, even back during his time in New Orleans. You know. I can't seem to shake this idea that maybe Leroy was overstepping. He was part of what Sharon was doing on her trip, or maybe he's trying to involve someone else we don't know in on the job somehow. I know you had it all planned out and limited the number of guys who had knowledge of what was going on. But is it possible that whoever you had break it down and create these new pieces has ties to Leroy? Is it possible that the guy you used decided to keep any of the stones for himself? As an insurance policy? So that we wouldn't retaliate against him or just to make his own profit?"

"What? No," Frank replied indignantly. "Nick, I've been using this guy for years. I trust him to keep his mouth shut. He'd never run the risk of doing something stupid like that. He values his life too much and knows exactly the fate that would fall on his head if he ever tried to double cross me."

"Okay Frank. Easy now. Maybe you're right. Maybe I'm just being paranoid. It's just that this necklace is a big deal. This guy in New York that was making all the noise. Well, he's been handled. And I know you've had the necklace locked up safe. Only you knew where it was, and..." Nick trailed off. Looking back and forth between the monitor and Frank.

"Nick, everything went according to plan. No deviations, no alterations, and definitely no others involved. I picked up the new pieces and the remaining loose stones this afternoon and everything, and I mean everything, is taken care of. No one would even recognize these diamonds were ever once all set in one necklace. The guy I had do this is a genius. I'm thinking whatever is going on with Leroy has nothing to do with this. As for Neil. Well, I can ask him. But his head isn't here anymore. In fact, that was one of the other things I wanted to talk to you about."

Turning his full attention to Frank, Nick frowned. "Yeah? Sure. What's going on with him? When does he start his new contract? Do we get to keep him around a little while longer now?"

"No, unfortunately. As you know, this is still his last night. The contract is a done deal. Now, he needs to get back to Los Angeles and start working. Neither of us expected it to happen this fast. They were nice enough to give him this week to come back and settle his affairs here. Not that he has many here to begin with. But this week has just gone by so fast. I haven't had a chance to come talk to you before now." Frank paused, trying to reign in his rambling and emotions before continuing.

"I guess what I'm trying to say is. Well, what I'm coming to ask is that I need a couple more days off. I know I've already taken those other days. I just didn't anticipate having to do this so soon again. I've arranged for Mickey and Danny to come over and to help him load up and move this weekend. But Nick. I feel responsible for the kid. I want to help get him back and settled. He's pretty much the only family I have left and I feel like I'd be letting my sister down if I didn't take care of him now. It shouldn't take me too long. Ron Harding is on the other end. He's taking care of all the business details and already has an apartment lined up for him. Now it's more just a matter of me driving him back over, unloading his stuff and getting him settled. I want to make sure he's got food, clothes. You know. All the things he's gonna need that he has no idea he's going to need. As soon as I'm done with that, I'm on my way back. He's family, Nick. I only want to see what's best for him."

Nick grinned. "Take a breath there, Frank. I get that. Family is everything. This is a big deal for him. And for you, too. So yeah, alright. Take the days you need. I think we can spare you around here. Michael can handle anything that comes up in your absence. As for Leroy, based on what you've told me, I'll leave him alone for now. Unless you hear otherwise. If you do, I'm your first call. Got it?"

"Of course, boss. I think you're worried over nothing. In fact, I'll go down and have a talk to the guys in the band right now. They trust me and won't hold back if something is going on."

As they walked back out to the outer office, Frank turned back to Nick. Attempting to fish for more information as to why Michael might have been following him earlier, Frank quizzed, "Anything else going on that Michael is working on that I need to know about?"

"No." Nick replied with a quick shake of his head.

"Alright. Good then. I'll go down to the dressing room now. All the guys should be there. If I find out anything new, I'll come back up and let you know. Otherwise, I'll see you as planned at your table for the late set."

Making his way down the elevator, Frank lets out the smallest sigh of relief. Knowing he wasn't out of the fire yet. He had to get through the rest of this night before he could set the rest of the plan in motion.

Not wanting to barge in, he knocked on the dressing room door, waiting until someone call out it was clear to come in. Pulling Clarence aside first, he explained what Nick saw on his monitors. Getting assurances from him they had nothing to hide, he turned his attention to questioning the rest of the guys. Revealing only a few pertinent details of what took place with the theft, he told them Nick was questioning any involvement or knowledge they may have had.

"Look guys. I know none of you had any part in this," he said, looking around at all the guys in the band. "We've just been getting hounded by the jeweler in New York. He's sure it was someone on our end. Despite all the evidence he has pointing at the courier. Yet, no matter how many assurances we give this jerk, he just won't drop it. Nick is getting nervous and I'm just the messenger."

Clarence stepped up to Frank and said, "I'm not liking this, Frank. You sure he's not trying to pin something on one of us? You know we all do our job and stay out of trouble. Well, some of us not as much as others," he said. Turning his gaze to Leroy. "But none of us had nuthin' to do with Ms. Monroe's necklace. Shoot, the closest we got to her was on stage. And that was such a whirlwind. It doesn't even feel like that even happened."

"I know Clarence. Like I said, I'm just the messenger." Pivoting to Leroy. "There has been some questionable behavior noticed. Do you have something you might want to share?"

Before Leroy could protest, Duane put a hand on his shoulder. "Just tell the truth, man."

"Alright," Leroy started. "Man, this is hard. Okay, well. Here's the deal Frank. I'm tryin' to get straight. After that con that Sharon pulled. Then Neil getting pinched by the cops too. And he had nothing to do with anything. And of course, none of us even knowing he was your nephew when it all first went down. It was all just crazy." Taking a breath, he continued. "It made me realize I needed to get my act together. Get off the booze. Away from the games.

With the help of the guys, that's what I've been trying to do. It's been rough. The worst of the detox happened while you two were out of town. So yeah. I guess that's why Neil doesn't know much about it, other than what he's seen this week. But why Nick is so concerned about me man? I don't know."

Frank took a minute to consider what Leroy shared with him.

"What else could you have done then that would have given Nick reason to question your behavior then? I don't understand if all you've been doing is detoxing."

Clarence interrupted, "I think I know. The day you and Neil left for Los Angeles, he started and was having a really bad time of it, too. We were off for a couple of days. No one heard from him, as we were all busy with our own stuff. When he didn't show up that first night we were back, of course we were concerned. It wasn't until late the next day, Duane got a hold of him. He promised to be here for the show that night and came late. But he showed up, man. Then Michael came in here between sets. He was asking all kinds of questions. What did we know about Sharon and the con she pulled? Were any of us involved? How did Neil fit in to all of this? None of us had any clue, man. All I can guess is that maybe that's where Mr. Costa got the idea that something more was goin' on."

"Okay. Listen to me. All of you. If Michael or anyone else comes back around asking questions, then you be straight with them. Tell them what you just told me. I'll also pass along this information and hopefully that will be the end of it. Leroy, I'm happy for you that you're finally getting things together. You're an outstanding player, man, and we'd hate to lose you."

"Yeah, especially since we're already losing one already," Duane chimed in.

The conversation pivoting to more discussion about Neil's newfound success and all the opportunities it was going to bring his way.

Accepting the well wishes on Neil's new adventure, Frank excused himself from the dressing room, telling the guys he'd see them all for the last set. "Remember. Nick, along with some other VIPs, will be in attendance tonight. Be sure to put on your best show."

Frank was back to feeling unsettled when he walked back out into the hall. Michael asking questions was not in line with the conversation he had with Nick. Trying to get his breathing under control, he started back to Nick's office. Once he explained to Nick what was going on with Leroy and that it was just a matter of detoxing, maybe he'd stop keeping such a close eye behind the scenes and turn his focus back to the floor. Nick was happy when he could watch the high rollers losing money. Then Frank could find some relief as he made his next moves.

Chapter 52

After relaying the information to Nick, Frank returned to his duties before watching Neil's last performance with the band. Even with the rest of the evening passing without any incidents or other questions, Frank was still on edge. Knowing that Neil's move to Los Angeles was going to be one of the last pieces of his plan.

The final set that night went longer than usual, turning into an all out party, almost rivaling a Mardi Gras celebration. No one wanting to say goodbye, toasts were made, drinks poured freely, and well wishes given many times over. The group finally parted ways as streaks of sun began its rise over the desert.

"I'm going to pay for this later," Neil slurred as Frank led him up to his apartment.

"Probably kid. But those guys have got your back, no matter what happens. And they are beyond excited for you and this next chapter you're about to embark on. Not that they need any reason to celebrate. This was definitely more than a good excuse for a party. Now, I want you to go lay down and try to sleep this off a bit. Mickey and Danny will be by later this morning. They'll load up the truck and the next stop will be Los Angeles."

"Are you sure you can take more time off, Frank? You've already done so much. I feel bad that you're driving me back over again."

"It's all good. Nick knows how much this, and you, means to me. Now go. The time to leave will be here soon enough."

Stumbling his way into the bedroom, Neil unceremoniously flopped onto the bed, not bothering to undress. Pulling the blanket up over him, Frank turned his attention back to his final preparations. Bag packed. Check. Money and other necessary papers. Check. Overwhelming sense of dread in the pit of his stomach? Oh yeah, that was ever present. But if he wanted to get back to his life, life as he had known it in New Orleans all those years ago, this is what had to happen. The world, and most importantly the Costa family, had to think he was dead. It would be the only way to break free from this mess he found himself in. His heart was heavy for the burden it would place on Neil. But eventually he would know the truth. And as the saying went, the truth would set him free.

Frank left Neil sound asleep in the apartment before walking down the block to the pharmacy on the corner. Using the payphone located outside by the back door, he placed one last call to agent Wendell. Without preamble, he said, "It's done." Hanging up before the agent had the opportunity to ask any more questions. Now It was up to the feds to do their job. If everything else went according to plan, by the beginning of next week, the world would think

Frank died in a terrible car accident. Meanwhile, Nick Costa and the rest of the family would be facing the rest of their lives behind bars.

Returning to Neil's apartment, Frank sat down in the well-worn armchair. He wondered how many people before him contemplated the meaning of life while sitting here? The thoughts of what he hoped life would have in store for him drifted through his mind as he dozed off.

Waking to the sound of banging on the front door, Frank opened it to find Mickey and Danny ready to move Neil's belongings. "Come on in, guys. Let me get some coffee started. I don't know how much help Neil is going to be able to give you guys with how he's feeling. But, as you can see, there's not too much that needs to go."

After rousing Neil from his stupor, Frank poured a cup of coffee and set down two aspirin in front of him. "Drink this. It should help take a little bit of the edge off. I'll take of care of showing Mickey and Danny what goes and what stays. You focus on getting the rest of your things into my car. We ride soon." Frank said with a grin.

Neil floundered in the front seat as he tried to settle in with the hangover pounding in his head. The drive to Los Angeles was painfully quiet. Frank was sure every bump in the road felt like a rock was being thrown against his nephew's skull. An hour outside the city, Frank quietly asked Neil if he's coherent enough to talk. Grumbling an affirmative response, Frank saw Neil attempt to sit up a little straighter in his seat.

"Listen kid. You may hear about an accident involving me after I drop you off. I just want you to remember what I told you before. Wait on the postcard. If it doesn't come, then you know what to do. Right?"

As if an electric current had shocked him, Neil turned to Frank more alert now, the realization of the seriousness of the conversation showing on his face.

"So soon? I mean, yeah, I remember what you told me. I just thought we would have a little more time together. Does it really have to be this way? I mean, surely there's got to be some other way. Just give Nick whatever he wants and be done with them, uncle Frank. Go back to New Orleans. Get back to your old life."

"I wish it were that simple. Really, I do. But other actions are in play now. And because of that, well, it's safest for everyone, most importantly you, if they think I'm dead. Besides, you'll be so busy getting settled, playing gigs, writing new material, recording, you won't even have a chance to miss me." Frank joked as he playfully punched Neil in the arm.

"Oof. That kinda hurt." Neil said, rubbing the spot on his arm.

Frank looked at him with concern in his eyes. "Sorry. Guess that hangover of yours is worse than I thought. But we're all good. Right?"

"Yeah, we're good. I don't like it. But I know it's what you have to do."

"Good. Now, rest a little longer. We're almost there. You're going to need all the strength you can muster for what's coming next."

As late afternoon rolled around, Frank and the guys had everything unloaded and moved into Neil's new apartment. Alan dropped by to make sure everything was in order for Neil and confirmed they'd start work first thing tomorrow morning. "You've got a bright future ahead. Looking forward to seeing where this journey takes you."

He said, satisfied Neil was as settled as he could be for the moment and prepared for what lay ahead of him.

Mickey and Danny were next to leave, wishing Neil luck. "See you back in Vegas," Mickey called out to Frank.

"Yeah man. See you in a couple of days." Frank replied.

Once the two were gone, he turned his attention back to Neil. Taking in his nephew and his new surroundings, he nodded. "Alan is right. You've got a bright future ahead. And I expect that soon I'll be seeing your name on the club circuit. I know you'll eventually wind up in New Orleans. Whether you see me in the crowd or not, just know that I'll be supporting you. Always."

Neil shook his head, trying to clear his muddled thoughts. Before he could respond, Frank grabbed him in a bear hug, squeezing as though he'd never let go.

"You got this kid." He said as he let go. Hurriedly, in an effort to hide the tears forming in his eyes, he put his sunglasses back on before quickly closing the door behind him.

Neil, left standing alone in his apartment, looked around. Taking in and processing all that had transpired. What a wild journey it had been these past few months. What an adventure was now waiting for him on the horizon.

Chapter 53

Driving back towards Las Vegas for what he hoped would be his last time, Frank found himself ruminating on whether or not he was doing the right thing. He knew it was best for Neil to be out of Las Vegas, that was a given. But as far as this next part of the plan, he knew this would put a lot of other people he cared about at risk. If anything happened to them, he wasn't sure he could forgive himself.

'Now is not the time to be having a crisis of conscience.' He chastised himself. 'You've got your deal in place with the feds. Neil is safe. By this time next week, you'll be on your way back home. Home to see your daughter. Home to your roots. To the life you left behind. You've crossed every t, dotted every i. Just one step after the other.'

Before crossing over into the city limits, he pulled over. Stepping out of the car, he stretched. Taking his time, he looked over the landscape. Seeing all the undeveloped land that was still available. Even though the strip was already crowded with casinos and what seemed like more being built every day, you could be sure to find a piece of desert where one could get lost. Or hide a body. Reminding himself that time was short, he got back in the car and headed for his safe house in town.

Arriving in Indian Springs, he pulled up to the idyllic little house he had bought shortly after arriving in Las Vegas all those years ago. What a contrast it was to his apartment back in the city. Here, despite what took place a few miles away in the desert, was the epitome of the American dream. A white picket fence surrounding a yard with what had the potential to be flower beds and green grass in an otherwise brown landscape if he been around more to take care of it. Inside the home, he found the perfect setting for a family. It offered three bedrooms, a kitchen, a living room and a dining room. How he would have loved to have shared this place with Neil. And eventually Remy, too. But now that wouldn't be possible. He was about to burn his last bridge here with the hope of returning to New Orleans and finally living out a tranquil life he so missed.

Returning his focus to what lay in front of him, now was the time to focus on the next task at hand. Pulling into the garage, he quietly closed the door, hoping to not draw any unwanted attention. He had met a few of the neighbors on the occasions their paths crossed. They knew little about him, as he had passed himself off as a pilot, in an effort to explain his long absences. Eventually, much later he hoped, questions would arise. Where did this mysterious neighbor go? Why didn't anyone see him coming around any longer? It wouldn't take long for it to become apparent to everyone, no one was living there anymore.

Stepping inside, he turned on as few lights as possible. Reaching the back bedroom, he took a minute to review all that he had already accomplished and what remained to be done. Here, in preparation, he had stashed what little else he would need to take with him, mostly cash and a few family heirlooms. Before leaving Los Angeles, he had made sure the few stones he left at Neil's remained hidden. He couldn't take any chances that Neil would find them before it was time for him to do so.

Having enough foresight, he held a few more back when he had gone to the safe deposit box. "Just as insurance," he told himself as he transferred those into the slit in the fabric of an open suitcase laying on the bed. The majority of what he kept of the remaining diamonds, along with a deed to this house, were ensconced in the safe deposit box at the local bank here in Indian Springs. He had made sure it was a place that had no connection to Frank Barnes or Frank Batiste. Remy Thibodeaux was the only name appearing on the account. A name no one would ever connect to him. As far as the bank manager was concerned, Frank was just a lawyer representing a client who wasn't wanting any questions asked and wanted to prepay the box rental for years to come.

Picking up his suitcase, Frank returned to the living room, taking one more wistful look around. Not one normally for nostalgia, he found himself surprised by the fact he would miss this place. Was it the idea of memories he had hoped to make here? Whatever it was, this was not the time to get lost in a fantasy, he chided himself. He had more important tasks at hand.

After loading the suitcases into the Ford Galaxie he had been storing in the garage, he checked under the hood to make sure rodents hadn't gotten in and chewed on anything necessary to the normal operation of the car. The last thing he needed was for anything to happen that might disrupt his carefully laid out plans. Satisfied that the car was in working order, he pulled it straight out into the driveway, leaving room to pull out the convertible, too. This had been the one step in the plan where failure was a distinct possibility. He had considered enlisting someone's help to get both cars into position, but knew he wouldn't find anyone he could trust enough to involve. No. This was something he had to do on his own.

Hooking up the tow chains, he gave them a final tug, making sure everything was secure. As he slowly drove away, leaving behind the family neighborhood and the possibilities it once held, he felt a tear roll down his cheek. Wiping it away with the back of his hand, he turned back onto the open road. It wasn't long before he found himself pulling up to his predetermined location a few miles outside of Indian Springs. Parking, he got out and disconnected the Galaxie in a spot where it wouldn't attract any unwanted attention. Especially from the local cops. Satisfied with the camouflage, he got back in the Thunderbird and set the next part of his plan into motion. This was the do or die moment. His hope now, as far as the world was concerned, was he had died in a terrible accident.

Chapter 54

The following morning, Nick Costa awoke to news of a fatal car crash in the desert, just outside of the Las Vegas city limits. The updates he was getting from the firefighters he had on the payroll indicated it had been a single car crash. From all appearances, they said, it was being reported to have been Frank's car, along with Frank inside.

"What the hell was the guy thinking?" He shouted as Michael entered his suite. "Drinking and driving like that? Late at night? I thought he was supposed to have been staying in Los Angeles for the weekend with his nephew? I'm not liking this, Michael, not one bit. Something is wrong with this scenario. I want you to get out there. Now! Find out everything you can. You hear me?"

"Yes sir, Mr. Costa."

"And while we're at it, stash this somewhere safe. It's making me nervous having this here." He said, handing over a box containing what Michael could only assume to be the reset diamonds.

"You got it, boss. Do you want me to let you know where that is once I've got it stashed?"

Nick looked incredulously at Michael. "Of course, you idiot. In fact, I want to know now where you plan on taking it. Before I even hand it over to you. I'm leaving nothing to chance right now. I've still got too many questions still being asked. Too many cops poking around too. Despite the fact our friend from New York, Mr. Ruben, has been handled, I still don't feel good about this."

"Right. Sorry, sir. I'll get the keys to the warehouse we've used before. I'm assuming that's where Frank originally hid it, so it should be safe if we use that spot again. Seeing as how no one has bothered to search that place before now. Only Redd and I, well, aside from Frank, know about it. If that was indeed Frank and his car and that is now a smoking wreck out in the desert. Then I guess it's just me and Redd now."

"Michael, don't start counting your chickens just yet. I'm not convinced that was Frank. The last time I talked to him, something seemed off with him. I couldn't put my finger on it then and maybe now I'm just being overly cautions. I found myself hoping it was just him looking out for his nephew. And the big break the kid just got. Then again, the concerns you raised about Sharon and all her trips to the cops have proven to be true. And now she's missing as well. No. There are just too many coincidences taking place for my liking. I want answers. Not more questions. Now, go. Get that taken care of. Don't come back until you have those answers for me."

Michael nodded. He picked up the box and backed out of the room as Nick turned his view back to the casino floor.

'No. Something is definitely not right,' he thought to himself. Pacing back and forth, he replayed his conversation with Frank in his head. Frank had been more wound up than usual, talking rapidly, trying to explain his need for more time off. While he didn't discount the fact that Neil had landed this contract, there were just too many coincidences stacking up for Nick's liking. Stopping mid-stride, he suddenly he realized it had to be the diamonds. That was it. Somehow, Frank had pulled one over on Nick. He should have looked at the pieces Frank had left, instead of just placing them in his personal safe. But he had no reason to suspect anything was amiss, so he hadn't.

Turning his attention back to the main floor, his gaze ran over the floor, as he tried to spot Michael before he left the building. Spotting him by the front doors, he called downstairs to have the doorman stop him before he could exit the building.

"Michael," he shouted into the phone. "Get back up here now. Bring the package with you. I think we may have been double crossed."

Sitting down in his chair, he found he couldn't stay still. Getting back up, he resumed walking the floor while waiting for Michael to return, as he considered all the implications. How could Frank do something like this? Nick had treated him like family all these years. Surely this wasn't happening. Was it the guy who Frank used to make the new pieces? Did he take out and hold back some of the smaller stones, trying to throw the blame on Frank? That had to be it. This guy saw what he had on hand and decided no one would be the wiser. Well, he didn't know Nick Costa. And he sure didn't want to know what fate would await him if Nick discovered this was what he had done.

Michael walked back into the office. "What's going on, boss?"

"Open the box Michael. Now," Nick demanded.

Opening the box, Michael set it on the desk while Nick pulled a jeweler's loupe from his desk drawer. Inspecting the necklace first, he noticed all the large stones were indeed the real thing. But a longer look at the small stones surrounding it revealed what he feared, they had been replaced. Oh, they had used decent enough quality diamonds, that would fool a first glance buyer. But Nick was no dummy. These were definitely not of the same quality as what had been in the original necklace, even if they had been cut down to a smaller size. He knew now he had been double-crossed. Not bothering to look at the bracelet and ring, his blood began to boil.

As his face began turning increasing shades of red, he gripped the edge of his desk, as if ready to flip it over. Attempting to regain his composure, he took a deep breath, before turning back and glaring at Michael.

"Leave this here. Get yourself out to the scene of the wreck. Find out all you can. Now. I want to know for certain the body in that car was indeed Franks. If you have even the slightest bit of uncertainty, you let me know. If it's not him, then I want you and Redd out there searching for him. I don't care what it takes. You find him and bring him back to me. You understand?"

"Yes sir," Michael nodded, knowing better than to ask any further questions. It wasn't often anyone saw Nick in a mood like this. But when he was, they all knew it was best to stay quiet. Do what they were told. Unless, of course, they didn't value their lives.

Leaving the office, Michael made his way back down to

the security office, finding Redd watching the bank of security cameras. Grabbing him by the arm and practically dragging him from the chair, he filled him in on the details of what had just taken place and his suspicions.

"You don't think Frank actually double crossed Nick do you? He wouldn't do that? With Neil landing that contract and all. What could he possibly be thinking?" Redd asked, rapid fire.

"I don't know man. I'm hoping that it is Frank in that car and it was just a tragic accident. Yet I don't have a good feeling about this. No, not at all." Michael replied, as they turned a corner and walked straight into two burly police officers.

"Gentlemen, I'm going to need you to come with me. And I'm also going to need you to tell me where we can find Mr. Nick Costa."

Chapter 55

It didn't take long for the rest of law enforcement, both the local police and federal agents, to descend upon the Crossroads Casino. While taking Nick Costa and the others into custody, they found the jewelry, laying in plain sight on the desk in Nick's office. Agent Wendell couldn't believe his luck. He thought for certain the necklace had gone up in the flames of the car wreck, along with his chances of making the case against Nick and the others. While he was no expert, he was sure these pieces had to be the missing diamonds. Even with them no longer in all their original glory, what he found should be enough for the jeweler to identify. Without Frank being there in person, he was going to hate having to rely on the written statement he had in his possession. And yet that would still be damaging enough when read in court. At least with that and all the other evidence he now had, he'd be able to put the Costa family away for many years to come.

Michael remained stoic during his repeated questioning, insisting he would only speak to a lawyer, remaining ever loyal to Nick and the Costa family. Redd, however, was tired of all the secrecy. It didn't take him long before he started to spill his guts, giving details even Frank hadn't provided. In doing so, he managed to work out a deal to take his family into witness protection. It wouldn't be easy leaving this lucrative life behind. As he told the interviewing detective, this supposed easy life wasn't that easy after all, when you took the time to think about it.

Clarence and the band were taken to the local jail and held for two days before being cleared of any charges. Despite all of Leroy's run-ins with cops, the band's alibi had been well documented, since they all had been on stage at the time of the theft.

Cleared of any involvement, Duane took this as his sign of it being time to move on. Going home, he approached Rosie and little Joe, suggesting a move to California. "I got a friend there now. I can ask him to put in a good word for us." He joked, before turning serious again as he picked up the phone to call Neil. He wasn't sure if Neil had been notified of Frank's accident and didn't want to have to be the one to break the bad news. Especially not over the phone.

"Neil, man. How's it going?" Duane said, his voice cracking.

"Duane! Good to hear from you so soon. It's going great. But what's wrong? You sound off, man." Neil replied.

Hesitating, Duane tried to think of how best to share the news about Frank. "Man. I've got some bad news. I don't know if you've been told yet. And I don't know any other way to say this but to just come out and say it. Although you may have already heard the rumors or the cops may have come found you there. But there was a dreadful crash a couple of nights ago. I'm so sorry, Neil, but it's being reported that it was Frank. None of us could believe it. We thought he was staying there with you there for a few more days."

"Um, I..." Neil stopped.

"Neil. I am so, so sorry. I can't believe you have to hear it this way. Dude. The Crossroads got shut down too. It seems that the Costa family stole the necklace that Marylin had been wearing, and well, a whole lot of other stuff, too. The feds arrested Nick. Then they took the rest of the security team into custody as well."

"Duane. Man. What about you guys? Clarence? The rest of the guys? Are you all okay?"

Surprised by Neil's lack of reaction to hearing about Frank's tragic accident, Duane looked at the handset before placing it back up to his ear again. "Um, yeah. We're all good. I'm home with Rosie now. The cops kept us a couple of days, but we were all cleared. As were you. I'm sure someone is going to be in touch soon with some questions. But are you sure you're okay, man? Your uncle, I mean, I know you guys just got back in touch. This has got to be a shock."

Pausing for what seemed like an awful long time to Duane, Neil only replied. "Yeah. I, um, I guess it just hasn't really sunk in yet. You know, he was just here. And I guess I've just been so busy these past couple of days that I barely know what day of the week it is right now. I do appreciate the call, man. Really, I do. Give Rosie and little Joe a hug for me, will you?"

Before Duane could respond, Neil hung up. Setting the phone back in the cradle, Duane turned to Rosie, who was looking at him with concern. "I'm not sure what just happened. Looks like California isn't the place for us after all."

"Everything will work out as it's supposed to, honey," Rosie said, wrapping her arms around Duane. "It always does."

THIS CALL WAS NOT what Neil had been expecting. He had overhead a story on the news, something about the Crossroads being shut down. But he hadn't heard anything about a reported car crash. The police hadn't been in touch with him either. Maybe they had reached out to Patrick Leary? But surely, he would have called Neil by now if that had been the case. Was this a part of what his uncle had been talking about on the drive over here? The memory hangover from that day resurfaced, along with a nauseous feeling similar to then, too. What was it Frank had said about a postcard again? All the thoughts and conversations they had over the past couple of weeks were weaving together in Neil's head. He was having a hard time making sense of anything.

Knowing he had mumbled something in response to Duane before hanging up the phone, he was unsure now of what he had even said. Everything was a blur. Finding his thoughts torn between wanting to rush back to Las Vegas and search for his uncle, or staying put and working on his music. He knew if he left now, he'd ruin his chances with the record deal, but at the same time, he couldn't face losing his uncle again.

"Think Neil. Remember what it was Frank told you that morning at breakfast." He scolded himself.

The letter. That was it. He ran to his bedroom, tossing clothes out of his dresser until he found the letter. Pulling it out, he held it in his hands, until he heard his uncle's voice in his head, as clear as if he was standing next to him. "Remember what I told you, kid. Only open this if you don't get the postcard from Tupelo by the end of two weeks."

Right, the postcard. That's what Neil was forgetting. Frank had alluded to the fact that something was going to happen. Had he been planning this all along? Why didn't I press him for more information that morning? 'I'm so stupid, he thought to himself. 'I shouldn't have let him leave like he did. If only he had stayed here a little longer, none of this would have happened.'

Calling Duane back, he immediately apologized for ending the previous conversation so abruptly.

"Man, I'm so sorry. I just cut you off. And, well. I don't know what to think." Neil lamented.

"Seriously Neil? You have nothing to apologize for. Man, I just told you that your uncle is gone. I wasn't expecting a soliloquy from you. You sure you're okay? Do you need me to come out? Or do anything for you here?"

"No. I'm okay right now. I'm pretty sure Frank had arrangements in place. Just in case anything happened to him. He mentioned something to me in passing one day about something like that." Before Duane could interrupt with questions he knew he couldn't answer right now, Neil continued. "But what about you and the guys? What are you going to do now that the casino has shut down? I mean, I know Clarence said he'd never leave. But you guys have got to work."

"Yeah man. That was one of the reasons why I called

you before. I know it's bad timing and all. And I hate to ask. Clarence, no surprise, has already landed another gig here. You know, he always had other bands trying to poach him away. He's agreed to taking Vernon and Joe with him. Leroy has decided to skip town. I'm not sure where he's headed, but he says he just can't stick around here anymore. As for me, well, I could go with Clarence too, but Rosie and I were talking about the possibility of a move instead. We weren't sure where. But if you've got it in you to put in a good word for me, we wouldn't be averse to coming to Los Angeles."

Before Duane could finish his sentence, Neil whooped. "Of course Duane! That would be amazing if you guys would move here. I don't know how much pull I've got right now. Let me get back to the offices tomorrow morning and I'll see what I can do. Oh, man. I'd love to have you join me on this journey. Were it not for you, and well, uncle Frank. I wouldn't be here right now."

Duane laughed as Neil ended the call, promising to get back to him as soon as he had news. Could it be things were going to work out for him as well, after all?

Chapter 56

The next two weeks went by exceeding slow and fast at the same time. While Neil kept himself busy at work during the day, the nights were when he found it to be the hardest to escape the lingering questions.

Alan had told him when he started, he wouldn't be playing any gigs just yet. "We need you focused on creating new material first. Get a few songs written, then we'll get you in the studio and get some tracks laid down. I've got a few ideas about sending you out on the road, but we'll discuss that soon enough."

Just over a week and a half after he received the news of the car crash and Frank's death, a postcard from Tupelo Mississippi arrived. The message was brief. *Wish you were here.* No signature, or anything else to reveal who had sent it. Neil was relieved to be holding it in his hands, knowing it was Frank's way of signaling to Neil that he was okay. While there was no indication of where he was or what he was doing, Neil found himself hoping maybe Frank had made it back to New Orleans. Of course, this still led to more questions. One being, with as much history as Frank had in the city and with its residents, would he be able to stay out of trouble? Or worse yet, would Nick's reach find him there?

Neil, armed with all these questions, still he didn't have time to find any answers. He had managed to convince the executives at Capitol records to give Duane a chance. As soon as he and the family arrived and settled, Neil and Duane set to work. Keeping even more busy, writing together and then recording the songs they just penned.

Alan came to them a few weeks later announcing, as promised, plans were being made and put in place to go on tour with some other up-and-coming bands. This would be a grueling tour, cramped conditions, playing no name bars and clubs, he told them. But Neil knew this was the dream he had spent all his time chasing, and now it was about to come true.

One night over dinner, while looking over the itinerary, Neil and Duane saw all the places they would be going. With stops scheduled in Arizona, New Mexico, Texas, they would make their way on to Louisiana. Neil could feel a pang of homesickness wash over him as he sat there, wishing they could schedule a stop in Arkansas. He desperately wanted daddy to come see him perform and to see that Neil had put in the necessary work, finally making something of himself and this dream. How long had it been since he had tried to reach out to him either by phone or by letter? The last time he called was to no avail. The old man was still nothing if not stubborn. Perusing the schedule again, his face lit up when he saw they would play two nights in New Orleans.

'Maybe. Just maybe, Frank will put in an appearance at one of those shows. Wouldn't that be something if he did?' He thought to himself. How would he explain that to Duane was still a question he didn't have the answer to. As far as Duane and the rest of the guys knew, Frank had died in the crash. Neil knew he couldn't break that trust that Frank had put in him. Not for anyone. No, if Frank did show up, then he would bear the responsibility of explaining it to Duane.

Returning home that night, he lay in bed with the recurring thought, how could he find the time while they were in town to locate his cousin Remy? He knew he had a responsibility to try to reach out to her and let her know she still had family on her dad's side. Was she even aware of that fact, or would this be news to her as well? Someone, that if she was interested, had known her dad and could share stories of him. But how could he go about finding her? That was going to be the challenge. Hoping he would have some downtime, he would try to drop by the Batiste family home. See if anyone living there knew where she might be. It was going to be a long shot, but one he knew he had to take.

Packing his bags, he tucked the unopened letter into a pocket in the suitcase. He knew this was something he had to be sure to take with him, no matter where he went. He didn't feel right leaving it at home, even if it was unopened. Even after being notified by the police, he was surprised to find no one else had come looking for him or asking about Frank. Yet he knew deep inside that he couldn't take the chance of anyone ever finding it, either. He had to do whatever he could in his power to protect his uncle. Even if he never saw him again.

Grabbing for an extra pair of socks that he found shoved far back in the drawer, he startled as a small bag dropped out onto the floor. Not recognizing it as something he had put away, he gently picked it up with two fingers, holding it out in front of him. Considering for a moment whether to look inside, he stuffed it back, unopened, into the sock it fell out of, and tucked it into the suitcase, too. "I don't know for certain what it is. I have my suspicions and yet I don't think it's something I should confirm right now, either. But somehow I think this needs to be kept close to me at all times." He said as he finished his packing, before turning his attention back to the future ahead of him.

Chapter 57

Summer had arrived in New Orleans, hanging heavy in the air. The months leading up had been long and nightmarish for Frank. As promised, he sent the postcard from Tupelo assuring Neil of his survival despite the reports of a fiery crash and his death in the desert. He hated to destroy that car, but it had been one of many necessary details to give credence to his demise.

Since arriving back in his hometown, he had been keeping a low profile, gleaning what news he could regarding the takedown of the Costa family in Las Vegas. After the FBI had raided the casino and their homes, Nick, Michael, and many other members of the family were left to face a long list of charges. Redd, he heard, turned state evidence. 'Good on him. At least one of them had enough sense to save themselves.'

Learning from yet another source that Nick figured out Frank's deception with the diamonds, he knew Nick still did not know where they could be hidden. Armed with the knowledge the remaining stones were still tucked away in the safe deposit box, he took solace in the idea that one day, they would find their way back to him. Or at least his family, if he was no longer around.

During the first few months after his return, Frank spotted a few of Nick's local henchmen out and about in the city. He was sure Nick suspected he had returned here and was still alive. He was also well aware he was living with a target on his head and probably would have one for the rest of his life. Or at least as long as Nick was still alive, even in he remained in prison. Nick had friends on the outside, willing to do whatever he asked. After three long months of hiding, only going out when absolutely necessary, he ventured out into the city again. He found a sliver of relief when it appeared even those that had been searching for him were no longer to be seen. Maybe the results of their crimes had caught up to them. He wondered if the police had finally swept them up, too. Frank didn't know and he wasn't about to go asking questions in an effort to find out, either.

During his self-imposed confinement, he received news of Leroy's death. He found himself saddened and certainly not believing the story of it being a drunk driving accident. He knew Leroy was finally serious about his sobriety based on his last conversation with him and when he heard he had left the band and Las Vegas for a move to Chicago. Frank was sure this was just Nick's way of sending another message intended for him and possibly Neil as well. No matter where you go or what you do, somehow they would find you and the consequences of that would catch up with you.

Frank was well aware, no matter where he was or who he became, he would have to continue to be careful. Always keeping an eye out. Having reached out to Jimmy to make sure he was still okay, he also found out the rest of the guys from the band had landed on their feet at another casino. This news did not surprise Frank. Even when the Crossroads was at its peak, other owners were always trying to poach Clarence and The Tru Tones.

The Crossroads had been taken over by another organization and was now under new ownership as well. The new owners came in and made so many changes that no one would have even recognized the Crossroads as having ever been the original casino that occupied the building. Times were changing once again.

Stepping off the streetcar, he took a leisurely walk around the French Quarter. The evening was sultry, anticipation of an approaching storm had people scurrying to get inside. As Frank approached the Sho Bar, he smiled to himself when he saw the sign for tonight's show. 'The kid did it. Just like I knew he would.' Seeing Neil's name on the flyer, Frank found himself thinking of his sister Celeste and how proud she would have been of Neil. How he wished she and Joe could have been here to help celebrate his success.

Opening the door, he found it already packed with wall to wall people. Winding through the crowd, he made his way to the bar and ordered a drink. Finding a dark corner, which he could disappear into, he knew he had to remain in the shadows for now. Tonight, the spotlight should only be on one person and it was shining brightly when he took the stage.

"Hey New Orleans! You ready to party!" A familiar voice calling out over the crowd.

Frank smiled and cheered with the rest of the crowd. They had no idea what they were about to experience, but Frank knew it was a party they wouldn't soon forget.

Acknowledgments

Acknowledgements for a second book always seem to read like a who's who of the author's life. And despite writing being a solitary activity, it really does take a village to get this from an idea in your head to actual publication.

One question authors always get asked is, "Where do you get your ideas?" Often there isn't really a good answer. But in the case of this book, the original inspiration for this story came from what some might consider an unusual place. The Neon Museum in Las Vegas is where the idea was conceived. If you've never visited there, I highly recommend it. The outdoor museum is full of old casino and business signs from years gone by. The tours they offer share an encyclopedic amount of information and history. From the designers who came up with and built the signs to the stories of the owners of the casinos and other fascinating tidbits of information. The tour is a breeding ground of ideas for anyone willing to listen and learn.

To the wonderful community of writers at Author Nation - you all are such an incredible group I'm lucky to be a part of. Whether or not you realize it. Seeing the support, whether it's backing Kickstarter projects, to cheering every step of the way from the first draft to when the book is published. I'm glad I have found you and look forward to what comes next for all of us.

To Dean. My heart. My best friend. You supported and believed in me from the very beginning. Especially at those points when I didn't think I could do this. Though you're no longer here, I know you're still cheering me on. I miss you each and every day.

To Amy. I won't embarrass you and get all mushy. Just know you are amazing and an inspiration. Keep chasing your dreams.

To Natalie and Amber - you ladies are amazing. Asking thought-provoking questions, sharing countless cups of coffee, and supporting me every step of the way.

To my cover designer, Ann. You captured the heart of the story in your art and also deciphered my rambling thoughts of ideas for what I was envisioning. Thank you. I can't wait to see what you come up with for the next book.

I've said it before, and it bears repeating. Thank you to all the teachers and librarians who showed me the worlds contained in stories, both fiction and non-fiction. You encouraged and challenged me with your teaching and book recommendations, and instilled a love of reading that will never die. You truly are unsung heroes.

Most of all, thank you to you, my readers. For investing the time to read this book. A book that for so long only lived inside my head. I hope you've enjoyed it. And if you would be so kind, drop a review wherever you purchased it, so others can find it too.

About the Author

M.E. Cooper has been making up stories since childhood.

Her stories transport readers through time and across continents. Drawing inspiration from her extensive travels, she brings vivid settings and rich cultural textures to each novel. Her work spans decades, seamlessly blending historical authenticity with deeply personal character journeys. Whether set in mid-century Las Vegas or the jazz-infused streets of 1920s New Orleans, Cooper's novels delve into the inner lives of her characters, exploring identity, memory, redemption, and the human spirit. When she's not writing, she can be found wandering through hidden alleyways in unfamiliar cities, always chasing the next story.

You can find all of her books at your favorite retailer. And if they aren't available there, ask them to carry her books. Or drop a line with any recommendations of where you think she should sell her books.

Drop by and visit her author site at http://me-cooper.net

There you can buy books direct, sign up for her e-mail newsletter, read short stories and get all the news on upcoming books and more.

www.ingramcontent.com/pod-product-compliance
Lightning Source LLC
Chambersburg PA
CBHW032349310726

48973CB00007B/1926